Sudden Turn

By Eden Monroe

Print ISBNs

Amazon Print 9780228625353
BWL Print 9780228625360
LSI Print 9780228625377
B&N Print 9780228625384

BWL Publishing

Books we love to
Authors around the world.

http://bwlpublishing.ca

Table of Contents

Prologue

No day should ever be called ordinary, and certainly not this one. Dazzingly beautiful, delicious even, the countryside was aflame in tangerine, gold, vermillion and maple sugar red, the sapphire blue sky the perfect partner in this spectacular autumn dance. The unseasonably warm temperatures buoyed the spirit, lightened the step and lulled last-minute mosquitoes into a false sense of security. But a major weather system was slowly bearing down on the city of Franklin and the surrounding countryside.

For most people, that Saturday was simply a relaxing, do-as-you-please day, the finish line following the sprint toward another weekend. However, for many there was work to be done, a burden as old as time, although not everyone considered their job to be drudgery. Certainly not Ginger Martel as she inserted fresh batteries into her micro mini recorder, happily anticipating the interview she'd be conducting in just about thirty minutes.

Cedric Gourney called himself the moose whisperer, the best big game hunter in New Brunswick. He promised to be an interesting, quirky subject. He seemed colourful and willing to be a step or two off centre, just the type of person she liked to feature in her weekly column, People Unlimited. She'd get some great stuff, she knew she would. She'd also have access to a treasure trove of his own pictures. If it went as well as she hoped it would, she'd enter the published piece in the annual Keith Hassam Media Awards competition, which also considered lighter fare in its line-up. She'd won in her category before. She was a dedicated freelancer with a flair for unearthing the unusual, and she'd stop at nothing for a good story.

* * *

Shane Elliott stopped at The Daily Grind for his usual cup of coffee. He knew he was feeding the cops and coffee shop stereotype, but he loved the stuff almost as much as he loved his job. Hostage negotiator. It was a career he'd envisioned for himself since he was a kid. So he'd entered law enforcement and had fifteen years in now, six of them in another province, before returning home and getting hired on with the local force. He was now a corporal with the Franklin Police

Department but had never lost sight of his goal to become a hostage negotiator. His opportunity to join the crisis negotiator team finally came with the retirement of Kenny Ferguson. Shane was a natural, and absorbed the negotiator training like a sponge.

The team had been busy lately because it had turned out to be a difficult year. People had to be having a really bad day in order for negotiators to do their thing, and Shane loved to help; to try to make a difference and save lives. That was the real rush. The only downside was that his beloved April hadn't lived long enough to see him realize his dream, gone half a lifetime too soon. After three years he still put flowers on her grave. Real ones. Pink roses, summer and winter, and he never missed a week.

Chapter One

Ginger found McNally Road with no problem, although it wasn't even a mile long and she didn't see any houses on it. Located on the outer boundaries, albeit within the far flung city limits, she assumed it would be fairly well populated given the trend toward suburbia. But no, these were wide-open spaces. She couldn't even find Cedric Gourney, because if he lived on McNally Road, he was well hidden. He'd given his address as One McNally Road, but the civic number wasn't in evidence unless it was obscured by the abundance of vegetation that crowded both sides of the unpaved surface.

She glanced at her watch as dark clouds began to scud across the mid-afternoon sky, the beautiful autumn day seemingly having folded its tent and left in favour of the heavier weather to come. It was now three minutes to the hour. She did not want to be late because she felt it was unprofessional to have to call and say she was lost. She would if she had to though, and that's the way it was beginning to appear. She recalled passing a narrow lane a short distance back. It was barely visible among the trees and bushes, but the absence of either a civic number or a mailbox at its entrance wasn't very encouraging. It probably led to a pit, or a clear-cut where logs or pulpwood had been harvested. Nevertheless, anxious to reach her destination, she decided to check it out, turning her small grey hatchback and accelerating once she'd finished negotiating the sharp turn. At the very least she could verify that it didn't lead to Cedric's residence, but then again she had to be close because a line of telephone poles marched determinedly through the trees.

The lane was barely the width of a vehicle, tree branches nearly brushing the sides of her car as she slowed for another sharp turn. Passing over a narrow bridge, she spied a decrepit mailbox with the name Gourney painted in sloppy green letters. She crept up the driveway to a ramshackle, two-storey house in weather beaten grey, even more forlorn looking than the mailbox. It appeared as though it had been constructed using mixed lumber scraps, creating a patchwork facade. A chill went up her spine, not because it looked rundown, there was just something sinister about it. She checked her reaction though, and warned it away. She'd visited worse looking properties and found regular everyday people living there. Challenging circumstances in life were sometimes at the expense of prosperity, and she would never look down her nose at anyone. She'd also had more than a few edgy interviews that had turned out fine and this one would too, so she shrugged off her reservations. Besides, her editor had given her the lead so how bad could it be?

As she pulled to a stop she saw three large German shepherds affixed to lengthy chains, long enough to give them full run of the large yard. They came bounding forward, barking in bass tones as if daring her to step out among them. She was not a lover of large dogs, at all, or for that matter, medium-sized ones. Attacked by a dog as a child and badly frightened, although only slightly injured during the experience, she still carried that deep fear. Even in her braver moments when she'd tried to pretend that everything was all right, the dog in question would sense her discomfort and react accordingly. And now there were three.

Before she could entirely process the presence of the dogs, she noticed a man she guessed to be somewhere in his fifties quickly making his way down a steep flight of stairs at one end of the building. He approached her vehicle, smiling broadly.

"You found me!" he declared, clearly pleased that she had arrived.

Ginger's smile came naturally, relieved that despite the creepy premises, including the guard dogs, he seemed to be friendly.

"It wasn't easy," she said lightly as she gathered her purse and the workbag that held her camera, tape recorder and notebook. "I must have gotten the directions mixed up. I was looking for you on the McNally Road."

His smile never wavered. "I told you I was off the McNally Road. I actually have my own little road because I like my privacy. If you'll look around you'll see I'm off the grid," he announced proudly. "I've got a big ole generator and that, along with solar panels, supply all the juice I need. I do have a landline phone though, which I guess you know 'cause you called me on it. Anyway, enough about all this. come on up and let's get started. I've got a million stories to tell you."

Again Ginger felt a chill tickle her spine and once again she dismissed it. Cedric looked welcoming enough. He was obviously happy that she'd come to interview him, but she definitely didn't like the dogs watching her as she got out of her car and started toward the house with their owner. As long as she was with Cedric though she should be fine.

Of medium height, he seemed to exude strength that belied his wiry build. He looked sinewy tough, a man who had apparently bested any number of wild animals. Her first impression was that he didn't seem like the type to back down, from anyone or anything, and could probably be a formidable opponent. He was being more than gracious now, although she was picking up on his nervous energy, which was not unusual to observe in someone about to be interviewed.

Once they'd climbed the stairs they entered what was obviously his living quarters. She had no idea what the first floor was used for because there were no curtains at the windows. In contrast the second floor had generous window coverings that blocked what was left of the light now that heavy clouds had taken command of the sky. Hmmm, curtains. It was definitely a feminine touch. She didn't see evidence of a female in residence, but it did help to relax her a little as she yet again shrugged off a sense of disquiet. Why this restlessness she wondered. It's just another interview, but she knew she'd be glad when she was finished and on her way home.

They passed through a small kitchen into a modest living room with one sofa and an mismatched armchair of indiscriminate age. The furniture was in relatively good repair except for a battle scarred coffee table standing wearily in front of the sofa, groaning under the weight of several picture albums and two cardboard boxes containing photos. She was right about that at least, it seemed there would be plenty of old pictures to choose from. Aware of eyes upon her, she glanced up and around at several bear mounts staring at her from various locations on the walls, expertly preserved by a highly skilled taxidermist. There were in fact five, in addition to a large buck deer with massive antlers and a gigantic moose that dominated the room, hanging majestically between two doors. This was a trophy room for sure, bears appearing to be far and away his favourite target despite the fact that he called himself the moose whisperer.

He was obviously proud of his hunting prowess. "Quite a collection, eh? What you see here are only a few of my best."

"The rest got away?" she quipped, often relying on humour to relax her subjects. Cedric Gourney did need relaxing, but she could see by the way his eyes darkened that he didn't appreciate the comment.

"Nothing gets away from Cedric Gourney," he stated, his smile slipping. "Once something's in my sites, it's not going anywhere."

Again she felt apprehensive. This time it galloped up her spine, but she immediately remembered some of the other quirky interviews she'd done in the past. Upon reflection they too could be called dangerous, but everything had worked out. You had to take risks to get good stories, but did that drive make her too trusting?

"Sorry," she apologized as she took a seat on the sofa. "I was just trying to be light, and it didn't work. You must be a good shot or you wouldn't have all these specimens," she said, indicating the game trophies with a sweep of her hand.

Retrieving her tape recorder and notebook from her bag, she set to work arranging them on what space remained on the coffee table. She was surprised when Cedric plunked down beside her as bold as brass, brushing her thigh with his own. She'd assumed he'd take the armchair.

"You know what?" she asked cheerfully, "I think I'll sit over there," and quickly relocated to the single armchair. "That way I can see you when you're speaking. If we're going to have a conversation I should be able to see your face. I think the tape recorder will pick you up a little better too with some distance."

If he was perturbed by her abrupt switch to the armchair it didn't show, his smile back in place. She guessed that like most people his favourite subject was himself; that would be his comfort zone. He just needed be settled a bit and so she got right down to business.

"All right then, Mr. Gourney…."

"Call me Cedric."

"Okay, Cedric. How long have you been hunting?"

"Since I was eight years old and could carry a gun safely. My father expected me to help feed the family, so as soon as I was old enough to know what a gun was I went hunting with him. Grant it, I was only carrying a .22 at that age, but it was loaded and I was ready. I didn't miss much, even back then. If I aimed at something, it came home with us for supper and my mother could make a meal out of just about anything."

"Such as…."

"Such as squirrel soup."

She pictured little fuzzy squirrels, wide-eyed and bushy-tailed and chattering in treetops, fiercely scolding anyone who came too near. She couldn't even think about them in a soup, but she had heard of such a thing. Being a city girl, her next meal was never further away than the closest supermarket, so she couldn't judge those who depended on the land for their sustenance. Cedric had obviously grown up poor.

"I've heard that's very tasty," she said, swallowing hard, but trying to meet him halfway.

"I've actually got a container of it in the fridge. I'll heat some up for you before you leave."

She was sure her mouth dropped open but she managed to keep her smile as his small dark eyes bored into hers. "Thank you," she said pleasantly, "but my stomach's a little off today. I'm not really eating much," which was the truth. The dish of devilled beef kidneys she'd eaten last night compliments of a darling senior interviewee had turned on her almost immediately. With her finicky stomach, she knew it was her first and last dish of devilled kidneys.

"Your loss," he said, his smile dipping slightly again.

"Right. So you got off to an early start with hunting, but I guess you took to it immediately. Have you done all of your hunting in New Brunswick?"

"Absolutely. I've hunted the woods in this province from one end to the other. I had a chance once to go to Newfoundland to hunt for moose but since I've had pretty good luck with the annual draw in New Brunswick, I just stay here. I like the hardwood moose best of all."

"Hardwood?"

"The ones who browse in hardwood forest rather than in swampy areas. It's all about the taste. My father taught me that while he was still around. The swampy meat can be stronger, hard to get the wild taste out of it."

"Where are you from originally ... Cedric?"

"From hereabouts. I like it here so I stayed here, logged, worked as a guide at a

16

few hunting lodges and that kind of thing. I've done pretty well for myself I'd say. I own the land this house sits on and everything you see around it, all two hundred acres. As I said, I enjoy my own company so I keep to myself and prefer living off the grid. I don't like anybody telling me what to do, never have."

She checked the tape recorder to see if it was still functioning properly. It was. She was delighted with the way the interview was going. Cedric would make good copy.

"So you're a loner. I'm not surprised, going by the amount of time you spend in the woods, or do you hunt with a party? You used to hunt with your dad, so you must miss that."

"Yes I do. My father died when I was nine. He was a cold, hard man, but I still missed him. After that I hunted with an older cousin of mine for a few years until we started to not get along so well. I didn't always agree with everything he told me. I mean I did when I was a little kid. When I started to grow up I wanted to do things my own way you know, like anybody would. As it turned out I was a much better hunter than he was and he didn't like that. Used to get after me about it all the time. He's dead now too."

"I'm sorry to hear that you lost your father and your cousin."

"My father died at work, and its been more than forty years ago now since my cousin passed away. His name was Randall … Rand for short. Terrible accident."

Cedric seemed to be a man of sudden mood changes, and she watched him closely. "He was in an accident?"

"Yep!"

"An automobile accident you mean?"

"No, a hunting accident. They said he died instantly, if there is such a thing."

"That's dreadful! Did he trip and fall on his gun maybe?"

"No, he walked right into my shot. Any fool knows you should never do that, but old Rand wasn't too smart."

Ginger knew she was staring, uncharacteristically at a loss for words and aware that he was studying her.

"You know you've got very pretty eyes, Ginger, and I love that name by the way. You should have brown eyes with the name Ginger, something spicy; fiery, but then again I've always been a sucker for big blue eyes. And your hair is so dark, like mahogany. Do you colour it or something?"

Momentarily knocked off centre she recovered smoothly. "No, this is my natural hair colour. I'd like to talk a bit more about your cousin if it isn't too difficult for you. That must have been really awful."

"Because I shot my own cousin? I was cleared of any wrongdoing if that's what you're getting at. Hunting accidents happen."

"I hadn't meant to suggest...."

"Good. He knew I had a ten-point buck in my sights and the stupid fool walked right in front of me. Who does that? Rand cost me that buck, and he was the prettiest buck you'd ever want to see too."

"But your cousin...."

"Look, it was an accident. I've already explained that I'm a good shot. What do you want me to say? I can't bring him back. He was an idiot anyway, so it wasn't like I didn't do the world a favour. No one missed him that I could tell, least of all me. He was getting on my nerves something terrible at the time."

Ginger's stomach was definitely off now, devilled kidneys or not. She'd talked to some cold people in her life, but perhaps Cedric Gourney now held the distinction of being the coldest. He'd killed a man, although he'd said it was an accident, but it was his cavalier attitude that was so off-putting. She had to change the subject, for her own good.

"Soooo....," she began again, still struggling, meeting his eyes with an effort. "What was your first big game trophy?"

"That would be that moose right over there." He pointed to the brown shaggy

19

behemoth. "Wouldn't you agree that he's a real trophy?"

"He is big."

"Look at the set of antlers on him! He was a cagey old fella, but I managed to drop him and I might add that I don't hunt only for the trophies. I hunt for the meat, and I throw as little away as possible. Don't put me in the same category as those trophy hunters in Africa who kill lions and elephants and stuff. I don't agree with that at all. I am a responsible hunter. Make sure you put that in your story. I don't need a bunch of bleeding hearts getting on my case because they were misled by something you wrote."

"Of course, I'll make that point."

"And I don't hunt illegally. I always have a license and tag my kill. I don't need the police after me, saying I'm jacking deer or something. Listen carefully to what I'm telling you, Ginger. If you don't tell the truth I'll sue your newspaper, so remember that when you're writing all this up."

His mood seemed to be deteriorating. Maybe he'd want to change his mind and stop the interview, but she hoped not because he was giving her some great stuff. Well, except for the shooting.

"I will be accurate, Mr. Gourney...."

"Cedric. I told you to call me Cedric."

"Cedric. What I write will be fair and balanced and I won't misquote you. That's why I'm taping the interview. It's not really standard practice, but it's the way I like to do it so I can guarantee there'll be no mistakes."

"You do it whatever way you want, so long as you print things exactly as I say them. Don't twist anything around to make the story more exciting like some do. That's what would make me angry. Very angry."

"I won't twist anything, I promise. So tell me, Cedric," she said, pointing at the mounted moose head watching her balefully through glass eyes, "what's the story behind getting that moose? Did you have to track him for a long while? Use your moose whispering skills? You said he was cagey, so did he play cat and mouse with you? Would you say it was a battle between two old adversaries, the hunter and the hunted? Had you tried to get him before and he outwitted you?"

"First of all, as I've already told you, if I aim at something, it falls. The exception was that beautiful ten-point buck that got away because the bullet that was intended for him ended up elsewhere."

She paused. He was taking her back to his cousin's death, so she'd give him a chance to clarify himself. It just couldn't be as cut and dried as he'd made it out to be.

"That must have been a horrible experience."

He was pensive for a moment. "He was the type of person you were better off without. I for one did not cry at his funeral."

The interview had taken a dark turn. She needed to try to shift direction back to the moose because she was picking up on his anger, even now. He looked like a man you didn't want to cross. She wouldn't drill down any further about the hunting accident, which didn't sound like a hunting accident at all.

"So back to the moose," she said, determined to lighten the mood. "Tell me about the hunt, how you came to get him."

As quickly as his face clouded, it cleared, once again wreathed in a smile. "All I can say is he gave me one of the finest hunts I've ever had. He could cover some ground let me tell you. I was watching him for months, learning his habits, where he liked to hang out. He was a hit with the ladies too don't think he wasn't. When he called, the cows came running and he didn't waste any time if you know what I mean."

He eyed her meaningfully, his lips curling in a suggestive grin. "You do know what I mean, don't you?"

She met his gaze head on. She was no shrinking violet and she refused to be baited. "I know exactly what you mean. Moose season takes place during the annual rut, so I assume that's what they were doing, rutting."

Something passed over those small eyes of his, but it evaporated so quickly it was as though she might have imagined it.

"Correct. They were rutting, and I'm not above doing a little of that myself from time to time." He threw back his head and guffawed. "I would appreciate it you wouldn't include that last remark in the paper because people might get the wrong idea. I do want you to include the part about the animals rutting. It's not a bad thing you know."

"Of course it's not. It's simply nature."

He smiled again. "Yes. Nature. So anyway, I was ready for the first day of moose season that year," he said, returning to his story of how he had bagged the mounted trophy they now shared the room with. "Moose season is only for a few days you know, so you've got to have some idea of what you're going to do. Be ready, and I was. I'd been whispering to him in my own way for a long time and I was in the woods waiting just as it was coming light. When it was light enough, I called him. Did I mention that I make my own moose call out of birch bark? Well I do, and I have to say it's the finest one out there. Works every time. He came a running and then, kaboom. It was all over."

"Did you ever have a run in with a moose when it wasn't hunting season?"

"I just told you a few minutes ago that I don't hunt out of season. Now, Ginger, this isn't going to work if you're going to try and trick me because I guarantee you, you'll never outsmart Cedric Gourney. Not going to happen. Ever. I think you'll find ole Cedric is too smart for you."

"Okay, sorry, let me clarify. I did not mean to imply you would be hunting if you happened to see a moose, I meant you being a moose whisperer and all, have you ever had a moose encounter say when you didn't have a gun? If so, what did you do? How did you handle that?"

"First of all, sure, I've had a bunch of animal encounters when I didn't have a gun, moose included. If you've been in the woods as much as I have you're going to run into an animal. Up north there's places where the moose are pretty thick and I was walking along this old game path late one afternoon in the fall. A moose stepped right out in front of me. He couldn't have been more than ten feet away." He glanced back at the wall-mounted moose, then back at Ginger. "He was almost as big as him but not quite; maybe two or three years younger. His ears were flattened against his head and the hair on his hump was standing right up straight."

"That means he was angry."

"That means he probably had a cow moose nearby. He was ready to fight with

24

anything that came across his path, but I wasn't a threat to him."

"What did you do?"

"I stared him down and spoke to him for quite a while. He got the message."

That sounded a bit farfetched, but it was his quote. "What was the message?"

"What was the message! Don't mess with Cedric Gourney, that's what the message was."

"And how would he know you were Cedric Gourney?" She could barely keep from laughing. "Or were you following this one too? What did you say?"

He bristled. "Look at my eyes, Ginger. Take a good look and don't look away. Come on, do it."

She found herself doing as he asked.

"Now tell me, would you want to mess with me if you didn't have to? That's what I said to the moose. I whisper to them and they listen. Anyway, I stared him down, said my piece and then I continued on my way to where my truck was parked. I didn't break a single bead of sweat. I don't get excited about things, but I do get what I want. That's why I've been so successful."

Ginger was starting to feel uncomfortable, especially after his repeated declarations about his determination to always get what he wanted. She could really do something with this story. Cedric was very quotable, but she had already taken a disliking to this guy. He had called his cousin an idiot? Cedric Gourney was an idiot of the first order. A chill crept over her as she ploughed ahead to her next question.

The roll of thunder sounded in the distance and the wind had begun to pick up. It seemed the weather forecasters were accurate with their storm prediction. She could see through the narrow gap in the curtains that the sky had darkened significantly.

"Let's talk about bears," she said, trying to inject light heartedness into her tone.

"What do you want to know, darlin'?"

"How about the first bear you ever saw?"

He pointed to one of the bears mounted on the wall. "That was the first bear I ever saw, right there. It took me awhile to track him, but I got him."

"I thought you had to bait bears. I was in a bear stand once and the bear came to us."

"Not me, I tracked this one."

"Seriously?"

"Seriously! I'm a bear expert too. I have baited bears, yes, working as a guide. That's the way it's typically done, but the bear you see up there was giving me trouble; raiding my chicken coop. So I waited for him and when he went into the woods I followed and that was the end of Mr. Bear."

"Oh I see. Do you whisper to bears too?"

"Nah, they wouldn't listen."

She truly did have to struggle to keep a smile off her face. "What advice would you have for other bear hunters out there, perhaps someone who was new to it and could use a tip or two?"

"Here's the best tip of all," he said with a wide grin. "Don't miss."

She did smile at that one and got the laugh out of her system. "That's a good point. And how many bears do you think you've bagged over the years, Mr. ... Cedric?"

"Quite a few, that's for sure, but then sometimes the bear almost gets me. One time a bear followed me for a mile or two. It wasn't hunting season, and it was way back up country and coming on dark. Now bears are curious creatures and it's likely he was only checking me out, but they can't be completely trusted because they are known to be unpredictable. So here I was in the middle of nowhere, and a bear a few yards behind me and getting closer all the time."

"What did you do, try to scare him off?"

"Yep! One trick is to pull the bottom of your jacket up over your head to make yourself look bigger, taller, and let him know you don't want him around. You can yell, throw sticks at him, rocks, whatever comes to hand. Most of the time they'll take the hint and leave."

"But not always, or I should probably say not in this case probably."

"You're right. Nothing was scaring him off and he just kept getting closer and closer and I knew my luck had to change or I was in big trouble."

"Oh my gosh, what did you do?"

"I knew there was an old camp not far from where I was and I also knew I didn't have very much time to make it there. He was getting closer by the minute."

"Did you run?"

"Worst thing you can do is try to outrun a bear because it can't be done. A bear doesn't look very streamlined and his walk looks awkward, but they can actually run about thirty-five miles per hour. They can outrun a racehorse."

"Really?"

"Really! Check it out if you want to, you'll see I'm telling you the truth."

"You could always climb a tree I suppose."

"That's true, but not as fast as they could. A bear can be to the top of a tree in seconds. They are supremely adapted to their environment, and when you go in the woods you're in their territory."

"So I take it you made it to the camp all right."

"I'm here aren't I? I made it with not a moment to spare and thankfully the door was not locked. It's a rule of the wilderness that camps should be left unlocked in case someone needs food or shelter. I got inside and got the door locked just as he was about to start nipping at my heels. It was a close call all right, and he was a big brute. Once inside I got a lamp lit, made a fire, found some food and settled in for the night. In the morning he was long gone and I continued on my way."

"You're brave."

"Nine-five percent of bears won't bother you. You just have to abide by their rules when you're in their home. If you do happen to see a bear in the woods, give them lots of room. If you're camping, be careful with your food. What I mean by that is don't eat in your tent if you don't want to have them come calling. For women I'd say don't camp in the woods during that time of the month."

Ginger felt her face colour at his frankness.

"Sorry to embarrass you, darlin', but those are the facts and knowing them might save your life someday."

"Have you ever encountered a mother bear with cubs?"

He nodded, obviously enjoying the opportunity to reminisce. "Just once and that day I did think I was done for. Again, I was out in the woods carousing a piece of land that I intended to cut logs on. I stopped by a thicket to light a cigarette and heard a blatt. I'd scared a cub who yelled for its momma. I could hear her coming like a freight train through the underbrush to protect her baby, heading right for me."

She felt her eyes widen, picturing the predicament he was in. "What did you do?"

"I spied a piece of wood lying practically at my feet and I grabbed it. When she reared up on her hind legs I swung, but I barely touched her. See this scar on my cheek?" he pointed to a narrow white line just above his cheekbone. "That's where she got me when she swiped at me with one of her paws. By that time I had the stick over my shoulder again and I unloaded on her with everything I had in me. I caught her right on the snout which is the most vulnerable spot."

"Why didn't you aim for her head?"

"Bears have thick, strong skulls that even rifle bullets might not get through. It would have likely broken the stick if I hadn't connected with her snout. My blow brought blood and she immediately dropped to all fours and took off, her cub right behind her."

"That's unbelievable! You're lucky to be alive. Would you say a bear is the most dangerous animal in the woods?"

"No, I would not say that. I would say a cow moose with a calf is by far one of the most dangerous. She'd kill you as quick as she looked at you with those front feet of hers, if she had the chance."

"Don't tell me a cow moose tried to kill you too."

"She chased me with intent to harm, I have no doubt about that. I did make it up a tree that time and that's where I stayed for a few hours until she and her calf decided to move on. I talked to her, that's why she left."

She could maybe see why his moose whispering worked. If she had to listen to him for any length of time she'd want to leave too.

"Why do you even go in the woods if it's that dangerous?"

He laughed. "It's not like that every time. I've been traipsing through the woods all my life and I've only had a handful of bad experiences. They're bound to happen."

"Once would be enough for me, thank you very much."

"Walking in the woods, being in nature, is a feeling like no other. I wouldn't trade my experiences for anything, and I don't intend to stop anytime soon."

Chapter Two

Ginger thought about her own time in the woods, how much she loved it, and knew she couldn't agree with him more. True, she was a city girl, had been all her life, but it wasn't like she didn't get out into nature. She was an avid hiker who took to the woods like someone who'd been born to it. Walking itself was a great all-around exercise, but there was nothing quite like a walk in the woods to soothe the soul. Doing the same in the city or even in the suburbs was a poor substitute.

"I can tell by the expression on that beautiful face of yours, Ginger, that you agree with me. Why don't you come with me some day and I'll show you the finer points of a walk in nature."

"I'm not a hunter in any way shape or form," she said quickly. "I don't judge people who do it because I know there are some who are trying to feed their families. But to kill something for the sport of it, to take the life of something that values theirs as much as I do my own, that I don't agree with."

"I didn't say we were going to kill anything, did I?"

"No, and thank you for the offer but I will have to decline. Now…."

"Why would you have to decline?"

"Because I don't mix my personal life with my work life."

He did not look pleased … at all. "It was just a friendly offer, don't go all snooty city girl on me now. Don't you look down on me!"

She forced a smile, more to defuse what could become a touchy situation than to show any real friendliness. "I'm not like that, so I don't do that. Again, thank you for the suggestion, but I think we should get on with the interview." She looked pointedly at her watch. "I'm sorry but I have something scheduled for this evening and our time is slipping away."

"We have all the time in the world, Ginger. Gee I love saying your name. I'll bet you're a spicy little thing too."

She glanced at the window and could see through the curtains that the sky had darkened even more over the past half hour. The wind had begun to pummel the branches of nearby trees as they scratched angrily against the side of house.

"Yes," he said, seeing her glance toward the window, "the weather is starting to get quite bad out there. I think you're going to find that you'll have to stay here for the night. As you might recall, you went over a bridge just after you turned onto my lane. If we get the amount of rain I think we will, that creek will jump its banks faster than you can say jackrabbit."

"Isn't it inconvenient to live in a flood zone?"

"I've got a four-wheel drive so that doesn't mean anything to me. You came here in a dinky little two-door and honey, you ain't going nowhere when that water starts to rise."

Fear spiked through her. Trapped? Here? With him? Yee gods! She reached for her tape recorder. "Maybe you're right, perhaps I should be on my way now if you say it's going to be as bad as that. I also have a day job and I'd have to be at work on Monday morning."

"You're not a full-time reporter?"

"No, but I certainly spend the majority of my free time at it."

He smirked. "That tells me you don't have a man taking any of your attention if you have enough time to work two jobs."

She flushed. "I am a professional, Mr. Gourney, and I would prefer to keep this on a professional level."

"What's your other job, can I ask you that much?"

"I'm an office manager," she answered tightly.

"Aw, now I've gone and made you mad, but I don't see why. You're asking me questions, why can't I ask you any?"

"Because you contacted the newspaper office and asked to appear in my column. To do that I have to conduct an interview which means I ask you questions."

"Fair enough, now turn the tape recorder back on. I was only joshing you about the flooding. It does, but not enough that you couldn't get through, even in your little car. Relax and let's continue with the interview. I'm just having some fun with you. I guess I've been on my own too long and I'm enjoying the company. Go ahead, darlin', ask me another question. I'm all ears."

"All right, going back to an earlier question, what would you say is the most dangerous animal in New Brunswick woods?"

"Me," he said with a straight face then laughed uproariously. "Okay, I'll be serious. The answer would be a bear or a moose under the right circumstances, but then maybe not. You also have to consider if the animal in question might be sick, as in rabies, in which case they behave out of character and will in all likelihood attack."

"What would you say is the animal people might be least likely to think will attack?"

He thought for a moment. "That would be the otter."

"The otter! Those sweet little things? I assume you mean the river otter."

"That's what I mean all right. They can indeed attack, and have. Again, check it out online. There are some vicious otter attacks on record. If they feel their young are threatened, or you're invading their territory, or they wake up in a bad mood one day, watch out. When you do look it up you'll see some of the pictures of otter bites and you won't think they're sweet little things anymore. Anything that has teeth and claws can do harm, like a cougar, and yes I believe they are out there because I've seen plenty of cougar signs. A lynx, bobcat … even a skunk or a raccoon can attack if they're rabid, any animal, so it's a very open-ended question. Really though, the larger predators are the most dangerous … any predator."

When Cedric wasn't acting like a fool he really was very interesting, with a vast wealth of knowledge. She knew this piece would have its colourful tone, but it would also be informative, in his anecdotal context. She would get the most out of it that she could.

"So you say you've seen signs that cougars are in New Brunswick woods?"

"Absolutely. These fancy scientists say no, but I say yes because I'm in the woods more in any given year than they ever will be. They come out of their office every now and then and take a walk in the forest. Then go back and write their hypotheses; say there are no cougars here. They're wrong."

"What cougar signs have you seen exactly?"

"Well for one thing I've seen actual cougars on more than one occasion, and I've heard them. Way back in the woods; remote areas of the province."

"Heard them?"

"Yes, heard them. They vocalize at night and let me tell you, darlin', once you've heard a cougar scream you'll never forget it. It sounds like a terrified woman's scream and it would stop your heart. I was camping one night and about three in the morning I heard a cougar scream not a hundred yards away, down by the river. A few minutes later it came again. Something had woken me out of a deep sleep and I figure it was that. I heard it a couple of more times. If that doesn't get your attention, nothing will. I guarantee it."

"What happened then?"

"What happened? Nothing happened. It went on its way I assume. I tried to go back to sleep, but a cougar scream will get you plenty juiced up. I was awake the rest of the night. The next morning I went to the river and there right by the water was a perfect set of cougar prints. It must have been getting a drink."

"Did you have a camera with you?"

"I wasn't carrying a camera with me but I do take lots of other pictures," he aid pointing to the albums and carton on the coffee table. "I travelled pretty light when I went into the woods. That was before digital cameras came out and now I do slip a small camera into my shirt pocket in case I see something unusual. You might know though I've never seen prints like that again."

"Have you seen any scat ... droppings?"

"I know what scat is, honey, and the answer is yes. I have."

"Did you bring some in for testing by biologists?"

"And do their job for them? Let them get out and go in the woods and find it for themselves. They're the ones who are getting paid the big bucks. Besides, I don't have to prove cougars are out there, they have to prove to me they aren't. So far they haven't been able to. I know what I know, and I know what's happening in the woods in New Brunswick, both with the woodlots and the animals. I make it my business to know."

"Do bobcats or lynx scream?"

"They have their own unique vocalizations, but nothing quite so hair-raising as the cougar. It's in a class all by itself in my opinion."

"Do bobcat and lynx kill deer?"

"I've seen where they've taken deer. A bear will too, and for sure will appropriate another predator's kill, like maybe a coyote pack that's been hunting. Again the so-called experts might disagree but I've seen evidence of it, and I doubt they have. I don't want it to look like I'm completely trashing them, it's just that I know more through hands-on experience."

"Right. And speaking of predators ... and prey, I suppose all animals have their alarm call ... or mating call for that matter."

"Ummm hmmm. Now here's a funny story you might want to use. I was walking in the woods one day and I heard these ungodly shrieks coming from a thicket, so I had to sneak over and see what the heck it was. It seemed like there was more than one animal and I was right. There were two."

"They were fighting?"

"They were mating."

"Oh. What animals were they?"

"Porcupines. I swear to God, that's what I saw ... and heard."

She laughed. "That's funny."

"Not to the porcupines, apparently."

"Have you seen many bobcats or lynx?" she asked, checking the tape recorder again for volume.

"A few, but they're both very shy. I consider myself lucky if I see either one of those animals because they're really beautiful."

What are some of the lesser-known animals you've come across in your travels?

"Let me see, there's pine martens, fishers, flying squirrels, badgers, things like that. I once came upon a deer giving birth. They like to get down by a brook where it's more secluded to have their young. They can better protect them there. This one was having triplets, which meant it was a good year. See, numbers can get low for whatever reason, including a brutal winter, but nature has a way of replenishing itself; balancing everything out. That is if something isn't hunted to extinction or killed just because they happen to be a predator and no one wants them around. That isn't fair. Sometimes a population can't recover from what man has done to it, like the caribou that used to be here in New Brunswick. They've been gone for many years now. You can't take more than what you're entitled to. That's the way I feel about it. I have always played by the rules with animals, never taken more than what was my fair share."

"Absolutely right," she agreed. "Do you still frequent the woods?"

"Am I often in the woods! Like I said, I make it my business to be in the woods from one end of this province to the other, and I know what's going on. And another thing, I have seen more than one wolf here in New Brunswick. Put that in your article and watch the tongues start wagging. The last time was about ten years ago. Again, if I had a camera I could have gotten a picture of his track. Believe you me, it was huge."

"You actually saw a wolf?"

"I did, but 'oh no, Cedric,' they say, 'you're wrong. There are no wolves in New Brunswick.' But I say, you miss a lot when you're not out in the woods on a regular basis. Just because the experts haven't seen them, doesn't mean they're not there. Any woodsman I know will definitely back me up."

"If you saw one would you shoot it?"

"No, I would not, unless there was a season for it. But the further I go along in this life the more I dislike killing animals. Maybe I will really get into cameras one day. I know some great places to get pictures."

"Shoot with a camera instead of a gun."

"There's nothing wrong with hunting, I'm not saying it's wrong or anything. I'm just talking about me."

"Okay. Now you've mentioned some very scary moments you've experienced in the woods. But you must have had plenty of other unusual experiences in life too. Can you think of any?"

The smile was back. "Yes, Ma'am, I certainly can."

"All right, would you care to share what was perhaps the most frightening? The one you wondered oh, what's going to happen to me?"

"Yep. I know exactly what you mean."

"All right then, can I ask you what that was?"

"You sure can. It was when I met you face to face."

She was thrown off centre yet again by this sudden turn in the conversation. "Oh, I mean...."

"I love it when you light up, Ginger. Just come here, I want to show you something."

"Ahh, no. I'm fine right here."

"Come on!" he coaxed her. "It's in this little room right here." He pointed to a door not five feet away, one of the two presided over by the giant moose. "It's not like I'm asking you to go to my bedroom."

"Mr. Gourney...."

"So we're back to Mr. Gourney. I told you, it's Cedric. You're Ginger and I'm Cedric. I don't want you to be scared of me, Ginger, so just come as far as the doorway because there's something you need to see to believe. I'm giving you permission to switch off your trusty little tape recorder and look at what I have to show you."

"Really, I...."

"You'll make me angry if you don't accept this invitation, Ginger. I think it will find a place in your story."

Stop acting like this, she reprimanded herself. People often had something they wanted to share during interviews, something meaningful to them whether it be a picture, an object.... Why behave like a ninny and refuse to look? So he was being a little frisky, so what? She'd certainly encountered enough of that, especially with some older men who sometimes seemed to think they had earned the right to misbehave. Cedric was likely harmless. Still, she'd be glad when she was done and on her way home because the wind truly had increased its intensity, rattling the windows. Look at what he wants you to see, get back to the interview and within minutes she'd be finished. Maybe there was another mounted animal in there, another one of his woodland treasures.

"Sure, what is it you want to show me?" she asked before switching the machine off and stepping away from the coffee table.

"Come and take a peek inside," he beckoned as he opened the door. "I think you need to see this before we go any further. I know you'll be impressed."

He stepped into the room and she made her way to the entrance, her jaw literally dropping. At one end stood an enormous bookcase, crammed with hardcover books. He was apparently an avid reader, but she couldn't believe what the surrounding walls were papered with. There didn't seem to be a spare inch that wasn't covered by newspaper clippings, and they were all of her and her stories. Her photo, featured in the column masthead, had been enlarged and comprised a major part of the display. She could only stare.

"Cat got your tongue?" he asked, obviously pleased at what he seemed to take as a favourable reaction. "What do you say? Do you like it?"

It was the first time she'd ever seen a shrine dedicated to ... herself. "I ... I ..."

"I'm a fan, Ginger, have been for years as you can tell from this room." He pointed to an empty frame leaning against the wall. "This is for the story you're doing on me, and this," he pointed to yet another frame "is for the place of honour in the living room, right over the sofa. I'm going to take down what's there now and put the new one up when it's ready."

Ginger's creep metre was off the charts. She'd always hoped she had established a following, people who enjoyed her work as she chose stories that would appeal to the paper's considerable readership. This was over the top though. She couldn't imagine in her wildest dreams why anyone would get so carried away about a newspaper column and the everyday person who wrote it.

"What will be in that?" she asked, pointing to the frame in question.

"Why a picture of me and you, what else? I've got a picture somewhere around here of me and big game hunter Chip Porter when he was in town. I was lucky enough to have my picture taken with him, but one of you and me together would be my prized possession. We could take like a selfie ... come on! You wouldn't deny me that would you?"

Without speaking she retraced her steps to the armchair and reclaimed it as though she had reached safe harbour, which was ridiculous because she was still on his turf. She'd wind this thing up and hit the road, storm or no storm. This had gotten too crazy.

He resumed his seat on the sofa. "You'll let me take a picture of us together, right? That's the real reason I bought a digital camera. I can't imagine you'd say no to the person who is probably your biggest fan."

"I really don't like having my picture taken," she said, stalling for time.

"But you're gorgeous! Those big blue eyes, that cute little hairdo of yours, the pink roses in your cheeks. And you're so tiny! I hadn't realized you were no bigger than a leprechaun."

If there was anything she disliked it was being called tiny. A leprechaun! Really! She didn't go around commenting on people's sizes. Oh, you're so tall! As if that had escaped the person's notice. Maybe people meant well, but why comment at all? And she certainly wasn't tiny at five foot six. Maybe smaller than him, but the whole thing was silly. She saw herself as quite average looking. She was not the world beauty he seemed to think she was. Maybe it had been awhile since he'd been with a woman.

"Okay, thank you for the support. We really appreciate that."

"We?"

"The newspaper. That's who I represent."

"And who do I represent?"

"The readership of course."

"That's it? The readership? I'm a lot more than that. I'm a fan. I don't think I've missed even one of your columns. You've been writing them for three years, eight months and two weeks. I'll bet no one else in your readership does that for you."

She smiled stiffly, an act of sheer determination. "Well, we like to sell newspapers and I am being sincere when I say thank you for that kind of support. We need more readers like you."

"You don't get it do you? Or are you being deliberately obtuse?"

He never ceased to amaze her. At first he came off like a country bumpkin, an aw shucks kind of guy, but he seemed to have the vocabulary of a well-read, intelligent man. He was difficult to read, and shifted moods faster than a race car driver shifted gears.

"I'm not trying to be anything, other than perhaps polite … professional," she tried again. "Now I'd like to continue with the interview. I only have a few more questions before we wrap things up and I'm on my way."

He stared at her in that unnerving way of his, his eyes glittering black glass. "Very well, but I warn you, Ginger, we are going to take that picture. I don't feel that's a lot to ask seeing as how I'm taking the time to bare my soul. I think if I improve your circulation, up your sales, that should be worth a little bonus. This is going to be a fabulous story and that tired old rag you work for could use a little shot in the arm from someone like me."

She busied herself turning the tape recorder back on.

"Did you hear what I said?" he asked, perturbed.

"Yes, I did."

"The New Chronicle is a second rate newspaper with a third rate editor behind the desk. Foster McDougall is as useless as they come. He'll never compete with the big boys here in Franklin. For one thing he won't print anything bad about any of his friends. One of his cronies got picked up for drinking and driving and there wasn't one word about it in the paper. Not one! Then poor old Lester Simpson, someone he doesn't like, gets nabbed for the same thing and he puts it on the front page; says it's because he prints the truth. It's enough to make you sick, but having said that there are good points about your little paper too, besides your column. It's going to take me a minute or two to think of what they are, but maybe it's the want ads. Stuff like that, but the way you guys report the news is a joke. It's so slanted it's disgusting."

"Really, Cedric, the New Chronicle may be small compared to others in the city, but it has a faithful following. I think you're being unfair in your criticism of it."

He hooted. "Unfair! Who are your followers, other than someone outstanding like me? I'll tell you who they are, a bunch of old biddies looking for the recipe of the week, or about somebody's vacation to Alberta, or Maine, or St. George. It's pathetic and I can't imagine you don't know that. Or who visited who for the weekend; who's home from the west for a week. It's

48

all in there. The only thing the New Chronicle is good for is wrapping fish, other than that....

"That's why I called and offered myself for a story in your column. I knew it'd be great. Things need to get livened up over there, wake some people up and I'm just the guy to do it. I'm not afraid to speak out, and you can quote me on all of this if you want. Go ahead, somebody's got to say it. Old Foster will probably have me arrested if you do print it, and if that ever happened there's no doubt in my mind that it would make the front page. That'd be good too because I don't mind loosening things up a bit."

She had to laugh. "It's not as bad as all that. For one thing I know you're a subscriber. So why would you subscribe to a substandard newspaper? I think you're just pulling my leg," and immediately regretted her choice of words.

"I'd like to pull your leg, but that's beside the point. Maybe I am just trying to get you going, but really, why don't you quit your job managing an office and take over the paper? Now there's what should happen! You'd be good at it, Ginger."

"I think you're misjudging Mr. McDougall just a little."

"Oh cut the crap!" he snapped furiously, surprising her yet again. "I go back a lot further than you do with Foster McDougall.

49

Foster's problem is that he doesn't have any cahonies, if you know what I mean. No backbone is I guess the way I should say it to a lady, but never mind. I'm glad you're here and I'm sure you're going to give the people a really good story. How could it be anything but good with me in it, right?"

Her smile felt frozen, and the best she could do right now was tough it out and finish.

"Right. So let's return to my earlier question of what the scariest thing you have ever had happen to you, other than in the woods."

"I told you, meeting you."

"Okay, besides that."

"Aren't you going to ask what was so scary about meeting you?"

She sighed, suddenly weary. "Okay, what was so scary about meeting me?"

"Your eyes. I've never been looked at like that before … I mean through eyes that shade of blue. That scares a man. It feels like if I got too close I could fall right into those things. If that isn't scary, I don't know what is."

She blinked, never having been told such a thing, unsure of how to respond, other than to keep pressing on through this foolishness.

"And now you're batting your eyes at me," he announced. "What are you trying to do to me anyway?"

"Cedric ... Mr. Gourney. I have to be honest and tell you I'm uncomfortable with all of this. If you're not interested in continuing with the interview, we'll stop and I'll go with what I've got. I think I have enough anyway to write a good piece. You've shared some very interesting experiences and insights with me."

"Don't get your girdle in a snap. Didn't mean to upset you. What's the scariest thing that's ever happened to me outside of being in the woods? It was when my wife almost died."

That was the first time he'd mentioned a wife. There were indeed female touches to the spartan décor, but she was pretty sure there was no woman on the premises now.

"Do you want to talk about it? I mean if you're comfortable doing so. I don't expect you to share those details otherwise."

He shrugged. "I don't mind talking about it because it happened a long time ago. My wife was only thirty-two when she had an aneurism and I was told she might not live the night. The thought of being without her was absolutely terrifying. We were best friends, buddies, since we were kids. We fell in love while we were still teenagers. We did everything together, and I mean everything. She was right by my side when I was hunting. In fact it was her that bagged that animal on the wall in back of you. She was as sure a shot as they come. I loved everything about her."

"And you almost lost her? That's dreadful, but I take it she survived her ordeal."

"She did. She was rushed into surgery and luckily they got it before any real damage was done, but it was a while before I knew which way it was going to go. Thankfully she survived, although it was a long road back before she completely recovered. I looked after her day and night, refused to let anyone else near her because I wanted to do it all on my own. I would take her out into the woods, on a good smooth trail, and push her in her wheelchair."

"Wow! You were very devoted to her. That's wonderful."

"I wanted her to be able to smell the woods, hear the birds, not just sit in a truck and try to get all that through an open window. Those trips in the woods did her a world of good and she came back a lot faster than they thought she would. They even said there might be some cognitive impairment, but we got very lucky and there wasn't. Not a thing wrong with her vision or hearing. I had my Annabelle back the way she was before she got sick. So to answer your question, almost losing her was the scariest thing in my life."

"I can certainly understand that. Had you been together long when that happened?"

"We were married when we were seventeen years old, Ginger. I guess when you meet the right one, you know. Why wait, right? We had a hunting wedding here at the house."

Ginger looked at him quizzically. "A hunting wedding?"

"That's right, a hunting wedding. We were married in deer season, all dressed in hunter orange, right here in this room. There was a picture of it in the paper at the time. Have you ever been married, Ginger?"

"Ahhh," she said evasively, again unprepared for yet another sudden turn.

"Am I getting too personal on you again?"

She nodded, trying to move on. "Did you and Annabelle have a wedding cake? Guests?"

"Sure, my mother baked a nice little cake for us and we had a few people here. It was a lot of fun. You should try it some time."

"A hunting wedding?"

"Any kind of wedding."

"Right, and now, back to your wedding. That must have been pretty unusual for the time. Now people do those sorts of things, but I guess you would have been considered a bit of a trend setter at the time, wouldn't you?"

He smiled. "I guess so, but it didn't matter. We thought alike, Annabelle and I. If she had said she wanted to get married on the moon I would have found a way to get there."

"She must have been from around here too, was she?"

"She and her parents moved here from where they lived uptown when she was in first grade. She was not happy to come and live in the country, but she adjusted real fast. She was good that way. She could go along with just about anything someone suggested. She was a big strong gal. Maybe that's why I think of you as tiny. I was used to a much bigger woman. She could handle any man."

The wind slammed against the side of the house in a powerful gust, the daylight continuing to fade. Thankfully she was nearly finished. She still had to take photos though and that in itself could eat up time. She'd been looking forward to looking through his pictures, but she'd forego those now if she could without offending him. An hour or two with Cedric Gourney was more than enough.

"Annabelle sounds like quite a woman. Would you like to mention the rest of your family too? Children? Grandchildren? It's entirely up to you if you don't want to make it too personal."

He shrugged again. "No big deal to me. We only had the one child, a son, Stilwell, named after my grandfather on my mother's side. My son never married so there aren't any grandchildren, which is too bad. So family get-togethers are a little thin these days. Don't have much of a Christmas list either now that I think about it."

"Forgive me for saying this, Cedric, but you seem to mention Annabelle as though she's in the past. Is she no longer part of your life? Again, if you'd rather not talk about it…."

"It doesn't matter to me. Annabelle's been dead now for quite a while. It was right around this time of year that she passed away unexpectedly."

"I'm very sorry to hear that. Did she have another aneurism?"

"No, I killed her."

Chapter Three

Shane settled the large takeout coffee in the console cup holder of his SUV. It would need to cool a few degrees before he could drink it. He wasn't one of those guys who liked his beverages scalding hot. The idea was to put out a fire, not start one.

He drove to the cemetery on auto pilot. With heavy weather moving in he'd decided to make an unscheduled Saturday morning visit rather than wait until this afternoon. It was not the time of week he usually brought roses to April's grave, but this was an important visit nonetheless.

Not surprisingly, the closer he got the more he thought about her and their life together as man and wife. They'd met young, fallen in love while they were still teenagers although they'd decided to go their separate ways when they finished high school. They'd both been agreeable to the split, knowing it was the right time to explore other possibilities; meet new people. He had gone to Dalhousie University in Halifax, just because it was a little further from home with lots of room to spread his wings. April hadn't been as adventurous, choosing the University of New Brunswick to pursue a nursing degree.

They hadn't kept in touch, other than an awkward encounter when they were home on spring break, running into each other at a local club. At that time she'd been seeing Jason Bennett and he'd had Tilda Halverston on his arm.

When he'd finished university, he wasn't ready to move back to Franklin. So he applied and was accepted into the Ontario Provincial Police, or OPP, where he underwent his police training. He'd spent six years working in Ontario before opting to return home, and he wasn't back long before he decided to look April up. He'd heard through the grapevine that she still lived in the city and worked at Bayview General. Most importantly of all, she was single. So they'd picked up the pieces and carried on as though they'd never been apart, until death had separated them for good three years ago.

Slowing, he turned into the main entrance of Sprucewood Gardens and followed the gravelled drive to where April's grave was located. He sat there for a few moments deep in thought before climbing out and going to stand beside the pink granite headstone that bore her name. He never visited her grave that he didn't think about the night she died.

He'd been at work when he received the news, and he'd never forget the sergeant stopping him in the hallway, asking to speak with him privately. It was urgent. His gut told him it had something to do with April, and it had. She'd been killed instantly in a wreck out near the highway.

He brought his thoughts back to the present as he stood looking at the headstone, then down at last week's pink roses, now withered and brown.

"Hi April," he began, dry-eyed, used now to talking to his late wife in this way. "This is a hard thing I have to say, but I've been doing a lot of thinking. It's time, April, time to let you go. I know that's what you'd want because we talked about it one time. We both agreed that if something like this ever happened to either one of us, we'd eventually have to move on. I never thought I could ever do that, but lately I've started to feel differently. It's time to move ahead with my life. I'll always love you, you know that, but now I feel ready."

A feeling swept over him. It was as though she was telling him she understood, but it was likely only him wanting to sense her approval. Not that he needed it, he understood that of course, but the time truly had come to let go of the past. When they'd agreed that if one of them was ever lost they'd move on with their lives, he'd figured they'd never have to worry about that. They'd grow old together, so no problem. Not a week after they'd had that conversation, she was gone.

Part of him still felt like he was abandoning her, but a bigger, more fundamental part of him knew he was making the right decision, as difficult as it was.

"April, honey, I won't be bringing any more flowers. I hope you understand. I'm lonely and I can't keep holding on because I know you're never coming back."

That's when the tears came. He knew this would be hard, but not this damn hard. He was speaking aloud, from his heart, a conversation he'd been having with himself for the last few months. It had taken almost that long to have the guts to come here and say it to his dead wife.

The tears continued as he went down on one knee in front of the monument, but there was not the endless wellspring there had been in the early days. After a few minutes he dried his eyes, thankful he had healed enough to be able to come here and do this. He'd wondered if that time would ever come. Now it had and so he stood, hands on the stone, and whispered: "I will always love you," one more time. He turned to go. He glanced back at the roses, wiped his eyes again with the backs of his hands, then returned to his vehicle.

He was surprised to feel a weight lifted from his shoulders. He'd done something he didn't believe he'd ever be strong enough to do, make the decision to move on. Some might say it was silly to make that announcement to a dead woman, but that's what he felt in his heart was right for him. He had decided to open up the space beside him for someone to come into his life. For many years that space had been occupied by his wife, both living and dead. Now he had done what he needed to do. The rest was up to fate.

Just as he was leaving he spied a vehicle moving slowly toward him, the battered old green half-ton rolling to a stop as Shane lowered his window.

"Hey, Hank. How's it going?" he asked the cemetery caretaker.

The white-haired man nodded. "It's going fine, Shane. It's only Saturday, are you bringing flowers for the missus?" he asked personally.

Shane and the caretaker had become pretty good friends over the past three years. Hank was often here either mowing or clipping or plowing snow when Shane made his weekly visits. Hank took his job seriously and kept the place in superb condition. He'd even been somewhat of a confidante to the young police officer,

60

lending an ear when Shane was at his lowest point. That's when Hank had laid a hand on his shoulder, letting Shane know he wasn't alone.

Shane looked away. Could he possibly share the nature of this visit with his kindly friend? He certainly didn't have to, it was nobody's business but his own. He wasn't one to open up easily, but he knew Hank cared about him, much like a father would a son. Lord knew he wasn't close to his own father. He hadn't even turned to him when April was killed.

"This is kind of a special visit," Shane began, actually wanting to talk, but not knowing how to begin. He looked off toward a lofty oak tree, it's widespread limbs shading a number of older graves on the west corner.

"It's personal, I understand," Hank said quietly. "Tell me what's on your mind only if it will help you get past something, otherwise you're not obligated to share it. You don't owe anybody any explanations, son."

"No," Shane protested quickly, "I guess I do need to say what's on my mind," and knew he could do so with Hank and not be judged.

Pulling onto the shoulder so other vehicles could get past, Hank put his truck in park and shut off the engine. The clattering rattle slowly wheezed to a stop as he did so. If ever there was a truck that needed a tune-up, it was this one. It had to be over forty years old and he guessed that Hank had been its owner for at least that long.

"Why don't you park over there," Hank suggested, pointing to the other side of the road, "and bring your coffee with you. We'll sit here awhile and talk. It might help to get a few things off your mind. Come on, I've got some time. Do you have a few minutes?"

Shane glanced at the illuminated dash clock. "Yeah, I've got plenty of time and I'd like that. To talk I mean."

Shane parked his vehicle and climbed into Hank's trusty old pick-up, settling in as they sat at the side of the cemetery road.

"You look like you're having a bad day. Old memories cropping up maybe?" Hank asked to get the conversation rolling. He always knew the right things to say to get him to open up.

Shane was silent for a moment. "You know, I remember the day of the accident like it was yesterday, or a few hours ago. It's burned into my memory like nothing else I've ever had to go through. Mum dying when I was a kid was no picnic either. I've heard it said that sudden death is worse, and it is. I guess I should know that too because as a police officer I've had to give so many death notices to loved ones.

That's a terrible part of the job. A cop never gets used to that no matter how many years they've been doing it."

"And then you end up inside the same nightmare."

"Yep. Nothing can prepare you for that, no training … nothing."

"That's right. But unless I miss my guess you have something of a different nature on your mind today."

Shane took a long drink of coffee before responding. "I do. I think it's time to let go, Hank. Not of her memory, never that, but I know April wouldn't want me living in the past like I've been doing. She'd want me to move on. I'm still sleeping in the guest room for heaven's sake because I've pretty much turned the bedroom we shared together into a shrine. All her things are still set out, just as she left them, including her picture. I never even changed the sheets from the last time we slept together. How crazy is that?"

"Not crazy at all. Those are the actions of a man whose heart has been broken. We do what we have to do to get through times like that, some of the awful things that are thrown at us. When my Edna died I used to hug her pillow every night and pretend it was her. I prayed to God to let her come to me in a dream, talk to me, but it never happened."

"And do you still do that?"

"No. I eventually healed enough to be able to move on. I did it for a while though, I guess you could say for as long as I needed to. It's been a lot of years now since I lost my wife."

"Did you ever remarry?"

"Yes, a few years ago. I met a lovely woman, Mary, and she was a widow. It's never really the same as your first love, but you can love again and that's the way it is with me. Mary understands where I'm coming from because her husband passed away a year or so after Edna did. She knows what loss feels like. How hard it is."

Shane took another swig of coffee before returning his attention to the caretaker. "That's what's going on with me, but I feel like I'm dishonouring her memory or something."

"You're not dishonouring her memory at all. Life goes on. Have you met someone?"

Shane shook his head. "Not really. There's this one woman though. I see her at the coffee shop from time to time. I think she works at an office near there. I've been thinking about asking her out, but I'm not sure. Sometimes I think I'm going to do it. You know, introduce myself and see if she'd be interested in getting together, and the next I think I'm just not ready. But one thing I do know and am trying to make peace with is that I've decided to move on, live my life. I have to leave April in the past, and as long as I come here every week with flowers it's like I can never break that tie."

"It's tough, but you're a young man. How old are you, thirty-two? Thirty-three?"

"I just turned thirty-six."

"Well like I say, you're a young man. You have to go on with your life. She'd want you to."

"That's what we talked about one time. It wasn't long before she was killed actually, but it's just that I feel so damned guilty. I feel like I'm breaking my wedding vows or something. I mean how do I stop bringing roses to her grave after I've been doing it every week for three years? How can I stop, just like that?" he asked, snapping his fingers for emphasis.

"That's how you stop. Just like that," Hank said, also snapping his fingers. "Life is for the living, not the dead. You will never forget your wife, but if you feel you'd like to move ahead, then that means you're ready. Ask that lady out that you've got your eye on, or not. But leave yourself open to meet someone else. You won't be betraying your wife. Just go ahead and do it. Don't expect that you won't have second thoughts, because you will, but you'll be all right. You'll adjust. Time is the thing in all of this, just like it is with everything."

"That's not all. I think I'll start boxing her things, but what do I do with them?"

"There's probably stuff her family would like to have. Her clothes could go to goodwill, just save a few things that are most precious to you and put them away. And take back your bedroom. She's gone and if you want someone else to come into your life, you have to make room for her … all the way. If you don't, she'll feel it. I promise you that."

"I can't pretend April never existed."

"I'm not saying you should, of course she existed. You loved her very much but the time you had together is at an end and I think you've made peace with that. There's a new life ahead of you now. You can honour her memory, but you don't have to live it. Celebrate her life, but live your own. If you don't, there's actually been two deaths, hers and yours, and that just isn't right."

"That's the thing, I do feel as though there's been a shift. I've got to stop reliving the accident, the night she died. I have gone over and over that in my mind a million times and I still do, although not so much lately. Not like I once did, but how do I stop feeling awful because I'm moving on without her?"

"Only time can fix that. I don't recall you ever mentioning children, were there any?"

Shane shook his head. "We talked about them but we weren't quite ready to start a family. We thought we'd get the house paid down a bit first, take a few trips before we got busy with children, that kind of thing. It sounds so selfish now, but in a way I'm glad there were no kids who'd have to deal with losing their mother, like I did."

"You've certainly experienced your share of loss."

"And I don't seem to get any better at handling it either."

"It seems to me you're handling everything just fine."

Shane was silent for a few moments, contemplative. "I don't plan to be back for a while, so what about April's grave?"

"What about it?"

"I can't just leave, I...."

"That's my job, and I promise you I'll look after her grave. She's in good hands, both above and down here on earth."

"Thank you," Shane managed gruffly, his coffee forgotten as he continued to stare out the side window. He was not in any hurry to take his leave now that he'd decided to have this conversation.

"Shane," the older man said quietly.

The two had long since been on a first-name basis. Hank often stopped his work to speak with Shane when he came for his weekly visits; supplying water for the roses.

"Shane," he said again when the younger man didn't answer. "I get the feeling you have something on your mind that you've been wanting to talk to someone about for a while, something you've kept to yourself. I know I'm going out on a limb here, but I'm guessing it has you all twisted up inside. I feel like you're carrying a heavy burden, other than the loss of your wife of course. If I'm right, I've got the time if you want to talk about it."

Shane looked away, his silence speaking volumes.

"I'm right aren't I? There's something you need to get off your chest."

Shane could feel tears begin to sting his eyes. Just when he thought he had expended all of his grief, there it was waiting in the wings, demanding attention. He thought for a moment, his awful secret springing to life inside him again, craving release.

"There is something that's bothering me," he said at length, deliberately understating it. In truth, the weight of what he was carrying around was eating him up.

"Do you want to talk about it? You know it would go no further."

Shane nodded. "I know that."

"Well," said the older man, "go ahead and get it out. You'll feel a lot better when you do, I guarantee it."

Shane knew what he wanted to say. It was time to free up the painful mass that was lodged somewhere in the vicinity of his heart. It was finding the starting point to get going was all, the right words to use. His biggest fear was that when what he'd been holding inside of him was finally exposed to the harsh light of day, it might make him feel even worse. And would it be fair to April's memory to talk about it? Nevertheless the bigger part of him knew that the time had come to get it all out, no matter how bad it sounded. If he was going to heal completely, then he had to start talking. He knew it was no coincidence that his friend the caretaker had arrived in time to put these events in motion. Now was the moment.

He took a deep breath and slowly released it. "There is something that I've never told another soul. I planned to let it die with me, but now it feels like I've got this poison inside. And here I am about to tell you. You're right I do need to get it out to be able to move on with things. And again, I'm a very private person so I'm counting on your discretion."

"And you have it, I swear," Hank reassured him. "What we talk about today, stays here."

"Thank you." Shane cleared his throat noisily before starting. "The last day of April's life is still very vivid to me. She was off for a couple of days and I had to go to work for six o'clock that night. I remember very well how the argument started. It was about a wet towel and burned toast. April wasn't at her best in the morning, and she could get pretty cranky. Whoever was up first made breakfast, so that day it was me. I decided on French toast, my speciality. Breakfast was almost ready when I went in the bedroom to get her she was in a sour mood. She lit into me about leaving my wet towel on the bedroom floor when I got dressed. She'd gotten after me about that before and I'd forgotten again. So she started raking me over the coals about it. She was right, I was a slob, well, at least about that."

"I have the same failing myself," Hank noted before Shane continued.

"Anyway, I forgot about the pan on the stove and the next thing the smoke alarm is going off and there went the French toast, burned to a crisp. And wouldn't you know it, I'd used the last of the eggs to make it. I had my mouth set for French toast, but unless I ate it black, it wasn't going to happen. That's when the real fight got underway. I was angry with her for the ruined breakfast, and she said it was my own fault. Our breakfast wouldn't have burned if I knew how to pick up after myself. Well, you get the picture. I raised my voice to her, which she hated. She ran for the bathroom and locked herself in."

"And that made you angrier."

"Oh yeah! I hated when she locked herself in a room, and I was good and pissed off by that time. So I went and got the screwdriver and started taking the hinges off the door."

Hank laughed. "You showed remarkable restraint, I would have kicked the door off the hinges."

"I stay focused," Shane said, attempting a smile.

"But you got in."

"I got in and by that time she was bawling her eyes out. If I hadn't been so mad I would have put my arms around her because I could never stand to see her cry. But that day I didn't care. Let her cry, darned good and hard."

"So did you have breakfast at all?"

"Nah, I just threw everything in the garbage and went uptown and got a takeout breakfast sandwich; drove around to try to cool down. A couple of hours later I got back and when I went inside, there she was in the bedroom still crying."

"Did you have many fights?"

"A few, but not bad ones. That day it seemed like we couldn't help but get on each other's nerves. Anyway, I got some tissues and sat on the side of the bed to try to make up with her even though I thought the whole thing was her fault. She threw the tissues in my face and started in on me all over again, which only ramped me up even more.

"We said some terrible things to each other, things that I regret to this day.

Before, I always got out of the house until everything blew over, but it didn't seem like the earlier two-hour cool off had done any good at all.

"Now I don't want to give the impression that April was difficult to live with, she wasn't. There were times when she got picky, and I've been known to have a short fuse sometimes. So, out I went again and this time I stayed out the rest of the day. I thought all we needed was a few hours apart. The way I had it figured, we'd have enough time for make-up sex before I went in for the six o'clock shift."

"Was she home when you got there?"

"She was home ... and still angry."

"What!"

"That's right, and to make a long story short she was giving me the cold shoulder. She said if I couldn't even come home to make things right between us before I went to work, she had nothing to say to me. Fine. I got showered and changed and left."

Shane stopped his story long enough to take a deep steadying breath, then continued.

"My gut was as tight as a drum when I drove away that night. I couldn't figure out what I'd done that was so terrible. It was a freaking wet towel, but then again I did let her have it pretty good with some of the things I said. I shouldn't have said them though and the more I thought about it, the

72

worse I felt. I should have put my arms around her when she was crying in the bathroom and said I was sorry for the wet towel. If I had done that I know she would have apologized too. It would be hard to tell which one of us was the more stubborn."

Just then late model sedan with an elderly man and woman inside crawled passed Hank's truck, greeting him with a friendly wave as they went by. It seemed everyone knew Hank. The couple parked and with careful steps made their way to a monument in the next section, carrying a floral saddle of bright pink and purple flowers. Hank and Shane watched absently as the couple made sure it was firmly in place atop the headstone, then stood silently looking at the grave.

"That's Mr. & Mrs. Webster," Hank explained, "and that's where their daughter Amelda is buried. She died a few years ago. She was their only child and they come every now and again for a visit."

Minutes later they slowly retraced their steps to the car, turned, then headed back the same way, raising their hands in farewell as they left.

Shane settled deeper into the seat and folded his arms. He knew he couldn't turn back now that he'd begun this intrepid trip down memory lane. He didn't want to. Nevertheless in the full light of day, his words falling on understanding, sympathetic ears, the whole thing didn't seem so bad after all. It sounded normal enough in the telling of it, something that almost every couple experienced from time to time. It just so happened that in his case it had a tragic ending.

He resumed his recollection of that fateful day. "I was feeling like a first class heel and I would have called her before I got to work, but I knew April well enough that she wouldn't answer. Let him suffer, she'd say and it's not that I didn't deserve it. So I did the next best thing. I stopped and bought a dozen pink roses, her favourite, then found a sappy card and added my own message to it. I planned to surprise her with it when I got off work the next morning. I was starting to feel a little better after having done that, but I knew the knot in my stomach wouldn't go away until we'd officially made up.

"It was a busy night, which was good because it didn't give me a lot of time to stew about what had happened at home, and I am a stewer. All I knew is that the next morning couldn't come fast enough. In the meantime I had a ton of paperwork to catch up on, and let's just say the natives were restless. There were plenty of calls to keep our guys and girls on their toes. That's why I wasn't surprised when the sergeant took me aside and said he wanted to talk to me. I figured I was needed for something, and I was. He told me about a car accident up near the highway."

"April's car," said Hank quietly.

"April's car, yes. I just gaped at him. All of a sudden I was all of those other poor people I'd given death notices to as part of my job. I came close to decking him when he told me she'd died in the accident, and that's a normal reaction too. You're so angry to be told something like that. I stared at him, until I was finding it hard to get my breath. I remember the words died instantly and with some of the horrific wrecks we see, those are actually two of the kindest words you can hear. As long as she hadn't suffered. I honestly don't remember many details from that night. It only managed to penetrate my brain the next day that it had happened on the road leading to the highway. A T-bone collision. She'd turned right in front of the oncoming car and was broadsided. It was a clear night, ideal road conditions and she was a good driver, a careful driver. I can't understand why that accident happened."

"It must have been a nightmare for you, Shane."

"It was that and so much more. The funeral was a blur. I remember arms holding me up when I first saw her casket; guys from work. Buddies. I was devastated, especially since the last words April and I ever spoke to each other were in anger.

The things we said to each other still rattle around in my brain like mad hornets, and they won't stop coming at me."

"Hopefully you getting some of this out will help. Do you think it might, now that you've taken this brave step and talked to me?"

Shane nodded. "I never thought it would help to talk about all of this, but I think it has. I felt like I couldn't even bear to say the words, but it's taking a lot of the sting out of it. I've just been so angry that I never got my chance to make it up to her. To tell her I was sorry for the things I'd said; hear her apologize for what she said to me. And because we didn't have that chance, it seems like she really meant what she said to me that day. I know I didn't mean what I said, but I couldn't tell her."

"Don't you think that three years is long enough to punish yourself?"

"I'll never stop punishing myself. I'll move on, but I never had a chance to make things right, and I never will. Life really bites you in the butt some days and it did that day. Little did I know when I bought those roses that I'd be putting them on her grave, not passing them to her. I burned the sappy card."

"Well, Shane, you've taken a big step today, you...."

"There's more."

"There's more?"

"Yes."

"Don't stop now then. Get it all out while you're at it. Make a clean sweep. What else is there, son?"

"She was leaving me that night. I've never told anyone that, but I found her note when I got home. She said she didn't believe I loved her anymore, so she wanted out."

Chapter Four

Hank was silent for a moment. "That would be a terrible thing to have to deal with. I'm sorry that was your experience, Shane. That's really rough."

"You can say that again. The guys at the scene could see that her car was full of stuff, but they never said anything to me about it. I guess they knew it was my business. Like I said, it wasn't until I went home later that I found the note and I was too humiliated to tell anyone about it. It just about flattened me, Hank. That's why I haven't been able to let go after all this time. I'm sad, but I'm also angry."

"And you feel like the whole thing is your fault."

Shane sighed again, feeling at least some of his tension begin to uncoil. "That's pretty much it. I kept going over and over it in my mind. I still do, as to how she could have felt that way. I'm not the most demonstrative guy, and I could be more sensitive, but I can't understand how she thought I didn't love her."

"Forgive me, Shane, if I ask the wrong questions, or seem nosey, but didn't you tell her you loved her?"

Shane folded his arms in front of him, a grim expression on his face. "I did, yes, of course, although I could have said it more often. Maybe my job has made me hard, I don't know. You see so much, but I can't imagine she didn't know I loved her with all my heart. I did everything I could for her. I'm not normally a sappy guy."

Hank grinned. "Sappy sounds negative, but I would say roses every week for three years is a man who loved his wife."

"Like I said, I didn't get a chance to give her those roses before she died, so I could damned well do it later although I know it's not even close to being the same."

"Why don't you go talk to someone about the load you're carrying around? It might help."

"I thought that's what I was doing."

"Someone professional I mean, someone who would know the right things to say to take away some of your pain. As municipal employees you must have access to psychologists through your employee assistance program."

Shane toyed absently with the plastic cover on his coffee cup. "Oh sure, but I'd say you're doing a great job. Look, I have the time right now, so could we keep talking? If it's not possible just say so. I don't want to hold you up too long because I know you've got a job to do."

"Hey, I'm retired and I don't have to be home for lunch for another couple of hours, so I'm good. As for my work here, what doesn't get done today will get done tomorrow. Nobody's going anywhere. They'll be here waiting for me tomorrow the same as they are everyday. I was going to clip around a few of the headstones, but that can wait. I'd just as soon sit and relax for a while longer, and I'm enjoying our chat. If it's helping you then so much the better. Maybe when we're done I'll hang out my shingle. Hank Peterson, clinical psychologist."

That got a small smile from Shane. "Sounds good to me, Dr. Peterson. If you were a practising psychologist charging by the hour, I'd make you rich with all of the stuff I've got tucked away."

"Fair enough, you get what you can off your chest. Don't bother sugar coating anything, and I won't pull any punches with you either. Deal?"

"It's a deal."

Hank cleared his throat. "So since I'm playing psychologist, I'll say that baggage from the unfortunate events in our lives starts to pile up after a while. It just keeps adding up until we're trying to move a mountain and of course we can't. So bear with me. I have to ask if you had a tough time growing up? You mentioned about role models. I know you said you were young when you lost your mother, and that would be hard for any child."

Shane's folded arms tightened across his chest. "I guess you could say it was tough. My world was never the same after my mother died, it couldn't be, and my old man didn't waste any time bringing home a replacement."

"He was probably in free fall."

"Probably," Shane agreed at length, "but he didn't treat any of the next three any better than he did the first. He was a jerk who always had a drink in his hand and everything was always somebody else's fault, never his. He was a self-righteous drunk who couldn't face the world without whiskey."

"Did he have time for you?"

Shane laughed bitterly, not intending to express amusement. "Shaney … he called me Shaney … do this, do that, and no matter what I did it was never good enough. He'd be sober for work, but as soon as he was home out came the bottle and he wasn't long getting oiled up. He was okay when he was sober, although all he thought about were women and his next drink. When the stuff started to kick in, there went his mood. I got so I hated the man, and that's the sad truth. My mother wasn't the warmest person on the planet either, but she treated me better than he did although not by much. She was also a little too free with her hands, always whacking me for one thing or another. He picked up where she left off when he got home. Not bad stuff, like they never abused me the way you hear about with some children, they were just always cuffing me. That gets to you after a while. I figured she had too much to deal with, living with my father and that's why she was mean. Still I didn't want her to die; especially not commit suicide. I'm glad I'm not the one who found her. I don't think I would have ever gotten over that. Her friend Lanna found her. I guess my mother opened a vein and bled to death. She must have done it in the morning after I went to school because Lanna came over around noon and she was already dead. They called me at school and told me."

"Your dad called you?"

"He had to take care of things. My grandmother, my father's mother, called and told me on the phone what had happened. I come from a long line of insensitive people. Anyway, I went to the funeral and it was an open casket but I refused to go anywhere near it. My father'd had a few so he forced me to look, but they hadn't done a great job on her so it was like looking at a stranger. That helped. I really missed her. Even though we weren't what you'd call close, she was still my mother."

"You said your father remarried."

"Three weeks after my mother died. I figured he'd been running around on her, that's what they were fighting about. That's why she did what she did, but he didn't seem to care. I never saw him act like he loved her so I figure he was glad she was out of the way. Saved him the expense of a divorce."

"Did his new wife treat you well?"

"She did not. He was about my age now when they got married, maybe a year or two younger, and she was twenty. He was a firefighter and he was good at his job, decorated and all that stuff, but he liked the women and they were always falling all over him."

"And the marriage didn't last."

"No. They got divorced, but they did manage to make it almost four years. He got married again not even a year later."

"Did she treat you well?"

"She was real sweet, used to make a big fuss over me. I liked her a lot until I woke up one night and she was in bed with me. She'd been drinking with my father and they'd had a fight or something so she decided to crawl in with me I guess. Nothing happened, that I know of, but I didn't care for waking up to find someone else in my bed. There she was, naked, her arms and legs draped over me. She never even woke up when I got out. I went to sleep on the couch for the rest of the night. It really shook me up."

"Did she remember it the next day do you think?"

"I don't think so, but I gave her plenty of space after that. She made me nervous, like she was going to pull something crazy or end up naked in my bed again. She was drinking way too much by then. They both were so I stayed over at my friend Carver Monaghan's house a lot. His dad was a cop and that's where I got the idea to be a hostage negotiator because that's what Mr. Monaghan did. It was called something else then but it was the same thing. I figured since I was negotiating on a full-time basis at home just to keep peace, I might as well make a career out of it. Carver's father took me under his wing when he knew I was developing an interest in law enforcement, helped me understand what to expect and that type of thing.

"By the time I was in high school my father was trying to get dried out and putting in a better effort with wife number three. She was an okay person I suppose but not very friendly and definitely not in the market for a teenaged stepson. By then I was practically living at Carver's house anyway, so I wished them well and kept my distance until I finished high school and went away to university. I will say that they came to my university graduation, and later when I graduated from police training, so I have to give them that. Once she figured I was out of her hair for good, she really got into the stepmother act. I just let it slide. I didn't need either one of them."

"But you had April in your life too during your growing up years."

Shane nodded sadly. "We were inseparable. We could relate, you know, because her parents were divorced and they were making her life miserable. They couldn't stop fighting even though they weren't together anymore. They still managed to put her in the middle because she was an only child. I think her parents loved each other even though they'd split up. It's like they say, hate is not the opposite of love. The opposite of love is indifference, and her parents were a million miles away from being indifferent toward one another. So we were kind of miserable together, but after high school our relationship fizzled out. It was like we had outgrown each other at that stage of our lives."

"But it sounds like you relied on each other when you were together. Knew each other's story."

"Minimally. Actually I knew more about her than she knew about me because I was too embarrassed to tell her about all of it.

God! Waking up to find my stepmother in bed with me? Hardly. Yet here I am telling you all this crap, stuff that I never even told my own wife."

"Sounds like you held a big part of yourself back, Shane."

"You're right I did," he said after some thought. "When you have a family history like mine, that's what you do. It wasn't like April didn't know me, I think she understood where I was coming from."

"And you said you were apart for quite a number of years before you reconnected."

"It was a long time, years. I'll never forget the day we got married. I've never seen a woman look more beautiful walking down that aisle to me. I couldn't take my eyes off her. I have never loved anyone the way I loved her, and that just might be the way it always is."

"I don't think so. I think you're taking a healthy step forward in choosing to leave a lot of your pain in the past. It sounds as though she loved you for a long time, and I doubt she would want you to grieve forever. You're young. You will love again."

"Funny how the sharp edges go off grief, but it's always a heartbeat away. Our wedding was the best day of my life, bar none. Having to go and identify her body at the hospital was without question the worst. Because it was a side-on collision there wasn't a mark on her. The doctor said she'd died from an aorta tear, which is not unusual in that type of crash. To look at her you'd think she was asleep. It was as though I was looking at someone else, you know, kind of like I was removed from the whole thing."

"And then after the funeral…."

"It was terrible. I took some time off because I wasn't fit to work, too distracted. Even though I'm not a drinker like my dad was, not to the same extent, I got into the bottle pretty good during that time. I'm not proud of that but I just didn't care."

"But at some point you laid the bottle down I hope."

"After about six weeks I threw it away for good, sobered up and went back to work. That was the best thing I could have done. Then it was just a matter of picking up the pieces … again. It seems like I've done way too much of that in my life, although I know I don't have to look very far to find people much worse off than I am. An average day in police work will show you that."

"Have you dated at all since your wife died? I think you told me you hadn't."

"Not at all but I have kind of had my eye on that woman at the coffee shop. There's something about her I like, but I don't know about getting back into the whole dating thing. I'm out of practice."

"It'll all come back to you once you get started. You have to get up the nerve to ask her out. Is she pretty?"

"I think she's beautiful. The prettiest eyes you ever saw."

Hank grinned. "Well, don't hesitate too long."

He unfolded his arms, stretching. "You're probably right, I should get after that. You know? The more I'm talking about this, getting it out, the better I'm feeling. I know I'm talking your ear off though."

Hank chuckled. "Don't worry about my ear. I'm glad we're doing this. We've gotten to know each other quite well since you've been coming here. I knew you were still grieving for your wife. I heard it on TV one time, on one of those talk shows, that you can get stuck in grieving and it isn't healthy. I agree there's a time when you need to let go."

"Yeah, I heard that too, but a lot easier said than done. But I don't want to grow old alone. I want to share my life with someone, maybe have kids some day."

Hank's cellphone rang. Taking it from his pocket he glanced at the caller ID then back at Shane. "Sorry, I've got to take this. It's my wife."

He was already smiling when he pressed TALK. "Hi Mary, what's up? Sure, no problem. I'll stop for a quart of milk on the way home. Anything else?" He winked conspiratorially at Shane. "And a loaf of bread? Got it. Yes, I'll make sure it's fresh. Yes, I'll check the date on the tag. Anything else? No? Okay, honey, see you in a little while."

He flipped the phone shut and slipped it back into his pocket.

Shane was watching him. "See? That's what I want, someone calling me to bring bread and milk home … or whatever. I'm sick of knocking around that big house by myself. I'm lonely and not just for sex. I could find that anytime, I want the whole enchilada. Someone to wake up next to, go to sleep with and you know? I was just thinking, since April died I haven't once left my wet towel on the bedroom floor. Isn't that the damndest thing?"

"Funny how life is."

Shane checked his watch. "Well I should let you get back to work, I've tied you up long enough telling you my life story. Maybe I should write a book and get everything out of my system. Isn't that what people do these days?"

"Like I say, I'm enjoying the break from work, but I understand if you need to get going."

"I'm in no rush, but I don't think there's anything else to say."

"Can I ask you a question?"

"Sure, shoot."

"What about your father?"

89

"What about him?"

"Is he in your life right now?"

"Not really, why?"

"Have you forgiven him for the way things were between you when you were growing up? From what you said it doesn't sound like you have."

"What's the difference?"

"The difference is that if you haven't done so, that will also hold you back."

"You sound like you know what you're talking about."

"I do."

"How?"

"Because my father and I had a terrible relationship. He treated my mother like gold, and my sister, but he didn't like me and took every opportunity he could to let me know it. It wasn't only the physical aspect of it, it was the constant putdowns and sarcasm. He never had a good word to say to me, about anything."

"Geez, why would he be like that to you?"

"He was like that because my mother had me before she got married, while she was still a teenager. He called me the bastard. He knew who my father was and he hated the guy, so he made me pay for something I had no control over. Said the guy was no good, and I was just like him."

"Where was your mother in all of this?"

"She idolized my father and she did try to intervene, but she let him away with way too much. She tried to make it up to me on the sly, apologize for him and stuff, sneak me treats, but she would never go head to head with him about it. I call him my father because he legally adopted me to keep her happy. But he actually told me one day, point blank, that he only did it because my mother asked him to, not because he thought I was worth anything."

"So what about your real father? Did you have a relationship with him, like when you got older and out from under your adoptive father?"

"He didn't want me either, wouldn't marry my mother because he said she got pregnant to trap him."

"That's terrible. Do you hate him?"

"No, Shane, I don't."

"What about your adoptive father? You must hate him."

"I don't hate him either. I pity him, but I don't hate him. Life is too darned short to run around hating everybody."

"Don' tell me you forgave both of them."

"That's exactly what I did. It didn't mean they were any less unfavourably disposed toward me. It meant that I let it go, for both of them. I walked away from it all in my mind, and my heart. I remember the day I did it and now I don't even think about any of that old stuff. Maybe you should consider doing that for your dad, for your own good. It works."

"Sometimes people do things that you can never forgive. What about that?"

"You forgive for your own good, not for theirs. It's not like you're letting anybody off the hook, it's for your own peace of mind. If you don't mind me saying, now would be a great time to do that housekeeping in your life. Maybe turn the page and wipe the slate clean."

"You make it sound so easy."

"It is, and it isn't."

Shane chuckled softly under his breath. "I'm going to have to ask you to explain that one. I get the part about it not being easy, not the other way around."

"What I mean is that the words are very easy to say, but you have to mean what you say when you say it. You have to make a decision that that's what you want to do, and you're going to make it work; going to let it go. You can do it. Do you imagine it bothers your father that he didn't do a better job where you're concerned? Does he try to make it up to you?"

"Yeah, I get that impression, but I let him know it's too late. He should have been there for me when I needed him."

"Let me ask you a question, Shane and I don't mean any disrespect when I say this, okay?"

"Okay. What's the question?"

"Are you perfect?"

"I'm about as far from perfect as you could get, why?"

"And when you mess up with somebody, wouldn't you like to be given a second chance?"

"Of course. Okay I get it. I should have a conversation with my old man, but it's a little late to go back and fix all of that crap. I needed him when I was growing up. I don't need him now."

"You need him now, Shane. That much I can promise you. He's your father and if he's willing to work at a relationship it would be in your best interests to try to meet him halfway. Believe me it will give you peace of mind, and you look like a man who could use a whole lot of peace of mind. You've been through some very rough waters, but of course people can move past their mistakes and do better. It sounds like that's where he is. Why don't you try making things right between you and your dad?"

"What, just call my father and say I forgive you?"

"Sure, something like that. Make a start at least and I think you'll be pleasantly surprised. I think if you and your dad talk man to man you can get a whole lot of things ironed out. It'll take a while, but right now you've still got that anger from your growing up lying in your gut like a sharp rock. I can't imagine you wouldn't want to get rid of it."

Shane laid his head back against the headrest and closed his eyes, trying to imagine what it would be like to have a civil relationship with his father. What would that be like, and did he even want it? Yes you do, a little voice inside him answered. Hadn't his father tried to be there for him when April was killed, and later, and he'd shut him out? Wouldn't even return his calls because, yes, dammit, he was still angry with him.

"I doubt he'd sit and talk like this, let me get all this stuff off my mind. He probably wouldn't want to hear what I had to say. He'd be looking at his watch the whole time; getting up to mix another drink which is what he'd really be thinking about. I know he was trying to quit, but I doubt anything came of it. He's probably the same as he ever was, totally into himself."

"You never know. Maybe you won't hear from him what you need to. If not, forgive him for what can't be, and move on. I'm telling you it works. I'm a living example that it does. I was bitter for a long time before I let go of it."

Shane turned to look at him. "You know, Hank, I've only known you from coming here to the cemetery. I know you've been retired for quite a few years, but I don't think I ever knew what you did for a living … besides this."

Hank laughed. "I work here for a small stipend, it's to help them out more than anything. Give something back. I was a high school guidance counsellor for forty years. My wife and I sold our home in the country and moved to the city after I retired to be closer to the municipal services. That's why I love being the caretaker here. It's like being in the country again every day."

"I'm not surprised counselling was your career, because you're very good at it. You always seem to know the right thing to say."

"So will you do it? Will you give your father a second chance?"

"All I can say is that I'll think about it. I've been really mad at him for a lot of years, but I can say one thing, I love my dad. Even though I push him away, I do love him."

"My guess is that you want him in your life, you're just not done punishing him yet. Think long and hard about it. You only have one father."

Shane's hands now lay loosely in his lap, relaxed as his earlier defensiveness had slowly begun to ease away. "You're right, I will think about it."

"So do you feel any better at all now that we've had this conversation? I've been very blunt with you about some things. If there's something that I think someone needs to hear, I'll go ahead and tell them. But I'll ask first if they're open to hearing what I have to say, just as I did with you."

"To answer your question, it's been great to have someone to talk to."

"Now I'm going to say something to you that might surprise you."

Shane held the older man's gaze. "What's that?"

"You've talked a lot about your late wife. You've maybe shared things you never thought you would, but I believe there's something else that's been eating at you since the day she died. Maybe before that."

Shane turned to look at him sharply, then looked away. "What makes you say that?"

"Just your reaction right now. Do you think you want to tell me what it is?"

"I think I've shared everything I want to share for one day, thanks."

"All right then. Think about it. If you want to talk you know where to find me. Or you could give me a call at home. I'll give you my number."

Shane raised his hand. "I don't need your number and I don't plan to come back here, thanks all the same."

"Shane, I feel like you're really close to saying what's stuck inside you, but I can't pull it out. You have to do that yourself."

Shane reached for the door handle. "Look, I've got to go. Thanks for the head shrinking."

"Why are you so afraid to face the question that's been burning you up inside?"

"Maybe I don't want to know."

"And maybe you do. Maybe you just don't think you can handle the answer, but you need to know."

Shane wrenched the door open. "Go to hell."

"No thank you, I like it here. It's only in facing things, Shane, that we can make peace with them. Again, isn't there a question you'd like to ask me but are terrified to?"

Shane leaned his head against the frame of the open truck window. "I'm sorry, Hank. I shouldn't have spoken to you like that. You're trying to help me and I had no business lashing out. You're right, there is something I've dreaded facing. Maybe I thought I'd never have to, but I need to know the answer before I can really move on. I just don't want to end up hating April. I loved her with all my heart and soul."

"I can tell you did. I would never question that. But I think you know I have the answer to the question you want to ask."

Shane nodded slowly, miserably. "I've guessed at the truth but I have to know for sure. I saw red roses on her grave one day and I wondered. It's haunted me for three years. Who put them there?"

"Shane why don't you get back in the truck, and sit down."

"Tell me."

"Okay, I'll tell you. You were like clockwork, Shane. I could always count on seeing you at the first of the week with your bouquet of pink roses. When you first started coming, before we began to chat now and again, I used to wonder who you were. If you were her husband."

"Who else would I be?"

"Well like I say I wasn't sure because…."

"Oh my God, no."

"Yes, there was another man who came a few times after she was laid to rest. He's the one who brought the red roses."

Chapter Five

Ginger gawked at Cedric, open-mouthed, her eyes as wide as saucers.

"You killed your wife!"

"Well, she's dead isn't she?"

"I don't know. You just told me you killed your wife."

"I did."

She was speechless for a moment then found her tongue. He was probably just grandstanding again to get a rise out of her. "You actually killed your wife."

"Can't you understand plain English? That's exactly what I did."

She held his unwavering gaze. "How?"

"She fell out of a tree stand."

Another hunting accident. Was this man a psychotic maniac or simply starved for attention? In any event her heart started to pound. "You pushed her out of a tree stand?"

"Come on now, Ginger. Don't go all tabloid on me. I bumped into her as I was trying to get past, that's all," he explained, validating her earlier assumption, although still shocking. "Our tree stand wasn't very big so not a lot of room, and with two good-sized adults up there it became a little crowded. Anyway, Annabelle lost her balance, fell into the framework and it let go is what happened. We were up about fifteen feet and she didn't have a chance. She didn't scream or anything, she just fell. She was as surprised as I was. Not a good way to go."

"What did you do?"

"What could I do? I could see that she was dead by the angle of her head. Her neck was broken. At least it was all over very quickly."

"I'm sorry, I don't mean to seem insensitive here but you talk about her death without any emotion. I can't even imagine what something like that would feel like. You must have been horrified."

He appeared to draw in upon himself, suddenly lost in the difficult memory. His wife had died by his hand. He hadn't been able to save her.

"I don't show much emotion because I've buried that day away so deep, I can talk about it as though I have no emotional attachment. But of course I do. She was my wife! I loved her! You used the word horrified, and that's what I was. It was like all of the air was sucked out of me and I couldn't breathe. Everything seemed to go into slow motion. We were two miles back in the woods and we'd come in on foot. I had no communication device with me, my wife was dead, and I had to get her body out somehow. All I could do was carry her over my shoulder to where my vehicle was parked. It felt like I went out of my body somehow and was watching someone else take care of things. I can still see the shocked look on her face, like she knew she was going to fall. It all happened so fast. I got hold of her sleeve, but the momentum of her fall pulled it out of my hand. I grabbed again, but all I got was air. I let out a roar I'm sure they heard a mile away."

Ginger felt as though the air had been sucked out of her; she'd never heard such a tragic story. "So what then?"

"I drove like a maniac, stopped at a house where I knew a doctor lived because we'd gone hunting together one time. He confirmed what I already knew, that Annabelle was dead. He called the police for me because I was shaking so hard I couldn't have held the phone."

"And the police came...."

"They came and they listened to my story and then they arrested me and charged me with manslaughter."

"Cedric! Did you tell them it was an accident?"

"Certainly, but I had no witnesses. Just a dead wife and they thought it was suspicious ... kept asking me if we'd had a fight or something. All I had was my word and when they dug up that other hunting accident involving my cousin, they weren't long slapping on the cuffs. I didn't care anyway at that point. The only woman I had ever loved was dead, and basically it was my fault. All I did was bump into her but she stumbled or something and pitched forward."

"So you went to court I assume."

"I did, and my lawyer couldn't get me off. What it came down to was they didn't believe my story. Like I said anyway, it didn't matter. They could have sentenced me to life in prison and I wouldn't have batted an eye. As it was I got eight years and I served them, got out, and came back here; decided to live the rest of my life as far away from everybody as possible. And from that day on I have never hunted with another person, and I never will again. It's too easy for accidents to happen."

"You invited me," she reminded him with raised eyebrows.

"And that invitation still stands. We could use cameras instead of guns. Would you like that better? See? I'm easy to get along with."

"I don't want to go at all," she said with a grin, "but thank you for the invitation. So, is there anything you'd like to say about your wife? Something in her memory?"

He sighed deeply and closed his eyes. "I miss her, still. This all took place a long time ago but never a day goes by that I don't think about her. I can only speak about the bare facts as I have here today. I can't drill down any deeper than that and keep my sanity. I'm sure you understand because you look like a soft hearted person."

"What about Annabelle herself? Would you like to tell me about her? Her likes, her dislikes, what she was passionate about, that type of thing."

"Annabelle was a sweetheart, so kind, so giving. She was always there for everyone and she didn't deserve to die the way she did. Her mother and father have never spoken to me since the accident. Her father threatened to kill me for what I'd done to his daughter, but in the end he settled for cutting me out of their lives. They didn't even want anything to do with their grandson; wanted a clean break and so I made sure we stayed away. I wasn't that crazy about them anyway. The smartest thing they ever did was have Annabelle, other than that they were stupid."

Ginger leaned ahead and retrieved the tape recorder, taking out the tape and flipping it over because the unexpected just kept coming with Cedric. She'd had no idea there was so much depth to this story. Incredible! A big part of her wanted to believe what he said was true. It certainly could be, but doubt was niggling at the back of her brain: two hunting accidents; two people dead. It was an uncanny coincidence and there was only Cedric to tell the story. Annabelle could never tell hers, nor could his cousin, Randall. The police had been convinced enough to lay charges in Annabelle's case, and he'd been found guilty of causing her death.

Reading her mind he tilted his head to one side, an ominous glint in his eyes. "So tell me, pretty little Miss Ginger, do you believe me or are you a skeptic? "

She had to think fast. "I can only record what you tell me. You say you didn't mean to do it."

"I asked you if you believed me. That's a straightforward yes or no question."

She sagely considered her present circumstances, completely at his mercy with three German Shepherd dogs waiting in the yard. That fact had been in the forefront of her mind since she'd arrived and been escorted into this house.

"Of course I believe you, Cedric. If you said it was an accident, who am I to question that? That whole thing must have been beyond horrible for you. Way out in the middle of the woods and have something like that happen. It would be difficult to imagine coping with that."

"It's hard to find those words and I thought I could never love again, never be interested in another woman. Then you came along. When I first saw your picture in the newspaper I said there she is. She's the girl for me. She's my new Annabelle, my second chance at love."

Oh God! He was a weirdo! And never mind that she was only twenty-nine to his fifty whatever. Cedric was starting to get antsy again drifting off into left field. Time to wrap this up and leave. Seriously.

The wind was now howling like a banshee, thunder providing a deafening backdrop along with the pounding of torrential rain so at times it was hard to hear and of course there was the inevitable lightning. At least he had a generator, so she wouldn't be stuck here in the dark with him should the hydro go out. She did not like electrical storms, especially driving in them, but no matter. The trouble was, just when she thought there was nothing more, he took a sudden turn into something that she'd be a fool to walk away from. Stories like these did not grow on trees.

"Thank you, but I'm afraid I'm already spoken for," she lied in an attempt to divert his amorous thoughts. "I'm married."

She wasn't prepared for his angry reaction.

"What! You're sleeping with someone?" Was that a smile? Was he kidding? "You should have been right up front about that at the beginning, not lead me on."

She knew she should not have told such a bald face lie, but it was appropriate in this case. Now she had to stick with it. "Well...."

"You don't look married to me. I think you're just playing hard to get."

Was this guy on something, or was he actually serious? In any event she had to put a stop to this, yet not shut him down completely as long as he was willing to talk.

"Come on now, let's just move on with the interview and not get side tracked. "Tell me something, Cedric, what type of person would you say you are?"

"Are you asking for yourself or for the paper?"

She pointed needlessly to the tape recorder. "For the story. It's a difficult question to answer. I get that. You've been very forthcoming so I think you understand yourself very well. How would you answer that question?"

He leaned his head back, shutting his eyes again and she could only imagine what was to come out of his memory bank this time. He seemed to have a very large assortment of them to choose from, along with an active imagination. He was a born actor.

"I would say I'm the type of person you should take seriously. I know my mind, always have, and if I want something I'm going to move heaven and earth to get it."

"And if you don't get your own way?"

"What kind of question is that?"

She crossed her legs at the ankles. "A reasonable one I think. What do you do when someone says no to you?"

"Like you, you mean?"

"Like anyone, in any situation. Generally people don't like being denied when they want something. As adults however we understand that sometimes things don't work out the way we want them to, and move on to something else."

"Let me ask you a question, darlin'. Have you ever wanted something so bad it's all you can think about? No matter how hard you try not to think about it, it's right there waiting for you when you wake up in the morning? It's the last thing you think about at night?"

"Of course. Everyone has experienced that."

"Well then you understand. That's how I feel about you."

"Mr. Gourney...."

"Cedric...."

"Cedric. I have to ask you to stop saying those things. You contacted the newspaper because you wanted us...."

"You...."

"Me, to do a story on you, and that entails an interview. The questions I'm asking you are for that purpose. So I would prefer we kept it on that basis if you don't mind. No disrespect intended," she added quickly with what she hoped was a reassuring smile. "Now I'd like to finish up here and be on my way. I have a bit of a drive and I'd like to get home before the weather gets too much worse."

He laughed, enjoying himself immensely it seemed. "You're a feisty little thing, aren't you? I like that. Okay, no harm intended. What was the question again? I don't want to get on your wrong side."

"The question was what type of person would you say you are, how would you describe yourself?"

"Asked and answered. I said I was nobody to be fooled with, and I'm not. If I had to describe myself to anybody, that would be it. Do you think I had an easy time in prison? No, I didn't, but they learned very early in the game not to mess with me."

"Okay," she said as another shiver chased its way up her spine. "You've mentioned your son a couple of times, tell me about him."

"Stilwell?"

"You have more than one son?"

"No, just the one. Stilwell is a chip off the old block, just like his old man. Tough as nails. I worked hard to toughen him up and he took to his lessons like only a Gourney can. We've had our tussles; some good old-fashioned fist fights. He came to his senses a long time ago though and now we're like two peas in a pod. He's learned not to cross me so I'd say he's a pretty smart man. But then again, sometimes he forgets that and I have to remind him."

"Would you say your son is your greatest accomplishment in life?"

"Nope!"

"Oh!" she said, taken by surprise.

That question usually resulted in a positive, feel-good response, always a great way to end a piece. Again, if there was one thing she could expect from Cedric Gourney, it was the unexpected.

"Well what then?"

He pointed to a huge bear mounted on another wall, arms and paws extended with two-inch claws, his mouth open and teeth bared in a furious snarl. Just looking at the thing gave her the willies. Not that it wasn't beautiful, it was just too easy to imagine actually facing off with the creature.

"That bear is my greatest accomplishment."

Back to the animals. It would be a toss up which meant more to Cedric, people or animals. She suspected it was the latter because he seemed to have more respect for wild things, although he bragged about routinely besting them in any woodland encounter.

"Why is he or she your greatest accomplishment?"

"It's a he by the way and it's my greatest accomplishment because I managed to stay alive. That thing meant to have me, all six hundred pounds of him. He was the biggest black bear I ever saw and he was coming for me. As you can see, I won," he announced proudly. "That's as far as he's ever going to get now, hanging on that wall. I smile every time I look at him."

"Right. Okay. If I asked you what was your greatest accomplishment that didn't involve hunting, what would you say it was?"

"I'd have to think about that. Next question."

"That's why I asked you about your son. The birth of a child is usually the most precious moment in a parent's life."

"It was a great day. Remember I said he was born during hunting season?"

"Yes, I do," she nodded. "And you were there for the baby's birth."

"Of course, there's nothing like a man holding his newborn son."

"Or daughter."

"No, I wanted a son. A little Cedric, and I got him. I had a gun in that boy's hands when he was three years old. I think it's important to teach a child the proper use of a gun when they're young so they understand not to abuse the privilege when they get older."

"I agree it's important to know how to use a gun if you're going in the woods with one. That's true."

She was finally getting to the end of her questions, although she'd not soon forget this unusual interview.

"Cedric, what advice would you give to hunters?"

She smiled to herself because what immediately came to mind was don't go in the woods when Cedric Gourney is there. That might be the most valuable advice of all.

"It depends."

"On what?"

"On the type of hunting they're doing."

"Okay, let's say it's the type of hunting you do."

"My goodness, there are so many things I could say, so many directions I could go to really make this work. Hunting has so many aspects to it. There's safety of course, there's intelligence and by that I mean being able to read animals; understanding them and their behaviours. There's also being able to find your way in the woods. Being able to read the sky as well as your surroundings so you don't get lost; how to take care of yourself in case you do. You can't be a fool and go running off in all directions if you find yourself turned

111

around. The first thing I'd say is don't get excited, or panic. Just get quiet, get your bearings and always bring enough stuff with you so that if you do have to spend a night in the woods, you'll be okay."

"Have you ever gotten lost in the woods?"

"I've gotten turned around, yes, but I always look for natural signs."

"Such as...."

"Such as if I take a bearing for north and want to stay that way, remember that moss most often grows on the north side of trees and rocks around here. I mean in the northern hemisphere. Keep a watch for that and you'll keep heading north. The important thing is to keep your head about you. It's not rocket science, but there is a learning curve to it. The guys or gals you have to watch out for are the newbies. They're the ones who come prancing into the woods with a gun that they may or may not know how to use properly; start shooting at the first thing they see. People like that are dangerous. And always wear your hunter orange. You know one time I was hunting and I heard something just up ahead and to my right and what walks out of the woods into the clearing but a young guy. He was probably about twenty years old or so, wearing a tan coloured jacket, carrying a gun. Said he was driving by and thought he'd go in for a quick hunt. That's a really good way to lose your life."

"You actually saw someone do that?"

"I actually saw someone do that. Where I've spent so much time in the woods I could tell you a bunch of stories that you might or might not believe, but they're true."

"Tell me one real fast, the abridged version."

"I'm thinking about a guy I saw one time, a big man, carrying a lot of extra weight. Anyway, he had his hunter orange on, but if you can believe it he was wearing black dress shoes with smooth leather soles. He'd tried to manoeuvre a small knoll, slipped on wet ground, fell and his rifle discharged. He took quite a tumble and he'd been holding his rifle with his finger on the trigger, apparently."

"Was he shot?"

"No, but someone else could have been because of his stupidity. And the danged fool couldn't get to his feet because of the way he fell. Along I come and he calls out and there I was trying to get him back up. I was able to get him on his feet after a while and I had the sore back to prove it. Hair-brained things like that are what cheese me off. Smooth-soled dress shoes have no place in the woods. If things are even a little bit damp there's a good chance you're going to slip and fall."

"That's an interesting story and I'm sure you've seen more than most. So what's ahead, Cedric? What are your plans for the future?"

"If I told you what my plans are, you'd probably throw that tape recorder at me."

Another unsettling twist.

"Do you plan to continue hunting? Maybe look for a bigger prize? There's still some wall space left in here," she said quickly surveying the room.

"The thrill of it is kind of gone for me. I'm planning to invest in a really good camera and take wildlife pictures. I could get some real dandies."

"You'd have the patience for it too because isn't that a prerequisite for hunters?"

"Absolutely and I promise you, I do have all the patience in the world for some things. For other things I have no patience at all."

"Okay, now, any last words? Anything you'd like to share that I didn't ask you about?"

"Seriously?"

"Seriously."

He laughed, watching her, obviously enjoying himself. "No, Miss Ginger, I think you've about covered everything. I feel like my soul has been stripped bare, all my secrets told."

"You could have refused to answer if you felt what I asked was too personal."

"Everything is too personal when you think about it, but then again it's just you and I talking, right? I mean you're not going to put this in the newspaper are you? I don't think I'd want you to do that. After all, I'm a very private person."

She stared at him. "Yes, it's going to go in the newspaper, in my column, People Unlimited. You contacted us indicating that you wanted to have your story told; that you wanted to appear in that column."

He threw back his head and laughed large. "Got you going, didn't I? Just having a little fun, darlin'."

She sighed and kept a smile pasted on her face. She'd had more than enough of this idiotic man.

He rubbed his hands together. "Now for the photos. You asked me if I had any that you could pick from, and I have a bunch of them. I've got two boxfuls along with the albums," he said, pulling the lids apart on the first large carton.

It would take a month of Sundays to go through those, and she wanted out. Now.

Sitting down he patted the spot beside him on the sofa. "Come on, darlin', cozy up here with me and we'll go through these together."

She had no intention of sitting next to him on what amounted to a love seat. She'd take some really great photos of him herself. That should satisfy him instead of going through these. She could suggest a follow up interview at a future date, one which someone else at the newspaper office could do if they wanted to. When she finally got out of here she was never coming back. This place was going to look terrific in her rear view mirror.

"You know what, Cedric? I was thinking, the story in itself is going to be quite long. There's only so much space allocated for my column, so if I can get some good shots, that will be enough."

"No way!"

"They'll be fine, you'll see."

Turning the tape recorder off she slipped it into her workbag and took out her camera, checking to make sure all of the settings were correct before she got underway. Okay, ready. She got to her feet just as he did and in two steps he was right in front of her, his face mere inches from hers.

"I want to read your eyes," he said gazing at her and taking her completely by surprise yet again. "I want to see if you're lying about having a husband."

She took a step back. She was practically smack dab against the chair and nearly tumbled backwards. She managed to keep her feet.

"Ahhh, I'm not lying."

She felt her face heat up. She was a terrible liar and this guy had likely picked up on that by her blush. Who wouldn't? It was a dead giveaway. She wasn't normally given to blushing like a schoolgirl, but she definitely had the guilty flush of a poor liar.

"Aha!" he exclaimed with a broad smile. "You are lying. This is my lucky day. The woman of my dreams is available after all."

"Okay, Cedric, we're not going to do this. Now, I have to take some pictures, so why don't you go stand over there in front of that moose and I'll take one. That should make for a nice shot."

"Sure. It's something I'm very proud of, so good choice."

He stood with a broad smile, pointing up at the unfortunate moose while she clicked away. She took another few of him in front of the giant bear he'd talked about in the story. Again she got some good shots.

"Okay, I think that should do it. They'll make great images to accompany the story."

"What? We're done?"

"Really, I do think I have enough. As I was explaining, there's only so much space and what I use up in pictures means less word count."

"Okay then, but I want you to promise me there'll be another story. A follow up or something and then I do have a ton of photos that I want to see printed. Hell, if people can write page after page of what they did on their summer vacation, there ought to be room for someone who has something interesting to say."

"Good idea. I will definitely speak to my editor first thing Monday morning. I'm sure something can be worked out."

"Sounds good, now I want you to take more pictures."

Her heart dropped. He wasn't going to give up without a fight was he, she asked herself helplessly. He had to be the most persistent, frustrating man that ever laced on a pair of shoes, or boots in this case.

"Okay, one or two more but then I have to leave. I have another appointment this evening."

"Liar! You said you were going home."

"I work from my home too."

"Whatever. So get that camera of yours ready because I'll give you the best picture you've ever seen. I don't think you were ready to take a walk on the wild side when you came here, were you, Ginger? But that's what you're going to get in Cedric Gourney's house. Okay, wait here a minute and I'll be ready for the picture. I guarantee that lazy editor of yours will want to put it on the front page because it'll be the best damned picture you ever saw. I'll be right back."

He left the living room and she considered flight. Get out of here while she could, but just as quickly remembered the dogs roaming the yard below. No, she had to play this out until she could leave on his terms. But then again maybe she could make a call on her cell and have someone come and meet her, but who? And how would they find her because she was definitely off the beaten track. Maybe she couldn't even get service here because of the hills that surrounded them, so it would have to be a 9-1-1 call. No, she could handle this herself, she just had to keep her head. It wasn't like he had threatened her or anything. He'd only made her uncomfortable.

She jumped as he marched back into the room a few seconds later carrying a rifle and a handgun.

"Didn't mean to scare you, darlin', but I think the best pictures would be with me holding these, you know, in kind of a I mean business, shot. Like don't mess with Cedric Gourney."

Her discomfort level rose exponentially as she eyed the weapons and the man who held them so aggressively.

"I told you, Miss Ginger that I was not to be fooled with. That's why they're both fully loaded and ready to go."

Chapter Six

Standing outside the truck Shane fixed his eyes on Hank through the open passenger window, his gaze never wavering. He didn't realize he had a white-knuckled grip on the frame. Another man had brought roses, red ones, to his wife's grave. He wondered if the guy who'd done that had been at April's funeral for all the world to see, but then he couldn't remember much about that day.

"Shane, get back in the truck, please. I know you want to hear what I have to say, need to hear it; are ready. I believe you always suspected that some things didn't add up, but I don't want you taking off and getting in an accident or something because you're upset."

"I have a little more self-control than that," Shane finally managed, realizing he was still gripping the window frame. He pulled his hands back and flexed them.

"Okay then, do it for an old man," said Hank. "I've just given you a punch straight to the midsection and if it was me I'd need to sit down."

Shane did as he was asked and yanking the door open climbed back inside Hank's truck.

"Are you going to be okay?"

"As okay as a man can be who just found out his wife was cheating on him. Was leaving me for the other guy, the one she really loved. Apparently. Yeah, I'm just great. Sorry, I shouldn't be taking it out on you. It's not your fault that my life just blew up in my face."

"Perhaps I'll regret telling you."

Shane shook his head slowly. "No, don't do that. You're right," he sighed. "I needed to know. Part of me did always suspect something, but mostly I've been in denial because I didn't think I could deal with the truth. I might not have been able to handle it when she died, but now it's different. It's not that it doesn't hurt, like hell, but would there ever be a good time to hear something like that? No. How often did he come to her grave?"

"Seeing as how I'm only here during the day, from nine until about four o'clock, I'd say only a few times. Of course I'm later some days, like today because I had a dental appointment, but I'm usually here if the weather's fine. I can't speak for any time other than that. But he only brought red roses once, as you saw, or anything else. There was always just your pink roses, or the floral saddle her parents bring on the anniversary of her death."

"Did you ever talk to this other guy?"

Hank sighed. "Just once. It was right after the headstone had been installed and I was working on April's grave. He was crying when he told me she was the love of his life; how much in love they were. I certainly remember that."

Shane could feel his blood pumping at high speed. "So my whole marriage was a lie, a sham. Boy do I get the duffus of the year award!"

"You can't say that, Shane. Sometimes people get off track and lose their way. I'm sure she loved you very much."

"Bullshit!"

"She must have, she married you."

"It was always me taking the lead in that too, but what gets me is that when she left that note, she made out as though I was the villain. I didn't love her enough, and all the time it was the other way around. I could have done better at times. I'm not exactly what you'd call open, but she expected a lot. Too much at times. Boy, we were the perfect storm, weren't we?"

"It may have ended badly, Shane, but there's no reason to believe she didn't feel love for you. It seems from what you said that you had a very good marriage ... well, at the beginning anyway. I don't think you can fake that, not for that long."

Shane nodded slowly as though thinking about earlier times; better memories. "It was very good at the beginning, but after five years we had started to drift apart. I didn't think for a minute though that there was anything so bad that it couldn't be fixed. Sometimes with our shift work we were like ships passing in the night, but I never thought of our marriage as being in trouble."

"It happens."

Shane's fists balled at his sides, struggling to settle himself down because it wouldn't accomplish anything to fly into a rage. That wasn't his style anyway, although that's certainly what he felt like doing; smashing something if it would take away this pain. Facing stuff like this sucked, but he knew it had to be done and so here he was, doing it.

"It happens, but I didn't run out and try to find someone else. I'm the bozo who thought we were going to be okay, never mind a few problems from time to time. I made a commitment for life to that woman, not just until she thought it was time to move on to someone else."

"This is very bitter news to get, and I'm sorry to be the one to give it to you. Maybe it's better that you heard it from a friend than be blindsided some other way because eventually it would have found you. The truth always comes out, sooner or later."

"If she had lived I'd have found out three years ago, and I have to ask you this, Hank. I know it's a long shot, but did you happen to recognize the guy by any chance? Had you seen him anywhere before?"

"As a matter of fact I do know who he was."

Shane was instantly alert. "I have to wonder if it's someone I know, a mutual friend of ours or something."

"I doubt you knew this guy. I think it's safe to let you know now about him because he's beyond reach so you can't go and get yourself in trouble. I wouldn't tell you who it was if he was still around. I fear you'd find him and let him have it, even though it's been three years."

"What are you saying? That he did the right thing and killed himself? Sorry, that was out of line...."

"No, I'm not saying anything like that."

"So who is he? Are you going to tell me?"

"His name was Jackson Russell."

"Was?"

"He's deceased now too, but not by his own hand."

Shane repeated the name to himself. "Jackson Russell ... Jackson Russell. That name sounds familiar to me somehow. Do you know where he worked?"

"I do know where he worked. I had a bout with skin cancer a few years ago and he was one of the doctors who treated me. Dr. Jackson Russell."

"That's where I heard the name! April was having problems with her supervisor and she mentioned once that Dr. Russell had intervened on behalf of the ER nurses. He'd been going to try to tame the shrew so that they'd have an easier time. She told me how nice he was. So the affair started at the hospital. It all makes sense when I stop and think about it."

"Some of the puzzle pieces are starting to fit?"

"They are, but you say he's deceased? How did that happen, and when?"

"It was in the paper and I recognized his name. There was a team of medical people who went to Peru to work in the villages, like a humanitarian mission. While they were there a massive earthquake struck and some of the team members were killed. Dr. Russell was one of them. I'm sorry for your situation and what they did behind your back was reprehensible, but he was a brilliant young doctor who left a lot of patients behind who depended on him. He was a tremendous loss to the medical community here in New Brunswick."

Shane puffed out a long sigh, not realizing he'd been holding his breath. "So, they're both dead. It is sad when you think about it. I don't believe it was divine retribution that caused their deaths, but it's too bad that things worked out the way they did. I was the innocent, unsuspecting schmuck in the middle of everything, the one in the way. Even though I'm sorry that two young lives are gone, and you really liked the guy, I'm still mad as hell at what they did. She betrayed me, and he helped her do it. That's what's staring me in the face. That's what I have to learn to live with."

"I would be shocked if you didn't feel that way, Shane. What was done to you was most unfortunate and I empathize with you. But since you've decided to move on with your life, I think it was good for you to have all the cards on the table; every single one. Meet this thing head on then put it away. You've had a lot dumped on you, but I firmly believe you won't be truly happy until you deal with it."

Shane stared straight ahead as though choosing his next words carefully. "I loved that woman," he said at length. "I was always glad we'd found each other again after so many years apart, and to think they were sneaking around behind my back doing their … thing. It's all clear now. I was set up that morning. True, April wasn't a morning person, but she wouldn't be placated that day because she didn't want the fight to be over. She was looking for an excuse to leave and I handed it to her on a silver platter. I've often thought too that maybe she intentionally caused that car accident. I thought at the time that maybe it was because she really didn't think I loved her. But no, I might not have been the most demonstrative guy in the world, but I loved my wife and I'm sure she knew it. That's why the whole note thing came right out of left field.

"I know she was leaving me, she made that plain enough, but could it possibly be that she regretted what she was doing? Maybe was so torn up about everything that she'd done to me, our marriage? So confused that she wanted to end it all rather than face the music, which she would inevitably have to do sooner or later?

"You'll never know that, Shane."

"No, I won't, will I? I'm still looking for a way to excuse her. I guess that's easier than facing the ugly truth. My wife was running around with another man and left me for him. She'd found someone she liked better. I was out and he was in. The truth doesn't get much worse than that, not for me anyway."

"There are some hard things in life to get through, and betrayal has got to be one of the worst, especially by someone you love."

"I still don't hate her, Hank. I think she was mixed up. I know that makes me sound weak, or whatever, but that's the way I feel."

Hank chuckled. "I've come across a lot of weak people in my life, Shane, and you're certainly not one of them. You're one of the strongest young men I know. Edna and I never had children, it wasn't in the cards, but you would have been the type of son I imagined we would have. I'm sorry to be the one to tell you all this but I sensed you needed to know."

"I did need to know, it just hurts to know, that's all. And here I've been hanging on to the memory of this perfect angel for three long years. Thought I was the one who'd hurt her, driven her away when all along the joke was on me."

He thought back to the times they'd talked about the future and the many dreams they'd shared. How could he have been so wrong about another human being? He who was highly trained to read people? To get into their heads and find out what made them tick. It was his ability to do so that made him a skilled hostage negotiator, yet he couldn't even see what was happening at home. His own wife had run a number on him, gotten into his head and turned him completely around. April wasn't a monster, but knowing what she'd done to him, made him seriously question his ability to be a sound judge of character; to know when someone was trying to outsmart him. How could he do his job, win the trust of whomever he was trying to deal with when his sense of trust in his own life had been shaken to the core?

He should have let go of this whole thing a long time ago, gone and seen someone to try to get his head straightened out about it. There had been too many unanswered questions; things that he hadn't been ready to face three years ago, and with good cause as it turned out. Thank God for Hank Peterson. The truth had come to him through someone he trusted when he was ready to hear it, and so he had. His worst fears had been realized, suspicion no longer had to lie inside of him and fester. Facing the truth wasn't easy, but it was the only way if he wanted to get past all of this and start over.

Hank glanced at him. "I can't tell you how you should look at things, but even in the worst of experiences there is a tiny thread of something to hold onto. In this case it's that there was a time when the two of you were deeply in love. Some people never know that, never get to have that feeling. That's what you have to remember. What you're feeling now; what you've been feeling for these past three years, the pain of loss, is the cost of love. For everything, no matter how wonderful it is or may appear to be, there is a cost. That's been my experience anyway."

"What's the cost of hate?"

"Never knowing love."

"How did you get to be so gall darned wise anyway?"

Hank chuckled. "I've lived a good many years and if I hadn't learned a thing or two along the way I would think I've wasted my time. The point is, when you get a few things figured out, it has to be passed on. I've seen your grief, what you've gone through these past few years when you visited her grave. You show great restraint, but all I had to do was look at your face to know you were suffering. That's why I'd find myself working a little closer to where you were so that maybe we could strike up a conversation from time to time; help with a few words of comfort and wisdom."

Shane smiled sadly. "You being here for me has meant a lot, but now that I won't be coming back, I guess I won't be seeing you anymore. So I want to take the chance while I can to say thank you, Hank. I wish you the best."

"And I wish the same for you, Shane. You'll spend a few more hours in this dark valley I suspect before you climb out and see the light. I mean really see the light and find a new path. Your radar has been down for a long time, so put it back up and let people know you're ready to move on; especially the women who'd like to meet you. You're a good-looking fella and I expect there's been a glance or two come your way that you haven't even noticed. Something tells me you will now though, onward and upward, son. And good luck with that pretty woman in the coffee shop."

Shane ran a hand over his short-cropped blonde hair and smiled. He liked the way Hank looked at the world and his words did bring him peace. There was also a lot of wisdom in them. When he said he'd spend at least a few more hours, days, whatever, in this dark valley, he was right. He still had to go home and face the place with new eyes. Knowing eyes, and while he'd intended to lovingly dismantle what amounted to a shrine for April, he knew now it would not be done gently. However he wasn't prepared for the anger that swept through him when he pulled into the driveway of the split-level that he and April had called home. He remembered the day they'd seen it for sale, knowing at first sight it was perfect for them. They'd submitted a generous offer so as not to lose it to another couple who were also interested. They'd been ecstatic when their offer was accepted. They took possession almost immediately because the property had been sitting vacant for a couple of months.

He sat in the car and stared at the building, because that's all it was now, a building. Not the house where love lived, or for the past three years, the cherished memory of that love. His eyes went to the welcome sign that April had tole painted herself, surprising him with it when he'd come home from work one morning. She'd worked for a month on that thing and had done a good job, but that was then. He was out of the car in two bounds, tearing it from the ground and breaking it over his knee. Welcome indeed! It now seemed that April had been very welcoming. He threw the pieces aside. He'd pick them up for the trash when he finished in the house because by the time he was through there'd be plenty of garbage ready for pick-up day. It was a good job he had lots of bags in stock, blue for garbage recyclables and the opaque he'd use for what he was sending to goodwill. Hank was right, he still had to finish going through his dark valley. While he was there he intended to clear the house of anything that had, until today, carried any sentimental memories of April.

He went indoors and everything looked different now, tainted somehow, as he stormed through to the master bedroom; their bedroom. Ha! When he'd been away on course a few months before she died, had she brought her lover to their home? Had they done it in their bed? A whirlwind of tormented thoughts hammered at him. She'd been working nights that week, but the one night she was home he'd called her and she'd sounded funny. Not herself somehow. He now knew why. And there was the night she'd called to tell him she'd agreed to work an extra shift because they were shorthanded. The night shift. It didn't take a genius to connect the dots on that one. All these little things that had niggled at him but that he'd shoved away because he refused to entertain any doubts about the woman he adored. Now they were waiting to be dealt with. And face them he would, exorcise what needed to be exorcised, and then no more. He had that kind of mind. When he made it up that he was done with something, he was done and that now applied to April. He could never forget that he had once loved her. He still felt some love for her if he was being entirely honest, but when he was finished stripping the physical aspect of their marriage from his life, he was most definitely done.

He stood looking around the bedroom, and the first thing he tackled was the closet. He stuffed bags with what she'd left behind before her flight to freedom. Shoes, purses … obviously items she intended to come back for later, including hats, scarves, gloves, everything. Next he scooped out the contents of the bureau. There was plenty going to goodwill.

Any pictures of her, or them together, were next and into the garbage they went. He'd thought to save a few things for her family after the accident. However neither of her parents, who'd both remarried and moved out of town, had expressed interest in any of it at the time. So out they went too. It was a credit to his willpower that he didn't tear her photos into a million pieces. Instead he placed them carefully in the bags for some unearthly reason, although he could no longer bear to look at them. She'd been done with him, so he was done with her. It felt freeing to finally make the break from the woman whom it seemed in the end had not been deserving of his love.

He had to wonder too, was the illustrious Dr. Russell her only lover during the five years they'd been married? Or was she willing to jump ship for the first man who came along? No one would ever have the answer to that question, would they? It also crossed his mind that maybe she and the good doctor had been involved for most of her marriage to him. The thought of that made him even angrier as he hauled the jewellery case toward him and pulled out the first drawer to empty it into an opaque bag. He stopped, the wind knocked out of him. He'd never looked in any of this stuff, simply kept it as part of his memory of her.

There in the back, behind some costume jewellery, was tucked her wedding band and diamond.

He'd been too numb with shock the night he'd gone to identify her remains, or even at the funeral itself, to notice that she hadn't been wearing her wedding rings.

Clenching the rings in his hand he sat on the edge of the bed and finally broke down, his shoulders wracked with sobs. The thunder crashing overhead emphasized his dark mood. If this was the last of his pain finding its way out of his heart, then it was leaving on a tidal wave. The claws of the diamond ring bit into his palm and he welcomed the pain, hoping it would pierce his skin good and deep; leave a wound that would always remind him of what he'd believed to be true love and what it was capable of.

With a roar of agony he threw the rings against the wall and they bounced back onto the carpeted floor, none the worse for wear.

"You whore!" he shouted to the empty room. "I was never unfaithful to you. I never even thought about it! This is the last time I cry for you, you lying, cheating bitch!"

Through tears he saw where the rings had fallen and could not help but remember the day they'd been placed on April's finger. First the diamond when he asked her if she'd marry him, and then on that special day when she'd become his wife. He didn't see himself as a sentimental man, but that day had meant everything to him. It had felt like a new chance at a happy life, an opportunity to get things right and not make the mistakes his parents had made in their farce of a marriage. And he knew he'd never cheat because of what he'd seen at home. He believed his mother had died because of it, not strong enough to stand up to the emotional abuse his handsome womanizer father had dished out to her.

And now the most bitter of all blows, his own wife had done the same thing to him. But somewhere in the haze of this last slap in the face he knew that not everyone was so disrespectful of their wedding vows. He knew some of the guys at work ran around on their wives. Some of them never even tried to hide it, but he also knew as many strong, loving couples who loved each other very much and never failed to let it show. It seemed he wasn't capable of finding that kind of love, either in his parents or in the woman he had chosen to be his wife.

Drying his eyes with his sleeve, he looked at the rings again where they lay. What to do with them? He had no intention of keeping them as a memento of what might have been, or should have been. No way. A clean sweep was a clean sweep. He decided the best way was to take them to the jewellery store where he'd bought them and have them sold on consignment, albeit for a fraction of what they were worth. He hoped the next bride who wore them would be more worthy of the vows she made before God. He glanced at his bare wedding ring finger. The pale strip had long ago faded. So after finding his ring, he picked hers up from the floor and put all three together. He'd stop by the jewellery store on the way to work and get rid of them. They were nice and they'd sell fast. He never wanted to lay his eyes on them again.

The jewellery box went into the next goodwill bag, as did all of her tole painting supplies and projects. Next came the bathroom and there sat the toiletries she'd left behind. Anything that had belonged to her was all part of the mental shrine he had erected in her memory. In truth they were long overdue for the trash bin because of best before dates. When finished with that he went through the remaining rooms and found countless other items that she had either owned or bought for the house. Except for cooking utensils and the like, they were all bagged for pick-up.

Next he went through anything that she'd ever bought for him. Even though there hadn't been that much really, it became part of the mass exodus until he couldn't identify one single thing that she had ever touched, other than functional household items. Everything else stayed, and that's exactly the way he wanted it. April was now officially out of his life and after every trip he made to the garage with bags, he felt lighter, more healed. It was painful, yes, any expunging usually was, but hanging on any longer to what he thought April was, what he needed her to be, would be a mistake.

He carried twenty-three opaque bags into the garage, glad pick-up day wasn't today, in this rain. When he'd finished, he knew he was now ready to move on with a clean slate. The cleansing was done and the place beside him was open for business. His radar was up so to speak, way up. Not that he was looking for anything serious for a while. The opposite was true. He would simply enjoy some female companionship from time to time. Could he make a mistake of the heart again he wondered, and the answer popped right back at him. Probably, but you'll get over that too if it should happen. One thing he promised himself he would not do if he met someone, was punish her for April's sins. It would be all too easy to do, but very wrong. No, he was angry, not jaded.

He looked at his watch. Time to take a quick shower and head into work. Normally he would have gotten some sleep before starting a night shift, but he was still pumped with enough adrenalin to see him nicely through the next twelve hours. And of course he'd stop for another cup of Joe on the way. It was Saturday, but he couldn't help but wonder if the woman he'd had his eye on might happen to be at the coffee shop.

Chapter Seven

Ginger looked at the guns and then back at Cedric. "Is there any real need to have them loaded?"

"What's the use of a gun if it isn't loaded?"

"Well … you're not out in the woods hunting, you're here at home."

He laughed, seeming to enjoy her discomfort. "It's at home that I need to keep them loaded most of all. A person never knows who's going to come skulking around, do they? Don't tell me you don't keep a loaded weapon in your home in case you have a home invasion."

It was clear that she and Cedric turned in much different circles, although he probably had a valid point given today's crime rate. "I live in a secure apartment.…" She realized her mistake too late. "I mean," she tried to amend but he was too quick, pouncing on her like the proverbial cat on a mouse.

"Oh? You said I, not we. I gotcha! I knew you were lying to me about having a husband!" he taunted her with eyes alight. "It's not nice to lie you know. Naughty, naughty!"

She couldn't think of anything to say, so she said nothing.

"Why did you tell me you were married if you're not?"

Ginger recovered herself. This had gone far enough. "Mr. Gourney, this is ridiculous. I'm not here to discuss my personal life, now I'm going to finish this assignment and leave."

"And go home to what?"

"That is my business," she told him and immediately regretted her tone of voice considering there were two loaded guns only inches away from where she was standing, and him holding them.

His eyes narrowed and she knew she had to do damage control. Cedric Gourney was quirky, eccentric, like so many of her other subjects, and that was fine, but he was taking things too far. She finally had to admit that he was a bona fide nut, and a potentially dangerous one although he always seemed to stop short of acting upon some of his outrageous comments.

"No, it's my business," he said sarcastically, "now, let's start taking pictures and I want copies of everything by the way. That's the least you can do for me since I've given you what will probably be one of your best stories ever. I should ask for royalties considering all of the extra copies you're going to sell thanks to me. I don't want to be greedy, but I shouldn't be giving you my life story for free. If it was a book, it'd be a bestseller."

Ginger wisely held her tongue. She was known to be feisty, but now was not the time nor the place, so she decided to play it cool. Using her best professional smile she checked her camera again. It was more for something to do rather than concern that the dials had somehow changed of their own volition.

"Okay, Cedric, why don't you pick up the rifle and hold it, and I'll get a couple of good pictures of that. Ready? Smile."

His mood shifted again as he reverted to his earlier cheerfulness. He did as she asked and cradled the rifle in his arms as she snapped away. She took several shots if for no other reason than to appease him, which hopefully it would.

"There," she said with forced equanimity, "that should do it. I have enough of everything for a great story."

"I want you to take more pictures."

She swallowed a sigh of exasperation as he laid the rifle on the table. He picked up the handgun, a very large one it seemed to her although she didn't know much about weapons, calibre, velocity or any of the rest of it. Why would he even need something like that for hunting?

Again he seemed to read her mind and it unnerved her. "I can see you're wondering why I'd need a handgun for what I do. Am I right?"

"Yes, I was wondering that. Is it even le....."

"Legal? Of course it's legal. All of my weapons are registered and I don't appreciate you even asking me that."

"Again, sorry. So what do you need it for?"

"I keep it on me for when I go walking in the woods. It's for protection, really. There's always a chance that a bear means to have you. It's not common, but it's been known to happen because there have been many unprovoked predatory black bear attacks in the last hundred years or so. It's what I was explaining to you earlier. What makes a bear dangerous is that they're unpredictable. That could be said about any animal I suppose, but bears in particular. So it's always better to be prepared. I don't want to become bear scat, now do I? What if I hadn't been able to get into that cabin the night that bear was following me? That's exactly what I would have been the next day. They can and will attack, although it's rare, the exception being of course a sow with cubs. She's quite likely to if she feels her babies are threatened in any way, and she makes that decision, not anyone else. You don't ever want to encounter a mother bear with cubs, or get one of those little goobers upset with you.

"So that's why I have this little baby," he said, running his hand lovingly over the gleaming barrel of the gun. "I call it my get out of jail free card, and I always have it with me now. I'd feel naked without it. It's a beauty, isn't it?"

Her smile was so tight it hurt. "Very nice, but I thought you hunted bear with a rifle?"

"As I've already told you, Ginger, a bear's head is mighty hard and a bullet from a smaller calibre weapon will bounce right off it. You need some firepower to make any difference. That's what I'm holding in my hand, lots of firepower. If I fired right now it would blow a hole right in that wall over there, but since I don't want a hole in my wall I won't do it. Now if I was to shoot into something, well that's a different story. It would likely stay inside if I made just the right shot. You know what I mean? Anyway, the noise would be deafening no matter what I shot. It'd really hurt your ears."

She managed a neutral expression, struggling to keep tell tale colour from flooding her face. She did not want him to know he was scaring her.

"Good to know. Why don't you stand over there," she said, indicating a spot beside a mounted bear head, "and I'll get one or two of you holding that gun."

He moved into place, raised the gun and pointed it at her.

She lowered the camera. "Please don't point that gun at me. I'm not comfortable with you doing that."

Again that slow smile crawled across his face although it didn't get as far as his eyes; nothing could warm them up. They reminded her of a cobra about to strike, and she shivered involuntarily, hoping he hadn't noticed. She didn't want to set him off again.

"Why?" he smirked. "I have the safety on. You're perfectly safe, and I think it would make a great picture; give the story some extra umph."

"I respectfully disagree. You're a hunter, the pictures with the rifle will work just fine. I think you pointing a handgun at the readers will be off-putting to them. I don't think they'd want that and it doesn't really work with this piece, but thank you anyway."

"Nah, I want a picture of me pointing a gun ... this gun. Sorry, there's some things I know everything about, and this is one of them. I hope some of those old fuddy duddys do wet their pants when they see it. That would be hilarious."

She gritted her teeth as she raised her camera and took several pictures of Cedric pointing the gun at her. His threatening expression alone was frightening, never mind having a loaded weapon practically shoved in her face.

She lowered the camera, pushing the OFF button. "There, all done, now I must be on my way. It's really raining hard out there."

He lowered the gun although he seemed reluctant to do so. He was obviously enjoying his favourite topic, himself, given his single-minded pursuit of it, including those awful gun photos. A whacko with a gun! Perfect! There was no way the editor would run those images. The expression on Cedric's face would scare people. It was a small weekly newspaper, not an episode of Armed & Dangerous. If there was in fact another story done on him she knew the editor would want her to do it for the sake of continuity. Nevertheless there was no way in creation she'd take that assignment now. Never!

Placing her camera into her workbag, she was thankful beyond description to be finally heading for the door. Once she was in her car and clear of this place she was going to breathe one humongous sigh of relief.

She started out of the living room but he somehow managed to get to the kitchen before she did, still holding that confounded handgun. A moment later he laid it on the kitchen table then turned to her abruptly.

"I think you should stay here with me," he said, almost playfully, and she could feel her jaw dropping. "I have a brand new washer and dryer, and everything in here is run off the grid. I've got the mother of all generators out back, the one I was telling you about earlier. You'd be surprised how much juice I get out of that. I could light up half the city if I wanted to."

Stepping to the other side of the room he pulled a pink woolly blanket off a washer and dryer pair. As he had described, they did indeed appear to be new. But what would make him think that would have any impact on her desire to leave? Unbelievable! Still, she played along to keep him from getting upset with her, anything to avoid escalating the situation. He'd already admitted to killing two people. He'd even spent time in prison on a manslaughter conviction. If she had ever known that, she would never have come. She and her editor were going to have a a conversation about that.

"They're lovely, Cedric, and I can see they're brand new. You do very well for living off the grid as it were. I will mention all of that in the story; how clever you are to be so self-sufficient."

"Don't you understand?" he demanded as though she were a complete dunce. "I'm saying they're yours to use from now on. You will never want for a thing."

What! "Ummm, again, thank you but I already have a washer and dryer at home. Now I must go."

He threw the pink blanket at the appliances where it draped haphazardly over the washer before sliding into a heap on the floor.

She started for the door but once again he stepped in front of her. "I think I'll keep you here with me."

"Mr. Gourney...."

"Cedric! I told you a hundred times to call me Cedric!"

"Okay, sorry, Cedric. I have to go. This was a work assignment and now the job is finished and I'm leaving. I only need to stay long enough to do the interview and take photos, and then it's over."

His eyes glinted. "You're done with me, is that what you're saying? You're leaving? Just like that?"

"Not just like that, but that's how it works. Now please let me pass."

He was still effectively blocking her path to the door, shaking his head. "I think you need to stay with me."

"Please stop kidding around, I have to go. I want to go."

"Okay, whatever you say," he said with his best hangdog. "Sorry. It's just that you're so pretty and well, a man gets lonely."

Her feeling of relief was palpable as she took hold of the doorknob, now that it seemed he was about to back off and stop his foolishness. At least he was going to let her go, but then she remembered the three German shepherds waiting in the yard.

"Those dogs aren't going to attack me when I go to my car are they?" she asked, trying to keep things light lest his mood deteriorate yet again before she was able to escape.

"They will if I tell them to."

A shiver ran through her and holding the doorknob, she struggled to remain composed. "Okay, then please walk me to my car so I can get there safely."

"Sure," he agreed affably, grinning. "You go first."

Opening the door she stepped out onto the landing, Cedric close behind. He sounded a loud whistle and the dogs, barking, bounded forward and started up the stairs. Their long chains provided them with plenty of leeway. Letting out a loud shriek she turned back, smack dab up against him. Just as the dogs were about to reach her, he gave a sharp command of Stay! Then Go! The dogs retreated, their nails clicking on the bleached steps before reaching the bottom and continuing out into to the now muddy yard.

Stepping away from him, Ginger was breathing heavily as she turned again in the direction of the stairs. Rain pelted her as she moved out beyond the awning, a flash of lightning illuminating the surrounding countryside. She hurried back under the awning to avoid getting drenched.

"Please walk me to my car and let me leave," she shouted above the gusts. "I do not feel safe going there by myself."

He laughed. "I don't blame you. It could be downright dangerous. Do you know a German shepherd has a bite of 238 pounds per square inch? A lot of big dogs bite hard, but these dogs are among the smartest in the world, and loyal to a fault. They make excellent guard dogs, nothing gets in here that I don't know about it, or out…."

Ginger also knew that any dog's over-aggressiveness was often the product of an irresponsible owner who trained them to behave that way. And dogs guarded their territory, it was an animal instinct as old as time. She was a stranger in their midst and if Cedric indicated to the dogs that she was a threat, either to him or their territory, it would not end well for her. She did not blame the dogs, but common sense prevailed in that she could not go to her vehicle alone. Her car was sitting just a few metres away, but she couldn't reach it on her own. As much as it galled her to ask, she needed him in order to get safe passage out of here.

"Cedric, I want to leave now. Please walk me down to my car."

"And what if I take the notion to set the dogs on you when you're halfway there? Do you think you can trust a stranger not to do that? It would be taking quite a risk wouldn't it?"

"I can call my editor to come and get me," she said, but knew Mr. McDougall was working the weekly BINGO at the Mariner's Hall right about now. Never married and without children, he had plenty of free time on his hands. Besides his busy job as a newspaper editor, he was involved in a slew of community activities and out of necessity often turned his cellphone off. There'd be no way to contact him, even if she could manage to get through. She guessed too that Cedric knew reception was a problem in this location, that's likely why he had an old school landline. Still, she could try to bluff him, although she knew in her gut that he was not easily outsmarted.

"Call your editor? That stupid old fart? Ha! A lot of good he'd be, but let me tell you something, darlin', don't even think about trying. You try to embarrass me and you'll wish you hadn't. Do you understand what I'm saying to you?"

"I think I do. You're threatening me!"

"Take it any way you want," he shrugged.

"I want to go, now!"

He didn't move from where he stood under the doorway awning. "Go ahead, if you dare. One whistle and you don't make it to your car. Do you understand that?"

Ginger tried to tamp down her panic. "I know I want to leave and you won't let me."

"Now don't get all excited, you belong here with me. How can I make you understand that?"

"I don't belong here with you," she said through clenched teeth. "I am a reporter doing a job and you are holding me here against my will."

He made a sweeping gesture with his hand. "I want you to stay, yes, but I'm not holding you here against your will. I told you to go if that's what you want to do."

"And you threaten to set the dogs on me if I try to get to my car."

"I keep telling you that you can leave anytime you want, Miss Ginger, but it's only right to warn you that you do so at your own risk. You came to my home and this is the way things are at my home. It's not my problem if you're afraid of dogs."

She was aghast. "Mr. Gourney...."

"Cedric! I told you to call me Cedric! Are you stupid or something?"

"I'm sorry!" Ginger answered just as loudly then lowered her voice when she saw his eyes catch fire.

There had to be some way to get through to this man, and even though she doubted he would respond to reason, she had to try. She'd say whatever it took to get out of here. "I'm sorry I called you by the wrong name and I'm sorry that I raised my voice to you a moment ago. That was very unprofessional, and I apologize. And now that I think of it, you're right. There is another story that should be written with everything you've told me. Since I'm a freelancer I can write for whomever I choose. That means as soon as I get home I could start looking for a really great magazine that I'm sure would love to do a feature on you because you're so fascinating. The story for my column will be a good one too of course, a big spread. I only interview interesting people. That's how I know yours will go over so well.

"Now, in all seriousness I have to get home to my office in order to do that. Gee, I could probably find more than one magazine who'd want to do a write-up on you. That means you'd become famous. Doesn't that sound great? Everyone far and wide would know all about you and your accomplishments; your knowledge."

She could see by the garish illumination from the outside light that his expression had softened. The idea of extended coverage appealed to him and she mentally crossed her fingers that she could finally extricate herself from this mess. When that happened, she would never get into another fix like this. But then just as quickly she realized that as a freelancer she was constantly stepping into the unknown to get a story. It was all part and parcel of what she did. You met people where they were, not have them come to you. It was always preferable to interview someone in their own environment, it lent colour and depth to the story; helped her understand her subject better. No, she was doing things the way they should be done, how could she know this one would turn out to be a psycho?

"You'd do that for me, really? You'd get me in magazines too? How many?"

"As many as you want, Cedric. If ever anyone deserved to be famous, it's you."

"I am a very interesting guy, and handsome. Wouldn't you agree that I'm handsome? Annabelle always thought so. She said I looked just like Rock Hudson from the old movies. Do you remember him? Maybe you're too young."

She almost laughed out loud. Rock Hudson! Cedric was about as far from the uber handsome Rock Hudson as you could get. Annabelle was either a very adept liar or she had been asked that question at gunpoint, or with the threat of having the dogs set on her. That's likely why she'd tell him such a whopper. It was why she was about to do the same thing.

"I remember who Rock Hudson was and you do look exactly like him. It's unreal! I was going to mention that when I first got here, but didn't like to say anything in case you weren't a fan of his movies."

If, as the old fairy tale predicted, your nose would grow if you lied, then she was about to see a major change in her profile. But if lying was going to get her out of here, then so be it. Stroke his ego. All she needed to do was convince him that her leaving would be of enormous benefit to him. She had to get him to see her safely to her car. Play the game until she got away and she could find her way back to civilization. Cedric had no idea where she lived, and she was usually only in touch with the newspaper office electronically. So when she got away, off she would go to the city proper where she lived. He'd just continue doing his thing out here on the outskirts. She never had to see him again. Nevertheless, lying to him as outrageously as she was doing now was a risk, but she had to take it.

"I like Rock Hudson's movies," he said, still aglow from her compliment. "I'm a big fan, and what man wouldn't want to look like him? So you think you could make me famous like him?"

"I know I could, all it would take is the right stories. I already have enough from what we talked about here today to accomplish that."

"You're saying all the right things, darlin'. There were a lot of people who judged me when Annabelle died, can you believe that? I think they need to see the real me."

"Sometimes people don't understand what others go through."

"I know, right? I knew you'd come around to my way of thinking, Ginger. See, you and I are a lot alike. I knew that from looking at your picture. There's something about your eyes that tells me those things. I've always been a sucker for big blue eyes. You've also got those long dark eyelashes, which you've been batting at me all afternoon. Don't deny it. I know you want me as much as I want you. You can't hide that kind of attraction from a man, but you like to play hard to get. You want to be begged is all. Besides, you still owe me that selfie, but don't worry, we have lots of time to get that."

She felt like gagging. First of all there'd be no selfie, and second of all … attracted to him? Ugh! How could she agree with him without him guessing the truth? But she had to keep up the ruse, so she pulled her face into a reluctant smile.

"Right, now Cedric, I'm sure you can understand that if I'm going to do all this work with other newspapers and magazines, I'll need to get to my office. But first I have to get to my car. I'm already late. I was hoping to have this story started by tonight. If I'm held up much longer it will delay the release of my column and I know you wouldn't want that."

"No problem, just write it up here and I'll drop it off at the newspaper office myself first thing Monday morning. I'll put it through the mail slot or something. Then you tell me what you need so you can start working on the other stuff and I'll bring it here for you. There, problem solved. You never have to leave this house again. I'll put your car in the garage downstairs and no one even has to know you're here."

She felt like screaming from sheer frustration. "I can't possibly do any of this without my office equipment because my copy needs to be typed and sent in-house via computer. If I submitted it in any other format it would have to be retyped and it wouldn't get done. Those are the rules and I have to follow them, just like everyone else. They're already short staffed at the newspaper office and they don't have time to do my work for me. I have to do it myself and it has to be done correctly. I can do all that in my home office, easy as pie, but not here. Not even close I'm afraid."

"I think it would work better doing it my way. I'll get you all set up, darlin', you'll see."

157

She could feel her blood beginning to boil as her patience, which she was never known to have an over-abundance of anyway, was just about at its limit.

"That's just not possible, I have to go and take care of it at home. That's the way it's set up and I have to do it that way."

"Aren't rules made to be broken, Miss Ginger? I break 'em all the time and the world is still turning. You need to loosen up a little, try something different for a change."

"Some rules can be bent a little, I agree, but not this one. Now I'm going to ask you very nicely to walk me to my vehicle and see me safely inside. Then I can go home and get to work on the rest of the publishing opportunities I told you about. Will you do that for me please?"

"If you leave, you walk to your car on your own."

"I can't, I'm afraid of your dogs."

"And you should be."

"Please! I want to go home!"

"Then try your luck with the dogs. That's the way it's going to be. You won't break your rules, so I won't break mine. You're staying here with me. Get used to it."

"Look, there are people who will wonder where I am if I don't go home."

He laughed. "Right, like who, your make-believe husband? That good-for-nothing editor of yours?"

"I … I have a boyfriend, a very jealous boyfriend. He knows where I was going and he won't like it that I'm late. He'll come looking for me and you wouldn't want to tangle with him, trust me. Neither will your dogs."

He laughed, enjoying himself. "You've got to be the worst liar I ever met. There's only one jealous boyfriend, darlin', and it's me. Now go on inside like a good girl and stop giving me grief."

She looked him in the eye. "I'm not going back inside, I'm going home."

Turning, he went back into the kitchen and returned with the handgun. He pointed the weapon in her direction. "And I say you're not going home if you can't get past those dogs on your own. Guess which one of us wins? Me. Now get inside or you're going to get an even closer look at this gun. Capiche?"

She could feel tears threatening, but refused to give in to them. Jutting out her chin she marched past him, going into the living room and reclaiming the armchair she'd previously occupied. There had to be some way to summon help, some way to call 9-1-1 on her cellphone. She didn't have to say anything, just activate that emergency service and the police would find her. All 9-1-1 calls were always checked out, so she'd have to find a way to dial that number without Cedric seeing her.

He was busy doing something in the kitchen when she called out to him. "Cedric, I need to use your washroom. Where is it?"

"It's right through the door at the end there, right beside the little room with all your pictures."

"Thank you, I won't be long."

She hoped he didn't become suspicious of her sudden conciliatory tone, but once inside she took her cellphone from her purse and with trembling hands activated 9-1-1. She was relieved to hear it ring. Her heart was in her mouth when her call was answered quickly. As loudly as she dared, she whispered: "HELP! I'm being held against my will," then gave the operator Cedric's name and address. She prayed they'd get here before this crackpot did anything to harm her. "My name is Ginger...."

She froze mid-sentence as a furious Cedric wrenched the door open, gun in hand.

Chapter Eight

Shane grabbed something to eat and took a quick shower but still had a couple of hours before his shift started at six. This day already seemed unnaturally long, and it had certainly been a few hours of great change. He'd always be grateful to Hank for his forthrightness. That had been a blessing in disguise, although he wouldn't try to pretend that his difficult revelations hadn't been some of the most painful words he'd ever heard. At the end of the day though he had to know the truth, needed to hear it and had made that challenging journey from suspicions to cold hard facts. Nothing could have prepared him for that transition, but it was something that had to be faced at some point if he hoped to live an authentic life and not one of make believe. He'd already had the make-believe kind with his marriage to April, next time around he wanted the real thing.

His willingness to try again surprised him. Somehow he thought he'd be bitter because of how his marriage had failed but he would have had to deal with it sooner or later anyway if April had lived. And now some random doctor had apparently lost the love of his life, although he was hard pressed to feel bad about that part of it. Nevertheless it was terrible that the guy had died trying to help people. Shane snapped himself back to the present and promised himself he would make a conscious effort to leave the past in the past.

Slipping into a clean uniform, he was dressed and out of the house before he had time to think too much about what he was going to do next. Score another point for Hank the quasi psychologist who'd succeeded in breaking through walls that Shane had erected so carefully around himself. So he would take a swing by his father's house and see if he was home. He had been thinking about his father for a while now. It had been parked right there in the front of his brain waiting for attention. He'd tried his best to ignore it, but today was the day he'd act on that intention. He was still in the mood for change, so he might as well continue to strike while the iron was hot.

There was a car in the driveway at his father's house, a two-story mock Tudor in one of the newer subdivisions. Shane had gotten his address online, so Weston Elliott didn't know he was coming. Shane had to admire the neatly manicured lawn, what he could see of it in the rain. Any fallen leaves had been raked and contained in a row of green compost bags stacked at the curb.

His father answered on the first knock and with a wide smile welcomed his son inside. His light blonde hair, which Shane had inherited from him, was now liberally threaded with silver but as always, closely cropped. Shane had gotten his grey eyes from his mother and judging from the few pictures he had of her, they were far and away her best feature. But while his mother had not been very tall, he and his dad were both over six feet.

"Well if this isn't a nice surprise, come on in. I was just sitting out in the sunroom reading. I was enjoying the sun earlier, but it's a different story now. This is some storm." He looked out the door past Shane. "I forgot to take in those leaves but I guess it's too late to worry about them now. I meant to set them in the garage. I cleaned them up once, I don't want to have to do it a second time if those bags get banged around in the wind. It's a big job raking."

"Yeah I've got a yard full of leaves waiting for me at home and I'll probably get to them tomorrow. We are supposed to get some rain with the high winds and I find it easier to rake them up when they're wet."

"With this wind, maybe they'll blow into the neighbour's yard and you won't have to bother with them at all," said his father, trying to break the ice with small talk.

Shane nodded, his attempt at a smile not really amounting to much. He followed his father into the house and was ushered into what he'd probably referred to as the sunroom. He took a seat in a generous rattan armchair beside a lemon tree with actual little lemons actually growing on it. The room overlooked a spacious back yard, the sliding glass door providing an unimpeded view of the wild weather outside. Weston Elliott, having fetched a cup of tea for both of them settled back into a matching armchair opposite his son. He crossed his legs and took a long pull on his tea before setting the cup on the small glass table beside him. "It's nice to see you, Shaney. I'm glad you've come. I've missed you."

Shane swallowed a flash of irritation. Shaney just brought back too many crappy memories. "Any chance you can call me Shane, Dad, and not Shaney?"

"Shaney's your name. It's what I called you when you were a kid and I guess it stuck. Sorry."

"And I used to call you Daddy when I was little, and as you can see I'm not a kid anymore. Shane. My name's Shane."

Weston sighed, as though steeling himself for the difficult exchange he likely suspected was coming.

"Okay, Shane, what's on your mind?" Weston asked as a clap of thunder sounded overhead.

Shane hadn't come to make old wrongs right. It was much too late for that. Hank was the reason he was here, their earlier conversation providing the impetus for the visit. He knew he'd have come sooner or later, as it turned out he'd come sooner than he expected he would.

"Just thought I'd drop by and see how you're doing is all. It's been awhile since we've talked. I thought maybe we could get back to doing that, you know, see each other now and then. Keep in touch. Maybe make up for some lost time, stuff like that."

Weston folded his hands in his lap. "I'd like that, son. I know I wasn't exactly father of the year when you were growing up. I have to live with the fact that I made a lot of mistakes with you; missed way too much of your life when you were young. I wish I had it all to do over again, but of course there are no rewinds for that kind of thing. There was a point when I decided to be a better man for you, but by then you didn't want to have anything to do with me and I never got to tell you. So I'm telling you now. I would have looked you up a long time ago but I got the impression you didn't want to see me. I hoped every day that you'd change your mind and we could get together and catch up. I don't blame you for feeling the

165

way you do. I didn't get it right as a father when you were a kid. Not even close."

Shane waved his hand. "I didn't come here to take inventory, I really didn't. I've let a lot of things go already, well, most of it anyway. I think the most important thing is that you're sober now … you are still sober aren't you?"

Weston smiled, reaching for the cup of tea and holding it aloft as proof that he now preferred something other than booze. "I'm still into unleaded as you can see. I'm sure you recall that by this time of day I'd be licking the bottom of the bottle. To answer your question, I haven't had a drink in nine years and every day I pray for the strength to continue."

"Do you still think about it?"

"What, having a drink? Of course I do."

"But you'll probably never touch it again."

"With the good Lord's help I won't, but it's one day at a time. As I sit here right now I don't intend to ever drink again, but I have to be more realistic than that. I only have to get through today, and then tomorrow … but I don't focus on it like I used to. I have an illness and I'm thankful, son, that you don't suffer from it too."

"I'll drink to that," said Shane, raising his own cup in a toast to sobriety.

"Anyway, it's good to be out from under all that. I was very hard on the people in my life. I've tried to make amends...."

"I know you did, Dad, and I wouldn't let you. I just couldn't see any good reason at the time to let you ease your conscience. I was pretty hard on you, I understand that now."

"And I was rough on you growing up."

"Let's call it a draw then, okay?" Shane asked quietly, then glanced around. "This is a great place you've got here. Some nice touches."

"If that's your way of asking if there's a woman in my life, the answer is no."

"Oh."

"After the last divorce I came to the startling conclusion that I'm okay on my own and decided to leave it that way, at least for a while. It's less expensive if you know what I mean. How about you? How are you doing now? It's been what, three years since April died?"

Shane nodded, not intending to go into any details about the whole April thing. "I'm still on my own too. Been thinking lately though that I should probably try to meet someone. I'm ready to move ahead with my life."

"I think that would be a good idea. I'm glad to hear you've come to grips with her death. That was such a tragedy, her taken like that. You'll go a long ways to find someone as good as her though, so I can see why you haven't even tried. She was an angel if ever there was one. So beautiful and sweet, very dedicated to you, Shane. You guys had the perfect marriage. I was always glad about that."

Shane studied his hands lying loosely in his lap. "No marriage is perfect."

"You two came about as close as anybody I know. You must still miss her terribly."

"I miss the good times, yes. I suppose it's the same with anything, but I'm finally ready to move past what happened and meet someone. I'm tired of being on my own."

Weston nodded, his eyes never leaving his son's face. "I can completely understand about that, and I'm glad to hear you're getting back in the game."

Shane cringed at his father's choice of words, but knew what he meant so decided not to take him to task. But unbidden, another thought came to mind. "Dad, do you ever go to Mum's grave?"

Weston dropped his eyes to his shoes, staring as though it was the first time he'd ever laid eyes on them and needed to commit every detail to memory. "No, I don't."

Shane felt a rush of anger but managed to tamp it down. This was not a blame game, and maybe for the first time he and his father could have a meaningful conversation without it ending in an argument. His appetite had been whetted by Hank Peterson's empathetic approach. He saw no reason why it couldn't be the same with his father, although Hank and his father were very different. Hank was quiet and thoughtful, while Weston Elliott always thought he needed to be the life of the party, but then again that had likely been the booze talking. It would be interesting to get to know the man who wasn't always drunk, something he hadn't had much of a chance to do growing up. He knew too that he had to meet him at least halfway because there had been some very harsh words between them on more than one occasion.

"Can you tell me why?" he asked, hoping he wouldn't ignite something explosive inside of his father. It was a delicate subject between them, given his reaction to the question he'd just asked him.

"I couldn't." Weston pulled a cigarette from a pack sitting on the table beside him, before turning to his son. "Mind if I have a cigarette? I mean the smoke won't bother you will it?"

Shane shrugged. "It's your house, knock yourself out."

"You don't smoke I take it."

"I had the habit but I kicked it a couple of years ago. So, why couldn't you? Go to her grave I mean?"

"It was just too hard for me to do that."

Shane resisted the urge to shake his head in annoyance. "It was the least you could have done."

Weston coloured. Shane had struck a nerve. "What, under the circumstances? Seeing as how I drove her to do what she did?"

"Yeah, something like that."

Setting his cigarette in the ashtray, Weston ran his hand over his face wearily before shifting to meet Shane's glittering stare. "There's stuff you don't know, Shaney ... sorry ... Shane."

"What, that you were running around on her and she couldn't take it?"

Weston retrieved his cigarette, inhaled deeply and blew a smoke ring before returning his attention to his son. "I thought you said you didn't come here to take inventory."

"I didn't. That question just leaked out, but now that it has...."

"It sounds like you have your mind all made up, but let me ask you this. Do you think you can deal with the truth? I mean about your mother and me?"

Oh geez! Not another deep dark revelation! Maybe there had been enough truth telling for one day. Why couldn't he have kept his big mouth shut?

"Come on, Shane, can you handle the fact that maybe I wasn't a villain? The one you always figured was in the wrong? I think it is time you heard the truth and if you've got the stomach for it, let me know and I'll tell you the way it really was, man to man. But if you can't take it...."

Shane braced himself for what was to come. "I can take it. Are you going to tell me that Mum was the one running around on you?"

"No, that's not what I'm going to tell you at all. What I am going to tell you is that your mother turned away from me, in bed I mean, right after you were born. She was never what you'd call enthusiastic, no matter how hard I tried, but after you came along she refused to have anything more to do with me as far as sex was concerned. She didn't even want to kiss me. She told me, right up front, that she had no interest in sex; didn't want to have any more babies and that I could do what I wanted as long as I left her alone."

"But you were drinking like a fish at the time, are you trying to say that was her fault? That she drove you to that? Come on!"

"Of course not, although I really didn't drink all that heavily when she and I first got together. Alcoholism is a progressive

171

disease and of course it got worse as I went along. I'm not blaming her for any of that."

"So that's why you turned to other women? You weren't getting any at home?"

"You can put a nasty spin on this if you want to. I was a healthy young man with needs, and I satisfied those needs outside the home, yes. I loved your mother, but she didn't love me, Shane. She just lost interest."

"What does that mean, lost interest?"

"I have no idea, she just closed off; refused to talk about it."

"There was no other man?"

"No."

"So why did she kill herself? Because of that?"

"I don't know. All I can think is that she was a very unhappy woman. She loved you though, I can tell you that."

"If she loved me so much why did she leave me like that? You'd have thought she'd stick around at least long enough to see how I turned out."

"You'd think." He stubbed out his cigarette. "The whole thing was a mess and you were the one who got short changed all way around. Kids don't ask to be born, but boy were you ever dropped into a dysfunctional family."

"How you're saying my mother acted doesn't make sense."

"Tell me about it. She just folded in on herself a year or two into our marriage. She was so hateful...."

Shane was sorry he had ever asked the question. Did everything involve a deep dark secret? Did every answer have to be a wakeup call? When would he ever learn not to ask, although it was healthy to clean out a wound and let the air at it. Allow it to heal. He'd always thought it was his father who was the bad guy. He was no prize dad, but he too had a lot on his plate. It was funny how you could think someone was a jerk your whole life only to find out they'd been a victim too. By his father's own admission though he was the author of his own fate to a certain extent.

"So now that we're on the subject, can you tell me why my grandmother and grandfather, my mother's parents, never seemed to want to have anything to do with me? It's not that it matters all that much now, but I've always been curious as to why it was like that."

Weston drained the rest of his tea then set the cup back down and folded his arms in front of him. The self protective gesture was not lost on his son. Weston, for all his bluster, was not comfortable having this conversation. Shane wondered what was coming next.

"Let me put it this way, your mother always considered herself lucky that she'd escaped from that house. You were the fortunate one, you never had to deal with them at all. Does that answer your question?"

"Why were they so terrible?"

"For one thing your grandfather Neilson was a religious nut and his wife was just as bad and by that I don't mean good Christian folk. I mean anti-government, anti-everything chest beaters who saw the world as their enemy. Everything was a conspiracy. Your mother did suggest we take you to meet them one time but I wouldn't allow it, not after what they'd done to her. I met her at a dance she had snuck out to. She was twenty years old and still living at home, under their thumb. She wasn't permitted to wear make-up, style her hair or anything like that. They forbid her to go out on dates and that included the dance where I met her, but she went anyway. To make a long story short, I rescued her you might as well say. They were the ones who screwed her up and they did a bang-up job. It made her impossible to live with. She had no desire to be with me but she couldn't bring herself to make the changes in her life that she might have wanted to.

"So you can thank me for sparing you … them, because they weren't fit to be around. Even if it was just that one thing, at least I did something right. I didn't want them getting their hooks into you."

174

Shane had to chuckle. "Well then thank you. I never knew."

"I guess it was easier to make me the bad guy."

"Mum was no picnic either a lot of the time."

"I know. She was angry, I was angry and piss drunk most of the time so you got dumped on from both sides and it wasn't right. You got a rotten deal, son. It's funny how someone can start out with the best of intentions and then everything goes off the rails."

"So you both wanted me did you? I was planned?"

"Wanted you! When I found out your mother was pregnant with you I was very happy, we both were, or I thought she was. But anyway, I must have passed out a hundred cigars the day you were born. I gave to people on the way to work, at the fire station, on the street, whatever. It's hard to understand how a man can go from the way I was that day to how we ended up, but I managed to do it."

Shane nodded, thoughtfully, trying to process what he was hearing. At least he was a wanted child and that in itself made all the difference. He always figured he'd been a mistake or something, an accident and that's why they never seemed to want him around. But they had wanted him, or his father had, but he didn't want to dig any deeper on the whole parent thing. Some stones were best left unturned.

"I really didn't come here to extract an apology for past wrongs. I've decided to let it be water under the bridge. I did have some questions, and I'm glad we've had this talk, man-to-man. It was long overdue."

"You may not have come here for an apology, but I'm going to give you one all the same. I think you know I've been trying for a long time to say I'm sorry, but you didn't want to hear me. I am sorry for the way things were, Shane. It wasn't fair. You were just a little boy and I should have done better. If I could go back and do it all over, I would make a lot of changes. So do you think we can get our relationship back on track, or I should say start over and get it right this time?"

He looked at his father, one a carbon copy of the other. He saw the hope in his father's eyes. "Sure, I don't see why not. Let's just take it from here. I'll give you a call in a couple of weeks or so and see what you're doing. Maybe we can get together or something."

"I'd like that, Shane, very much. And you'll never guess what. I took a bunch of cooking lessons online and now I'm pretty handy in the kitchen. How about the next time we get together I cook a nice meal for us? And if you're seeing someone by then, you could bring her along too and I promise not to poison either one of you. How does that sound?"

Shane smiled with more warmth. "It sounds great, Dad. I'll be in touch."

As he backed out of the driveway he felt as though even more weight had been lifted from his shoulders as the layers continued to be peeled away. This full disclosure thing was really working out. He had something else on his mind too that he decided in that moment to act upon. He was on a roll, so why not get everything cleared up at the same time?

It had struck him while he was cleaning out the house that he no longer wanted to live at number fourteen Osprey Lane. It was a great house and they'd made a lot of renovations to get it the way they wanted, but now all it held for him was bad memories. And then there was the shrine thing. He decided he didn't want to look at that room one more time, let alone the rest of his life. He had to get rid of it.

That meant he had to start looking for another place, but then again wouldn't that be a great project? Maybe he'd get a fixer-upper and give himself a whole new hobby to work on. This time he'd go for location first and either rebuild or renovate. That's exactly what he'd do! He'd look for something a little further out this time, not way out so that he'd have a long commute every day, but something doable;

something on the river would be nice. Wouldn't that be great to wake up to every day? Wow, he was getting more into this by the minute and when he swung into the real estate office parking lot he was glad to see that the OPEN sign still in the window.

Fifteen minutes later he'd made arrangements to list with the same agent who'd acted for the original sale. Back in his car he made his way through massive puddles as he headed to Remington's, the jewellery store where he'd purchased their wedding bands. He couldn't help but think how happy he'd been the day he'd picked out the three-ring set. He'd spent a fortune, but then again there was this spectacular future ahead of him so why not splurge? Ha! He knew it would be a long time before he'd be ring hunting again.

When the little bell dingled over the door and he stepped up to the counter, he had no second thoughts when he pulled the rings out of his pocket. Unwrapping them from the piece of paper towel, he laid them on the counter. Walt Remington, the owner, smiled and nodded as though he remembered the pieces, but looked sad that they were no longer needed. He likely wouldn't remember April's accident.

The consignment price he gave Shane was ridiculously low considering what he'd paid for them, but he understood they were now second-hand. Still they were worth quite a lot.

"I'll have to clean them and polish them up, but I think they should sell fairly quickly," Walt told him. "They were one of our finer sets. In fact it was the only one I had like it. The diamond ring was so unique, the main stone surrounded by actual miniature emeralds, not just stone chips."

Shane nodded. "Now should I check in with you or will you call me?"

"We'll call," Walt assured him, and Shane wished him a good day as he left.

He didn't feel as bad as he feared he might after disposing of the rings he'd given to the woman he swore he'd love for the rest of his life.

Yet another layer had been stripped away and he glanced at his watch. He still had a half hour before the start of his shift so he might as well stop for coffee. Rather than use the drive thru he decided to park and do a walk in, rain and all. Maybe he'd see the beautiful brunette with the incredible blue eyes who seemed to like coffee as much as he did.

Sure enough, there she was sitting at a corner table, but his spirits took a slight nosedive when he saw she was not alone. Sitting beside her was a man and a good looking one at that, and he was holding her hand. Okay then. That answered that question; it was a dead end. She was a real looker so it shouldn't come as a surprise that she had a boyfriend. It had to be a boyfriend because she wasn't wearing a ring. He'd checked that out quite a while ago, but a woman as pretty as her could get all the male attention she wanted when she batted those eyes. Not that she'd given him any indication that she was either available or interested. It had been him all the way. Okay, shot down in flames, he told himself as he ordered a large coffee to go and retraced his steps without so much as a second glance at the table in the corner. You win some and you lose some, and the coffee shop girl was definitely lost to him.

No problem, he told himself, there's a lot of fish in the sea and another one would come swimming by sooner or later. Until she did he was plenty busy, especially with this new house project he'd placed on his radar. He got excited just thinking about it. Besides, he wasn't in a rush to meet anyone. It wasn't like he was desperate or anything, it was just that she had really caught his eye.

His coffee had cooled to an enjoyable temperature as he settled behind his desk and pulled a report file in front of him. There was always paperwork. It was funny when he wanted a career in law enforcement he hadn't thought a thing at all about paperwork, a necessity no matter what line of work you chose. None of the recruitment posters had ever said a thing about that either of course, but it went with the territory. He lifted his head as someone knocked on his door.

"Hey, Shane. A 9-1-1 call just came in. It sounds like we might have a hostage situation in the works. A woman says she's being held against her will."

Chapter Nine

Cedric grabbed the phone from her with his free hand and threw it across the room where it crashed against the wall and clattered to the floor. "Who were you calling?"

"No one."

"Don't lie to me! You were talking to someone and I want to know who it was."

Anger surged through her at the temerity of this man. "It's my telephone and I can use it if I want to," she threw at him recklessly.

She doubted he'd shoot her for making a telephone call, but that was a loaded weapon in his hand. Or more to the point he had told her it was loaded. He'd probably told her that to get her going. He knew she was here representing the newspaper. Wouldn't he naturally assume that someone knew where she'd be? People who'd be waiting for her and come looking for her if she didn't return by a reasonable hour? That wasn't exactly the case, but he didn't know that. He was full of himself, yes, but she doubted he was as crazy as he was making himself out to be, although.....

"You were sneaking to make a call behind my back, in my home, and that makes it my business. You had no right to do that."

False bravado pushed it's way to the forefront. She'd had enough of this! She'd played relatively nice up 'til now, but she wanted to leave and she'd bet that if she really pushed him he'd give in and walk her to her car. She'd explain to the police that it was a misunderstanding if in fact he did let her leave. That everything had been sorted out.

"Cedric, listen to me. This has gone far enough. I'm leaving. Now!" she announced as she brushed past him, retrieved her phone from the other side of the room, and slipped it into her purse.

Marching to the door she grabbed her workbag where it sat on the kitchen table. Pulling the door open she looked back at him. "I have told you very nicely I want to go, and you have no right to prevent me from doing that. There will be consequences if you do. Now I know those dogs are under your command but I'm advising you to see me safely on my way."

He didn't budge. Her bluff didn't appear to be working, and she guessed from the dumbfounded look on his face that not many people had spoken to him in that way. He looked like a man who didn't take well to having anything demanded of him. In the blink of an eye the look of astonishment was replaced with anger. It was storming outside all right, but if the fury now shining in his eyes was any indication, what was being unleashed by Mother Nature wouldn't hold a candle to what was about to happen indoors. In that moment she knew real fear. She had poked a very bad-tempered bear, and it was about to attack. Hadn't he told her himself a short time ago that what made a bear so dangerous was its unpredictability? He'd also called himself the bear man and he was well named given his unpredictable volatility. She knew from now on she'd be wise to play by his rules and not antagonize him any further. It was already plain that she had lit a lethal fuse, and she braced herself for the explosion. She didn't have long to wait.

He crossed the room in two steps and caught her by the hair. It was cut in a short style, but he managed to grab a fistful. "You would dare to speak to me like that? No one speaks to me like that and lives. No one! And if you're thinking this gun isn't really loaded, think again because it is. Would you like me to show you?"

She shook her head slightly, not easy given his punishing grip. The pain was white hot. Any movement at all made it worse. Now might be a good time for an apology. She was sure her 9-1-1 call had gone out; she could hear them, but she wasn't entirely sure they could hear her. Thank God Cedric hadn't had presence of mind to destroy the device, so its signal was still a clear beacon. She might have had a hard time finding him, but the police would track her down pretty fast and maybe once they arrived on the scene she could get out of here relatively unscathed.

"I'm sorry, Cedric," she lied, wincing. "I was calling my sister and I should have told you what I was doing. That way you'd know it was nothing more than a friendly call. Again, I'm sorry I upset you. That was not very professional of me."

She yelped as he tightened his hold. "I don't believe you. You're lying to me, I can smell it off you. One minute you're telling me what you're going to do and what you're not going to do like you own the place, and the next you're falling all over yourself saying you're sorry."

"That's because I had no idea it would upset you. How was I to know that? I didn't think a simple telephone call would get you so angry or I wouldn't have done it."

"What is your sister's name?"

"Naomi."

"Are you close? Is she like your best buddy or something? I don't want her coming to my house bothering us and I

185

heard you give her my name and address. What was that all about if you weren't trying to get her to come? I'm telling you if she does show up you'll be sorry and so will she, because those dogs haven't been fed in a day or so. I keep them hungry to keep them on edge. That's the secret to any good guard dog. So tell me, is she coming here?"

"No, she's not. I was just telling her where I was and that I'd be home soon, and yes, we're kind of close. She is my sister."

"Why would you say you're going to be home?" he screamed at her tugging her hair so hard she was sure it must be close to being ripped out. "You're staying here!"

"I'm sorry," she sobbed. "I didn't mean any harm. You're hurting me! If you want me to talk you have to stop hurting me."

He held on, pressing the gun against her temple.

"Why wouldn't she know your name? When I opened the door you were saying this is Ginger. How would she not know it was you calling if you're so gall darned close? You're a liar!"

She shifted her weight and even that slight movement produced a fresh wave of pain. "I don't know," she managed, "I said my name is all. I do it all the time. I really didn't think about it, but I'm sorry if you think I disrespected you."

"I'll bet you are, with a loaded gun at your head. You know it's funny. A woman is all brave when they're telling you what to do, then as soon as she sees what it's going to cost her for shooting off her mouth, she gets all apologetic. That's the way it was with Annabelle. She was going to leave you know, told me she wanted to start a new life; that she wasn't happy with me. She threatened to walk out that very door that you thought you were going to. I changed her mind in a hurry though, just like I changed yours. Do we understand each other now?"

"Yes," she squeaked.

"Do you know what I'm saying to you?"

"That Annabelle's death wasn't an accident?"

"Oh but it was. Such a horrible accident." She could hear the smirk in his voice and it made her blood run cold. "But she didn't leave me, did she? And why, because I didn't give her the chance? I know how to handle women who try to get away, women with a mouth."

The truth struck her like an icy wet rag to the face, and her fear shot to a new level. Dear God, he had murdered Annabelle. The woman he said he was so in love with. And what about the cousin? She could only assume he had crossed Cedric in some way too. Was she next?

He brought his face closer to hers and his breath smelled sour, fishy. She fought the urge to gag and managed to keep from doing so with an iron-willed effort. With his hair trigger temper things could get much worse, fast. She refused to let her mind wander to what he might have in mind since he'd removed all doubt that she was his prisoner. Maybe before the whole thing was over she would wish she was dead. It might be more merciful. She needed help.

Her thoughts turned traitorous, taunting her with stories she'd heard of botched 9-1-1 calls, operators who'd assumed the call was a prank and did not activate a response. They were few and far between, but she knew it happened; the operator reprimanded when it was proved the call for help had been real. She shoved such thoughts from her mind. She knew the police would come, but where were they? First they had to find her, she told herself. There was the inevitable travelling time of course and it had only been a few minutes. They couldn't materialize out of nowhere. She prayed like never before that help would arrive soon. She was trapped with a madman, one who had invited her to his lair. She couldn't get there fast enough because she wanted a good story, and she certainly had one. She had enough explosive stuff from Cedric to write a whole series of stories, but that candour came

188

with a price. Would someone else now write the story about her death? Stop! she mentally warned herself.

He continued to hold onto her hair and she gritted her teeth as he propelled her across the room to the same armchair she'd been sitting in to conduct the interview. Releasing her as suddenly as he'd grabbed her, she went off balance. Her thigh collided painfully against the arm of the chair as she tumbled sideways. Quickly righting herself, she sat in the chair and continued to watch him closely. If she looked away, she might be in for yet another nasty surprise.

He set the gun on the coffee table, then with remarkable strength in those sinewy arms of his yanked the chair around so that it was facing the entrance to the kitchen. She was too terrified to move. It crossed her mind to kick him where it would hurt the most, but even if she did manage to disable him, there was still those damned dogs waiting downstairs. It even flitted dangerously across her mind that if she could get hold of the gun she could make him let her go. She'd even shoot at the dogs if she had to, frighten them away long enough to get to her car. Her keys were pressing into her leg through the front pocket of her slacks and she knew if she ever got the chance to reach her vehicle safely, she'd burn rubber to leave this house of horrors behind.

Her adrenalin, in anticipation of putting her plan into action, pumped molten hot through her veins. But once again he read her accurately, and she guessed that was what made him such a good hunter. He had an uncanny ability to read his quarry. Whether two-legged or four-legged, he stayed one step ahead. He was a survivalist, a very skilled one, and unfortunately for her, she was his prey.

"I can read your eyes, darlin', so don't even think about kicking me," he said much too easily. "You wouldn't have a prayer of getting to that gun before I do, disabled or not. I doubt you've ever fired a handgun, let alone get used to the weight of it in your hand as quickly as you'd need to. You wouldn't be able to hit the broad side of a barn. And then there's my pals, Reaper, Jaws and Terminator. All I'd have to do is make it to that door and they'd be on you. I doubt you'd even get the gun aimed, so kudos to a brave little plan but it would be a special kind of stupid to try it. Capisce?"

She looked away, not wanting to meet his eyes.

"I said, capisce?"

Again she didn't answer.

With a lightning move he grabbed her chin, snatching her face around until she had no choice but to look at him. "I said, capisce?"

"Capisce," she said as nausea rose in her throat, a wave of revulsion as she was forced to look into those cold, snake-like eyes.

Just as suddenly as he'd grabbed her, he let go, straightening to stand. "Don't move a muscle," he warned her. "I have to use the little boy's room but I want you to stay in that chair."

Again she considered flight in her desperate need to get away from him, but once again he was one step ahead of her. "And I have the perfect way to keep you honest. Trust me, you're going to love it … or maybe not." He chuckled. "Remember now, don't even twitch a muscle."

Going to the back door he held it open and whistled one short shrill burst and within seconds three very large German shepherds barrelled into the kitchen. He didn't fondle them as he undid their long chains, but rather commanded them to settle down.

"These animals are not my pets," he informed her unnecessarily from the kitchen, "they are working dogs. Their territory is the yard; I've only brought them indoors to do this job."

She wondered what that might be, to tear her apart? He'd warned her not to move. That was never so easy to accomplish as it was in this moment. She'd already turned to stone, frozen with terror as the three dogs followed him into the living room. On the command of HALT! SIT! they sat a shoulder's width apart, their eyes fixed on her. One whisper, one twitch and they'd likely attack.

"I would advise you not to look them in the eye," he said, "it will only make them more aggressive. They have a very high prey drive. It's all about the chase and capture for them, and they'd be just as happy to play that little game with you. Now sit tight and try not to get on their nerves. Do not fight me or disrespect me in any way, and don't even think about escape. I can only control them so far and then nature takes over. If I even so much as raise my voice, you're hamburger." He thought for a moment. "I'd say the dogs would be a great addition to the story you're going to write. The stories.

"Now I don't have to tell you that I'm very angry with you at the moment. They're picking up on my mood, so don't do anything that might displease me any further. Don't move a muscle, not even a little tiny one."

Cedric left the room and closed the bathroom door behind him. The dogs, now understanding they were the ones running the show, began to growl threateningly, low in their throat. It was an ominous warning.

She vacillated between wanting to look at them, to know when the attack would come, and not wanting to stir them up any more. She began to pray like she had never prayed before. She was not one to pray, at all. Given her current situation however it would have been great to have had a closer relationship with her Maker seeing as how her life was now in His hands. She sent silent prayers heavenward, careful not to move her lips and possibly precipitate further aggression.

She'd always enjoyed the many adventures she had as a freelance writer. She couldn't imagine anything she would rather be doing in her spare time than chasing down an interesting story. Because of her writing she'd flown in helicopters, been to sea in rescue boats, been chased by an angry ostrich, fed baby emus, steered ships and in general had a load of fun. Add to that the countless number of fascinating people she'd crossed paths with and had the enjoyment of picking their brains. It had been a heck of a ride so far. But then like everything else in life, her luck had basically run out. She was in deep trouble.

Just then her cellphone rang in her purse sitting on the floor by the coffee. The strident sound made her jump. The dogs itching it seemed for any small encouragement for a fight from their quarry, were now on their feet growling ferociously.

The more the phone rang, the more excited the dogs became. She wondered what moment they would pounce. She dared not take even the tiniest of glances in their direction.

She thought she would pass out from dread, a miniscule amount of oxygen reaching her lungs because she was literally afraid to breathe. Finally her phone fell silent. Still Cedric did not emerge from the bathroom. What was taking so long? It wasn't as though having him guard her was the better choice, but at least she might be able to reason with him. His canine partners didn't appear to be approachable at all. She thought of speaking soothingly to them, but no, it was Cedric they would respond to and he had clearly identified her as the enemy. It was apparent they understood very well they were to guard this prisoner and it seemed they were itching for her to make the wrong move.

She felt an overwhelming need to take a deep refreshing breath for her oxygen starved lungs but was too afraid to do so, the dogs so close she could literally smell their breath. She wondered if there were any missing persons in this neck of the woods and if so, was she next?

With tiny frequent sips she was managing to get the air she needed, but she could see out of the corner of her eye that the dogs were still on their feet. She was tempted beyond all reason to issue the command of sit. Maybe it was the lack of oxygen that was getting to her brain that made her think that would be an option.

Her cellphone sprang to life again and she hoped the dogs didn't notice that she involuntarily jumped at the sound. They did, now dancing in place and barking loudly. They seemed to be waiting for the command to attack. That couldn't have been more clear than if they were able to speak and confirm her suspicion. He said he kept them hungry and now she was offering up two prayers. The first was to quiet the dogs, distract them somehow. The second was that whomever was calling on her phone would stop; hang up, leave a message or whatever. And it didn't help matters that in addition to the ringing, her phone was also set to vibrate. That seemed to elevate the dogs' excitement even further.

Again the phone stopped ringing, so there was prayer number two answered. Now if the dogs could just lose interest. She'd done a story once on animals and little known facts about them, and a dog trainer confirmed during the interview that dogs can actually smell fear. Boy was she giving them a full blast right now. He'd also told her it was the same thing with bees.

She heard the toilet flush and even though it went against everything she knew to be right and prudent, she was actually relieved that Cedric was going to be back in the room. She would try harder to reason with him, pretend to understand him, find some common ground that would spare her life. Enough had been said and done here today that proved he was unstable, but would he kill her? Who knew? He did enjoy scaring her.

"SIT!" he told the excited dogs, and they sat, although they never took their eyes off her. She didn't even have to look to know that, she could feel the intensity of their stare deep in her soul. It would be like staring down the barrel of a loaded gun if she dared to look into those eyes. As if that wasn't enough, the real thing was sitting on the coffee table only a few feet away.

"Was that your cellphone I heard ringing just now?"

She was terrified to move, trembling like a leaf. She didn't want to make him any angrier than he already was.

Unexpectedly he whistled to the dogs and they followed him to the back room. She did breathe deeply then, faint with relief, as she heard him close the door behind them. Tears threatened as she gulped air freely to try to restore at least some of her equilibrium.

"Yes, that was my phone."

"It has a stupid ring by the way. Why would it ring like that? It's annoying."

"I agree it is annoying and I've been meaning to change it but I haven't gotten around to it yet. That particular ring is called Spin Time if you can imagine," she chattered on still trying to find some good humour in him.

As off-putting as he was when she'd first arrived, she'd give anything to have him in that jocular mood again. Perhaps she'd be lucky enough to talk him into letting her go. And now with the dogs in the backroom she might have a fighting chance. But she knew as soon as she dared to entertain the thought that it wouldn't work. Her legs at the moment were like wet noodles. Her adrenalin which had minutes ago been pumping at warp speed, seemed to have eased off and she felt weak in the aftermath of that fight or flight push.

"I wouldn't have a cellphone if they paid me to take one," Cedric offered companionably. "They're nothing but a nuisance. A person can't be left alone for a second that someone isn't trying to talk to them."

"I agree," she said. "I wouldn't bother with one either only that it helps me with my work if I need to call someone on the road. It's saved me on more than one occasion, like if I was lost or didn't get the directions right. So in that respect they're good, but other than that you're right. They are a nuisance."

Thunder crashed one almighty crack overhead, the wind now hammering the house. Mother nature was in the foulest of moods. When she decided to throw a tantrum, she got into it pretty good.

"Looks like the storm is still overhead," he said glancing toward the window, "and you know what that means don't you?"

He hesitated so she rushed to answer him, still trying to humour him into a better mood.

"No, what does that mean?" she asked, forcing playfulness into her tone.

"It means we get to ride out the storm together. I love a good thunderstorm. Like any other force of nature, it's always more fun when you get to share it with someone. You, Ginger Martel, are that someone. We'll get under the covers and let everything flash and boom around us. That's what Annabelle and I used to do. It was like our own little corner of the world and nothing could touch us as long as we stayed hidden."

The thought of being under the covers with him soured her stomach in a way like nothing else ever had. In trying to improve his humour she had talked herself right into his bed. Way to go, Martel, she berated herself. Being in bed with him would be like crawling into a snake pit. As phobic as she was about snakes, that suddenly seemed like the better option. You knew where you stood with the snakes.

"You really are going to like it here, Ginger. I'm sorry I was so stern with you earlier, but you gave me no choice, disrespecting me like that. I can't put up with that kind of behaviour, from anybody. Now that you've settled down and see what the rules are, I think we're going to get along fine. Don't ever cross me, darlin'. I know I seem harsh, but I think we understand each other better now, don't we?"

All she could do was nod, her scalp still on fire as dread spiked through her like one of those lightning bolts lighting up the yard. Maybe if the dogs stayed in the house for the night and he was a sound sleeper she could get away, although it had really begun to settle home that she was probably well and truly stuck. So much for the 9-1-1 call.

"Look at me, honey, with those big blue eyes of yours and tell me you love me; that you feel the same way I do."

She steeled herself once again not to show the revulsion she felt. She'd been told she had a very expressive face, wore her heart on her sleeve. She offered another silent prayer that it wouldn't betray her now as she struggled for what she hoped was a passable smile.

"I came here, didn't I? Would I have done that if I didn't care?"

He knelt in front of her, his face now inches from hers. "Kiss me, Ginger. I've been waiting for this moment for a long time. Now that you agree we should be together, forever, I think it's only right that we seal it with a kiss. Annabelle said I was a very good kisser. She loved to kiss me, long and slow."

Her stomach was now in full revolt. All she could smell was fish, and felt an involuntary gag boiling to the surface. He inched closer, leaning in until their noses were touching. Oh God help me, she thought desperately. She'd sooner kiss a toad.

He obviously wasn't into closed-eyed kissing because his attention suddenly swung to the window and he shot to his feet. "The police are in the yard! That's who you were calling, wasn't it! You're dead now, bitch!"

Chapter Ten

"You have no right to hold me here," Ginger yelled, secure in the knowledge at least that there were police on the premises, although she knew this was far from over. "I've told you again and again that I want to go home. You have to let me leave!"

"No! This is where you're supposed to be!" he shouted back. "You agreed to come here and be with me. You told me not five minutes ago that you wanted to be here and now you're changing your mind again. You women are all alike. You can't be trusted to do what you say you're going to do."

Picking up the gun he assumed a shooter's stance, aiming straight at her head. "I'm going to kill you right now because you betrayed me. You lied to me about why you were in the bathroom. You told me you were talking to your sister and I believed you because I love you. I never thought you'd do something like this to me."

She fought for composure, not knowing what second he might pull the trigger. "Cedric, please. Put the gun down and let's talk about this," she pleaded. "I called the police, I admit that, but only because you wouldn't let me leave. All I want to do is go home. If you let me walk out of here I won't ever tell a soul what happened. It will be our secret. I swear that's true."

"You're not going anywhere now," he said, still drawing a bead on her head. "How many times do I need to explain it to you? After Annabelle died I swore I would never let another woman betray me, then I met you. I took a chance. But you tricked me so there's no way I can let you live. You're a bitch, just like all the others. A two-timing bitch! You're no good, so why would I let you live? Hmm? Give me one good reason that isn't a lie."

The tears she had successfully kept at bay now shimmered on her lashes. Shaking violently, she felt as though she had been pulled into a whirlwind of emotions. She fought for mental clarity, searching her mind for the correct words to keep him from pulling that trigger. He had killed before, and didn't they say it got easier after that? She was probably done for anyway, because it likely wouldn't matter what she said now, he'd take exception to it. If she told him she wanted to get away from him he could become even more agitated. If she said she wanted to be with him, that she did love him after all, it was doubtful he'd believe her because of his obvious hatred of women.

Her cellphone began to ring again and Cedric aimed his gun at her handbag, the intended victim being her phone.

"Wait!" she shouted. "I don't want you to get shot, Cedric. If they hear gunshots they might start shooting at the house. We both might get shot."

"They're the ones who are going to get shot. I'm a better marksman than they are on any given day. I've dropped a buck at three hundred yards, got him right between the eyes so what chance do you think the boys and girls in blue stand? No chance at all. Just like you."

The phone continued to ring.

"I don't want to get shot so if I answer the phone and tell them everything is okay, then they'll leave. Isn't that what you want? That would solve the problem right there and no one has to get hurt. I made a mistake, but I can fix it. Let me fix it … for us."

His attention swung back to her, his eyes boring a hole through her forehead. The gun was still pointed at her head. "Keep talking."

She plunged ahead, encouraged. "They have to follow up on every 9-1-1 call, it's the law. They have to do it but once they find

203

out everything's okay, they'll leave. They're only checking this out because I made that call, which I admit was a mistake. I want to make things right if you'll let me. This can all be over very quickly, Cedric."

"It will be all over very quickly if I let you answer that phone and you tell them to come in here. If you don't believe me, darlin', go ahead and tell them to come and get you. They won't get any further than that door. They'll never get me, not in a hundred years. They might think they will, but I know they won't."

The phone had stopped ringing, but started again until she felt she couldn't bear the strain.

"Please let me answer that, Cedric. I'm telling you they won't leave until they know I'm all right. I have to answer it. I will fix everything, okay?"

"That's what I want, but how do I know you won't give them some kind of signal? You were the one who called them, and now you say you're going to get them to go away. Why would you do that?"

"Listen to me! All they have to do is determine I'm okay, that I haven't been harmed in any way. If they know I'm safe they won't have any further reason to stay. That's how it works. If I'm fine, what reason would they have to be here?"

"I know how stuff like this works, so stop talking down to me."

Ginger took a deep breath. Her phone had stopped ringing, only to start up again and she knew this wouldn't go on all night before some action was taken. "It's the only way, Cedric if we want them to leave. Just let them see that I'm fine and that the 9-1-1 call was a mistake. A misdial."

"I heard you talking to them, if it was a misdial you wouldn't have been giving them your name. Stop lying to me!"

"All right. I won't lie to you anymore. I misunderstood your intentions that's all. I'll tell them I thought you were trying to force me to stay but I was wrong. I'm here of my own free will."

He lowered his arms. "Answer the damned phone then and tell them exactly what you just told me. And don't try to get cute with some of your lies. I've killed before and I can kill again. Killing don't mean anything to me, darlin'."

With one hand he retrieved her handbag and threw it on her lap, her phone still ringing. She knew she had to somehow let them know the danger she was in, but still placate the madman in front of her; let him think she meant what she was about to say.

"Hello," she said, struggling to compose herself.

"This is Constable Prescott," said a male voice, speaking in low tones as if to prevent being overheard by whomever

205

might be standing close to her. "Who am I speaking to please?"

"This is Ginger Martel," she replied, longing to tell the caller exactly what was happening.

But to what end? Would they storm the building? The very thought terrified her. Cedric was right, he was an expert marksman and the first person to die would be her. The idea that innocent people might also lose their lives if force was used was almost too much to bear.

"Ginger. Is everything okay in there? We heard shouting."

"Everything's okay," she lied, hopefully not too convincingly. "There was just a little argument but it's over now and everybody's happy."

"Okay. Why don't you come on out into the yard so that we can see you're fine and then we'll go. All right?"

What to say now? "Ummm, I think I'll stay a little while longer, you know to keep talking. We're trying to work things out between us."

"Is he your boyfriend?"

"No, I'm fine."

"Is it just the two of you in there?"

"Yes, everything's all right."

"Are you able to come out?"

"No, I'm fine."

There was the slightest hesitation on the other end, and she believed the constable understood her subtle message. "Does he have a gun?"

"Yes, I'm fine."

"Is he forcing you to stay?"

"Yes. You're right, it is a bad night to be out so I'm fine right here. Thank you very much but my friend says you can go now, everything's...."

Cedric snatched the phone from her trembling fingers and heaved it across the room. It hit the wall and landed on the floor face up, the screen immediately going black. It appeared he had disabled the device.

"Good, you did good, Miss Ginger. You had a chance to yell for help and you didn't, so that's good. I'm glad you didn't start screaming or something like some women would. If you had I would have shot you dead right then and there."

"I told you that's what I was going to say, and I was trying to say it when you took the phone away from me."

"And that's why you're still sitting there sucking air." He grabbed her purse, throwing that too and it thumped into a corner. Some of the contents spilled out upon impact. "You do as I tell you and we're going to get along just fine."

Moving closer to the window he cautiously peeked through the narrow gap between the curtain panels. "Dammit! They're still out there and they don't look

207

like they're going anywhere. What did you say to them anyway that I couldn't make out? I couldn't hear what they were saying to you. Did the two of you cook something up to try to outsmart me? Was it a cop? I want to know what you said to whoever was on the other end of the line, and I want to know now. What did you say!"

"Nothing! You could hear every word I said. They wanted to make small talk about the weather and I just went along with it. What did you expect me to do? I had to pretend like nothing was wrong, didn't I? Isn't that what I told you I'd do? If I hadn't, they would have been suspicious. I had to play the game."

"You're the one that started all this, calling the police! Every time I think about that it makes my blood boil. I might still put a bullet through that pretty little head of yours yet. Shooting's the easiest way to get rid of someone, but there's other ways too. It's ridiculous how easy it is to take someone out, especially if they're not expecting it. I've given you fair warning. You might have thought you could screw around with Cedric Gourney, but I'll bet you've changed your mind now. I guess I got you educated, didn't I? You uptown girls are all alike."

She nodded miserably. It was a little comforting to know the police were only a few feet away, but what now? Surely they wouldn't start shooting, because they'd probably guess she'd be the first to go. Cedric would see to that. Her stomach was coiled in a tight painful knot. It even hurt to breathe.

And when would he let the dogs out again? Bring them into the room with her because he knew how much they terrified her. If he did that she wouldn't have to worry about being shot, the dogs would take care of her easily enough. If ever there was an impossible situation, this would rank right up there with some of the worst.

The wind still shook the house, thunder crashing around them in a seemingly never-ending crescendo. The steady downpour drummed on the steel roof in a deafening roar. It was a moment or two before she realized that Cedric's phone was ringing. He looked at her as if she was somehow responsible for that too.

He crossed the room in two strides and snatched the receiver from its cradle. He held it to his ear, not loosening his grip on the handgun. He was still pointing it in her direction although at the moment he was not taking direct aim. He didn't say anything, just listened to see who was on the other end.

"Hello?"

"Who's this and how did you get my number?" Cedric demanded.

"My name is Shane, who am I talking to?" he asked in a calm voice with a soothing, downward inflection.

"This is Cedric Gourney. Why are you calling me?"

"I thought we could talk, Cedric, just us two."

"I don't have anything I want to say, whoever you are."

"Cedric, it sounds as if maybe your day isn't going so great. Is that right?"

"Are you one of those police negotiators?"

"I'm calling because I thought maybe you had something you wanted to get off your chest. You know, something that's bothering you so this whole thing can end peacefully. I don't think you want this, not really."

"Doesn't matter if I want it or not, I've got a lying scheming bitch sitting across the room from me and she's pushing my buttons. How would you handle that, other than wanting to blow her brains out for what she did?"

"How I would handle it is by talking," came the negotiator's laidback voice. "There's always a way to talk things out."

"The time for talking is past. There's nothing anyone can say now that will make any difference."

"Talk to me, Cedric. I want to hear what you have to say. Let's try to work this out so that nobody gets hurt. At the end of the day I know we both want the same thing and that's for everybody to go home to their families safe and sound. You're a fair guy, let's try to resolve this between the two of us. What has to happen for Ginger to be able to come out?"

"Ginger doesn't want to go anywhere. She's perfectly happy where she is. I heard her say it to whoever called on her cellphone. She said that everything is fine and you all could leave. As a matter of fact I want you off my property. Now."

"We can't leave right this minute, but absolutely we'll pull back. The main thing is that nobody gets hurt. Let's end this peacefully. I believe that's what you want too."

"Nobody cares what I want."

"I care."

"Okay, people might care, but they don't listen. That's how this whole thing got started in the first place. I want things to be a certain way and she does nothing but push against my plans."

"Okay, tell me about your plans, Cedric. I want to hear about them."

"Well, mister negotiator…."

"Please, call me Shane."

"Okay, Shane, all I ever wanted was to be happy with a woman, to have someone who loved me and wanted to be with me. I thought I had that with my late wife and she went and died, but before that she was getting ready to leave me. Told me I held on too tight when all I was trying to do was protect her. Make a good home for her. I treated her like a queen and she up and says stuff like that. It wasn't fair."

"And Annabelle was your wife's name."

"Yes. Her name was Annabelle. Her second name was Rosebud, if you can believe it."

Ginger noticed the gun was lowered as he talked. It seemed as though he'd forgotten all about her, at least for the moment, caught up in reminisces about his darling Annabelle. Cedric loved his women to death it seemed.

Shane's voice was as smooth as velvet, low and steady. "That is an unusual name, and was she like her name?"

"She was. She wasn't pretty, not like my new girlfriend. I might as well say it but I'm not the kind of guy who worries about things like that. I loved her anyway, but now that I have someone beautiful I've got to say I like it better. She's a lot easier to look at."

"And your new girlfriend is Ginger?"

Cedric actually smiled. "That's her name. You should see her, and you probably do because she's in the New Chronicle every week with People Unlimited. That's her column and I have never missed even one of her stories. I am her biggest fan."

"She's a reporter?"

"Yes, and she came to talk to little ole' Cedric Gourney if you can believe it."

"She came to do an interview with you?"

"That's right and I gave her enough stuff for a book."

"So what went wrong? Did she ask you something that upset you?"

"She did a perfect interview. She's very professional you know, but she thought she could just waltz in here, ask me a bunch of questions, take pictures and then leave. It doesn't work that way. I call the shots, not some little snit of a reporter."

"She wanted to leave when the interview was over?"

"She gathered everything up without so much as a by your leave and wished me a good day."

"And what would be the problem with her wanting to leave?"

"Because she doesn't understand the rules. I can't let her go after I went to all the trouble of getting her to come here. I've been in love with her for quite a while now. Since the first time I saw her in the paper. I have clipped out every picture there ever was of her in the newspaper. I made a special room in tribute to her, but it didn't seem to make any difference. Most women would have been flattered, but not her. She thinks she's too good for me. That's really what the problem is here, her attitude."

"Her attitude?"

"That's what I'm talking about, her attitude. She just kept on saying she wanted to leave. She even tried to leave once, but she didn't get very far."

"Is she okay, Cedric? Is she hurt in any way?"

"She's still in one piece but I won't lie. I pulled her hair some, pushed her around a little bit. She didn't like that at all. Sometimes you've got to be a little rough with them so they know you mean business. You see, I've got all these plans for us. She doesn't know it yet but I can make her happy, she just has to learn to mind me. She's got to lose those independent ways of hers."

"Independent ways?"

"That's what I'm talking about," Cedric explained, unaware that Shane was using a basic negotiator skill, mirroring, essentially imitating the hostage taker in an effort to comfort and relax him. "She wants to do everything her way and not listen to someone who knows better. She also has to learn to love my dogs but right now she's still scared of them."

"Tell me about your dogs, Cedric."

"I've got three of them. They're the best guard dogs you'd ever hope to find."

"And what kind of dogs are they?"

"Let's just say you fellas would love to get your hands on them because they'd be superb police dogs. They're shepherds, but I don't treat them like pets, oh no. I have them strictly for protection, like if anyone comes too near I let them go. I have them in the house at the moment, on guard duty. If I even think someone is getting too close, out they go."

"So you're telling me you've got them restrained right now? They're in the house with you?"

"I am telling you that."

"I'll ask you to keep them in the house with you so we don't have any problems with our officers, okay? We don't want anyone to get hurt here tonight. We want everyone to stay safe and get things resolved peacefully."

"Can I tell you what I think?"

"Absolutely. What do you think, Cedric?"

"I think the world would be a much better place if we didn't have any police."

"How would that work?"

"Everyone would take care of themselves," said Cedric, responding to Shane's questions which were designed to get him to open up and talk. The rationale was that when a hostage taker was talking, he wasn't shooting. How or what questions forced the hostage taker to use their mental

215

energy to solve the negotiator's problems. "We wouldn't need anyone walking around in a uniform thinking they were better than everyone else. Forcing people to do things they didn't want to do. Now what do you think about that?"

"I'm sorry, I respectfully disagree. Why do you feel like that?"

Cedric shrugged, the gun seemingly forgotten although Ginger knew she dared not make a move. Things could escalate again, fast. Best to let the professionals handle this. She could tell that the negotiator was trying to calm Cedric although she couldn't hear what was being said. She knew he would try to keep Cedric talking, and it was obviously working. She'd done a story on a police negotiator a few years back, and it was one of her better pieces. She couldn't think of the officer's name right off the top of her head, but she was fascinated by the techniques they used, the crisis negotiation skills they possessed. At the heart of it all was communication between the negotiator and the person in crisis, the hostage taker; building a rapport and displaying empathy. It was important to gain their trust as the negotiation toward a peaceful resolution progressed. She knew it took enormous patience on the part of the negotiator as they stepped into a variety of crises. They had to think fast on their feet, stay with the suspect verbally and defuse volatile situations. To the uninitiated it would seem like they were making small talk when they should be barging in and taking control of things, but that's how people got killed. The idea was to settle things down, let the suspect run out of steam and she hoped it worked now.

The more she thought about it the more she recalled what that negotiator had told her, such as active listening which is both an affective and effective skill. In the initial stages at least it was all about information gathering, and Cedric had already unwittingly inculpated himself in the crime that was being committed. It was as important to maintain an open dialogue, as it was to be respectful. Let the hostage taker know that his concerns were not only being heard, but addressed. Actually, isn't that what everyone wanted? To be heard and respected? A situation like this was the extreme for sure, but it also applied in many ways to everyday life.

She had been very impressed with the hostage negotiator she'd interviewed. Kenny Ferguson! Yes! That was his name. He had been a very nice man, a dedicated professional and while he may not have said so, he'd helped many people. She knew it wasn't the Ferguson fellow on the phone with Cedric, because the idea behind the story was Mr. Ferguson looking back just prior to his retirement. Ferguson had pointed out there were three on the crisis negotiation team in Franklin, and that someone was being trained to take his place. She couldn't recall the names of the other team members.

She forced herself to recall the story details. Such as the purpose of the negotiators' efforts were to convince the other party that there was an alternative way out, the possibility of an amicable solution. Yes, Cedric would be arrested, but he wouldn't be jumped the minute he walked out the door like you see on TV. And of all days for something like this to take place. They were still in the middle of a violent storm of which she was painfully reminded as another clap of thunder shook the old house. It truly sounded as though the heavens themselves were about to rupture and fall in on top of them.

In her initial panic she'd been afraid the police would make a forced entry, but now realized they wouldn't do that as long as she was still inside. The relief was almost palpable.

Cedric glanced in her direction as though he'd actually forgotten she was in the room. He loved to talk, especially about himself, and at the moment he was caught up in his gripes about the world. Then astonishingly, he winked at her. Boy, whoever was on the other end of the line was good if he could diffuse the likes of Cedric Gourney. She had certainly not been very good at it so far.

"Cedric, are you still with me?" Shane asked after a few moments of silence on the other end of the line.

He turned his attention back to the phone. "I'm still here. I was just distracted by the beautiful woman sitting in my chair. You should meet her."

"I'd like to say hello, so why don't you send her out so that we can resolve all of this before the weather gets any worse? This is one heck of a storm."

"She's staying here with me. She's nice and dry in here, you're the ones who are out in the storm getting all wet."

"Are you sure she's all right? Why don't you put her on the phone so I can hear her tell me that for herself."

"What, you don't believe me? You think I'm a liar?"

"Not at all, but is it possible to hear her voice? Let her come to the phone for just a second?" asked Shane, trying to establish the safety of the hostage.

Cedric waved her over to the phone with his gun hand, and she obediently walked across the room to the telephone. He held it to her ear as though she wasn't capable of doing that. She glanced at his eyes, and the warning in them was as clear as day. Don't try anything.

"Hello?"

"Ginger, this is Shane. How are you doing?"

She had never heard a man's voice like that in her life. Well modulated and softly deep it served its intended purpose, which was to calm people down. It also had to be the sexiest voice she'd ever heard. In the midst of this horrible experience, it was like a breath of cool fresh air and somehow she felt as though she was going to be all right.

"I'm doing okay," she managed, but she was sure he could tell she was frightened.

Too bad she wasn't like one of those movie heroines who let nothing bother them, she thought ridiculously. Stalwart in the face of whatever came their way, never showing any emotion. Taking care of business. But she wasn't built like that. She was a strong woman, but often rightly accused of being overly sensitive. This would likely scar her psyche forever; give her nightmares.

Cedric yanked the phone away from her ear and pointing to the armchair, indicated that she should return to it and gave her a shove in that direction.

"See, I told you she was all right."

"I'm glad to hear that. Now how are we going to end this thing before it goes any further?"

"You all go home, that's how it ends."

"We have to stay, Cedric, but we have pulled back as far as we can. I can tell you everyone's in their cars right now because it's raining so hard. So that's the best we can do. I know you don't want this to drag on, do you? I think you want it to be over soon too."

"I do want it to be over. I never wanted it to start at all, like I already said. I've been doing a lot of thinking, even since we started talking. You're asking me what can we do to end this. Well, Ginger has to stay here with me. She has to agree to do that, so it's all up to her, not me."

"How would that work for her do you think, staying somewhere against her will?"

"She'll learn to love me."

"How do you think that's going to happen? Do you think maybe she should leave and then make up her own mind about what she wants?"

"Then she might not come back. No, I want to marry her, so that's how we can end this thing. You get a minister to come to the house and marry us, otherwise she dies."

Ginger almost fell out of the chair, and might have, but for its spongy depths. Marry him! She'd rather walk over broken glass, barefoot. She wouldn't marry Cedric Gourney if he was the last man standing. Ugh!

"And then what?" the negotiator asked.

221

"Then she'll be my wife and she will have to stay by law and do everything I tell her."

"Do you think married people don't have a right to do what they want?"

"Sometimes I guess."

"Right. Sometimes things don't go like we planned. It doesn't mean it's the end of the world."

"What did you say your name was?"

"Shane."

"Shane, I'm tired of being alone. I mean not having anyone, a woman to cook and clean. I liked being married and I was good at it."

"It's no fun being alone, I hear you. Ginger came to do a story on you, do you think it's right to hold her there if she wants to leave?"

Cedric was silent for a moment. "Maybe not. It's just that she's so beautiful. I don't think I could ever find a woman like her again, and she's already right in my house. I've been waiting for this for a very long time. Women who look like her don't grow on trees. That's why it would be a shame if something happened to her."

"I hear you and I know you want to do the right thing. Let her come down those stairs and get into her car and leave. She didn't ask for any of this."

"I'm not a bad man, Shane. I know this looks like I'm a total loser, but I'm not."

"This whole thing has been a big misunderstanding."

"That's right."

She couldn't believe it. The negotiator was actually turning Cedric around. She could see it in his body language, the way his gun hand now hung slack at his side. When she got out of this place she would get on her knees and kiss the ground, rain and all. She wouldn't care. And the next thing she would do, and she hoped it would be possible, was to meet the hostage negotiator and thank him for helping her. He'd been on the phone with Cedric now for a while. Still she guessed it was a relatively short time to defuse a bomb. She musn't get impatient.

If only there wasn't another shift in Cedric's mercurial personality. There were mental health issues that she was obviously unaware of when she'd agreed to come to his house and do this interview. How was a person to tell the difference between someone who was off the wall colourful and those who had serious problems? Usually not until she'd talked to them, which was the case here, only then it was too late. Was she to start doing background checks on everyone she interviewed? Impossible, and therein, she had to admit, lay the danger.

A sound caught her attention, like a door closing in the back part of the building. Were the police trying to sneak into the house after all? No, she immediately rejected that notion. She couldn't imagine they'd do anything to jeopardize her wellbeing seeing as how Cedric was armed and had proven himself to be dangerous. It couldn't be the police doing that, not in the middle of a hostage negotiation, but she had definitely heard something.

She was surprised that Cedric didn't seem bothered by the sound because she knew he'd heard it too. He had to! Then she heard footsteps, and a cough. Dear God! There was another man in the house!

Chapter Eleven

Shane knew it would unnerve the hostage taker when he saw police gathered on his property. The scene had to be secured, make sure that not only any civilians in the surrounding area were safe, but also the police, as well as the hostage and the hostage taker himself. The perimeter had to be maintained for two reasons, to make sure nobody came to help the hostage taker, and to prevent his escape. There were a lot of moving parts to do this right.

Shane was part of a hostage negotiator team with Reg Stackhouse and Dominick Stears, although he would have to take this one alone because both other men happened to be off. Reg was in the hospital recovering from a ruptured appendix. Dom was in Fredericton on course but could be summoned if this thing dragged out for any length of time. But a good hostage negotiator was never in a rush to wrap things up. Shane and his colleagues worked to keep tensions and emotions at a low level, and that's where patience came in. A negotiator had to have that in spades. Pushing too hard could escalate matters. The last thing they needed was a hostage taker under pressure who started going off in all directions. That's when people could get hurt. No, it was stalling and effective pauses that worked brilliantly in hostage situations, the negotiator unflappable and persuasive, yet assertive when called for.

"Cedric, are you still there?" Shane asked after a prolonged silence.

"I'm here, I'm just thinking about what you said."

"That this whole thing has been a misunderstanding."

"Yes, that. I agreed with what you said, but maybe I'm the one who's being misunderstood. Did you ever think of that?"

"Of course I did. Tell me how you think you've been misunderstood."

"What did you say your name was again?"

"Shane. So tell me how you've been misunderstood, Cedric."

"Maybe it's just women in general that I don't understand. I'm misunderstood by them."

"How do you think you're misunderstood?"

"Take what's happening right here for example. I idolized this women, was ready to offer her the world. I want to give her a

226

home and the love of a good man and she repays me by pushing me away."

"How do you think she's feeling about all of this?"

Pause. "I don't know. Maybe I could have taken more time with her."

"Maybe she would have looked at things a little differently."

"I don't know. You could be right, but look, I have to go. I don't feel like talking on the phone right now. I've got to think it over, try to decide what I want to do. This whole thing is giving me a headache."

"Okay, do you think we could maybe talk a little longer?"

"No! I said I want to go." Cedric suddenly hung up, ending the connection.

Shane sat back, flexing his shoulders. Things seemed to be headed in the right direction, but it was very early in the process. From what they were able to determine, Ginger Martel had come to the property to conduct an interview with the moose whisperer as he was known. Of all the half-assed.... Police had already been talking to Foster McDougall, the editor of the New Chronicle. He confirmed that he had indeed suggested she do an interview with Mr. Gourney, despite the fact that he knew him to be highly volatile.

The police were also familiar with Cedric Gourney. There had been an incident several years ago when he'd held a telephone repairman at gunpoint for the better part of an hour because the man had ventured onto his property. The telephone company had advised Mr. Gourney they were terminating service to him because his telephone lines had been tampered with; their equipment damaged. When he refused to speak with them a rep had gone to his home. Cedric had apparently set the dogs on him. The man had managed to climb to safety into a nearby tree at which time Cedric held a gun on him. The company, not able to raise their repairman, had contacted police. That situation had been resolved quickly, and Cedric had gone to jail. He was unpredictable and dangerous. It angered Shane that the woman's editor knew all this and didn't warn his reporter.

And of course Cedric had done time in federal prison for manslaughter in the death of Annabelle Gourney. Cedric had played it all innocent, of course, but the pathologist found incriminating marks on her that suggested otherwise. So he'd been convicted in her death.

Shane would wait a minute or two before calling Cedric back. Perhaps his mood would have shifted again when they reconnected. If so he'd have to quickly adjust, but always with what was referred to as tactical empathy. That meant understanding the feelings and mindset of another person in that moment; what's behind those feelings. There was no cookie cutter approach to these things, ever. A split second decision could mean life or death for the hostage.

When he called his number again it was a cheerful Cedric who answered. "Where have you been, Shane? I thought you weren't going to call me back. I was actually getting kind of lonesome sitting here. You see, I don't mind my own company, never have, but it's always nice to have a woman to talk to. Sometimes I like to talk a lot and other times I don't. Right now I'm feeling downright gabby."

"You say you're sitting there alone?"

"Yes, all by myself."

"Where is Ginger?"

"Gone. She left me. Isn't that just like a woman to do that? One minute they're here and the next they're gone."

"Cedric, where did Ginger go?"

"Let me clarify. She's not gone yet, but she will be soon."

"Where is she going to go?"

"Nowhere hopefully. Except maybe if I shoot her dead. You know I'm an expert marksman, right? If I aim at something, I hit it. Make no mistake about that. So unless you guys get off my property right now I'm going to put one of these bullets to very good use."

Because of his criminal record, Cedric was prohibited from owning firearms. He had them anyway though and that certainly upped the ante.

"I'm sorry, but how can we do that when we don't know if Ginger is going to be safe?"

"What if I told you she wasn't safe with you guys here?"

"She's not safe with us here? We're not doing anything to harm her. We want her to come out."

"What else do you want? I know there must be something else."

"You're right, there is. We want you to put down your gun and come out yourself so that this whole thing can be over with no one getting hurt. It seems like that's what you want too," said Shane, employing a powerful tactic known as labelling: inviting the hostage taker to reveal himself. Acknowledge their feelings instead of having them act them out instead. "I can't imagine this is the way you wanted to spend your Saturday evening, but this can be over and no one gets hurt."

"Is it still raining out?" asked Cedric changing direction.

"Yes, it is, but the storm should pass soon."

"I don't want to get my gun wet."

"That wouldn't be good for a gun, so it'd be better if you put it down inside the house and come out with your hands where we can see them."

"You say it's still raining."

"Yes."

"You wouldn't lie to me would you, Shane? I'd look out the window to check for myself, but I know you'd shoot me if I did that."

"It's still raining, Cedric. I'm not lying to you. I will not lie to you. You can trust me with this. They say the rain should pass before long, but it is raining right now."

"I don't want to get wet in the rain. I hate getting wet in the rain."

"We'll have a raincoat waiting for you, I give you my word."

"Will they put handcuffs on me?"

"We have to do that for everyone's safety. It's procedure, so don't take it personally."

"Then I'm not coming out."

"Sorry, can't budge on that one. That's what's going to happen but I can promise you that we won't put them on too tight and hurt your wrists. We don't want to cause you any unnecessary pain. How does that sound?"

"I have big wrists."

"We have big cuffs; we can make them as large as they need to be. So you have nothing to worry about."

"That's good to know. Shane, can I tell you something that has bothered me for a long time? I mean would you actually listen to this story, and care?"

"I promise you I'll listen, and care. What do you want to tell me?"

"It's about a dog I used to own."

"Okay. Did something happen to the dog?"

"Yes."

"Tell me what happened to the dog."

"It disappeared. I knew my father had taken it and done something with it. He said he didn't, but my father lied to me, a lot. I was just a little kid but I knew he lied. Did you have a good father, Shane?"

He wasn't expecting that one, but he had to avoid emotional involvement.

"It's a big job being a father. So did you get your dog back?"

"No, not ever."

"Maybe the dog was sick and your father didn't want you to know."

Again there was silence on the other end of the line. "Yeah, maybe. I never thought of it like that. Maybe he didn't want me to see that Digger was sick. That's good, Shane. You're good. I'm getting the impression you care. At least someone does."

"So tell me, what is Ginger doing right now?"

"Do you think something happened to her while I was off the phone? Like maybe I strangled her or something? If I shot her you guys would have heard it because I'm holding a .357."

"Can you tell me how she's doing?"

"She's doing fine."

"What is she doing?"

"Just lying there looking up at the ceiling."

Shane took a deep breath. Was the hostage still alive? Had he strangled her like he'd just hinted? They hadn't heard any screams. If there were dogs in the house as Cedric had indicated, they would certainly have reacted to a commotion, yet they'd heard nothing suspicious from within.

"What do you mean she's lying there looking at the ceiling?"

"Just like I said."

"Is she sleeping?"

"You might say that."

"Has something happened to her?"

"You might say that too."

"Can you take the phone to her and let me hear her voice? I need to know she's okay."

"Nah, I'm on a landline, not a cordless. The cord won't stretch that far."

"How am I supposed to be able to talk to her if the cord won't stretch that far?"

"I would have to bring her to the phone."

"Good idea, I need to hear that she's all right."

Silence.

"Cedric?"

"She says she doesn't want to talk to you. Like me, she's all talked out right now."

"Can you get her to talk from where she is?"

"She can't do that."

"Is she lying or sitting?"

"Lying."

"I need to hear that she's all right. Why don't you ask her to get up and come to the phone? I only need to talk to her for a second. Just hear her voice."

"I said she can't talk right now."

"Why can't she talk?"

"You want to hear a woman talk? That's all they do sometimes is talk."

"I need to hear Ginger talk. Just for a second. Let her come to the phone please."

If the worst had happened; if he had in fact killed the hostage then it would be a much different scenario. The Emergency Response Team who routinely dealt with barricaded persons, would make every attempt to resolve the matter peacefully. Failing that they would indeed enter the building, deploy tear gas if necessary and end this thing. But as long as there was a chance Ginger was still alive, negotiations would continue.

Shane understood the importance of maintaining the trust and respect of the hostage taker throughout. He knew that to the uninitiated it might seem as though he was mollycoddling the hostage taker and it'd be better to burst in with guns a blazing. Attempt a rescue. However, past tactical mistakes in that regard in early policing had proven that to be an unwise decision. Skilled hostage negotiators had saved many lives; deescalated situations that could have otherwise been disastrous.

Known to be cool under pressure, Shane still felt the weight of the situation although in no way could he convey any type of fear or anxiety. He had to keep his composure at all times because if his mood or behaviour changed; if he became nervous or indecisive, that would reflect negatively on the hostage taker. Just as a horse becomes antsy if there is an antsy rider on its back, the same was true with humans. An upset negotiator would make for an upset hostage taker. Not good. Stability was key.

"Cedric, talk to me about Ginger."

"What would you like to know? She was beautiful, really beautiful. She had the best and biggest blue eyes I have ever seen. That's what I fell in love with right off. It's all about the eyes as far as I'm concerned. Oh sure, there's other good stuff too, of course, but I could have looked into her eyes for hours. But, as it turned out she didn't want me looking into her eyes. What could I do? I know you know what I mean. If you see a beautiful woman you want to look, right?

You can't blame a man for looking. In Ginger's case, I wanted to touch her too. And if she drew the line at looking, then you can imagine how she felt when I tried to touch her. It was a no go."

Shane was well aware that Cedric was now speaking about Ginger in the past tense, and that wasn't good. But then Cedric seemed to like playing games. He was not stupid and not above playing with someone's mind.

"Why won't you let me talk to Ginger?"

"Because she can't talk, or else I would."

"And why can't she talk?"

"Let's just say her talking days are over. But when she writes the story on me I guess you can hear what she says then."

Back to the present tense. He had to hope the reporter was still alive.

"So she's going to write a good story on you is she? What is the story going to be about?"

"About me, who else? She's going to tell about all the close calls I had in the woods, especially with moose or bear. Did you know I was almost dinner for a big ole' black bear one time? Snapping at my heels he was. That's how I came to buy the .357. It was because of that night. It was a close call and I've had a few of them."

"So she's got all her notes and everything."

"She took some notes but she also used a tape recorder. I didn't care how she did it as long as she got it done. And she took a lot of pictures too. She didn't like the one with me pointing the gun at her. She was freaking out that it was loaded but what good is a gun if it's not loaded? Not one danged bit of good at all."

Now Cedric had returned to the past tense. He had to establish contact with the hostage. Ginger Martel was an innocent victim, and Cedric Gourney was emotionally unstable at best. That was a bad combination. Everything was still quiet inside, no barking. It sounded as though the dogs were as aggressive as their owner. Hopefully the thunder was subduing them a bit, although it depended on the dog.

He'd had a dog once, Barkley he was called for obvious reasons. That dog could tell when a thunderstorm was thirty miles away. He'd start whining and searching for a place to hide.

A lightning bolt split the sky bathing the yard in unnatural light. This was a corker of a storm system, the rain continuing to fall in a torrential downpour whipped around by strong winds. It didn't seem inclined to fade anytime soon.

"Cedric, I need you to put Ginger on the line. Do it for me now, please."

"She's sleeping."

"Then wake her up if you don't mind. I want to speak with her."

"How many times do I have to tell you she can't talk?"

"What do you mean she can't talk?"

"Anymore is what I mean."

"Why can't she talk anymore?"

"I'll call her and we'll see if she answers me."

"Okay, do that for me."

"Ginger! Oh Miss Ginger! Do you walk to talk to Shane, darlin'?"

Silence.

"What did she say?"

"Nothing. She said nothing."

"What is she doing?"

"Just lying there looking at the ceiling. She don't want to talk."

"She doesn't want to talk, or can't?"

"Both."

Shane covered the phone and took a deep cleansing breath, flexing his shoulders. "Just give me a minute, Cedric. I'll be right back with you."

It was a deliberate pause because his gut told him Cedric was playing with him, or at least he was hoping that was true. He was a cat and mouse type of guy, and he could only imagine what Ginger was enduring at this moment.

He took another deep breath before reconnecting. "Hi, I'm back. Tell me about Ginger."

There was a momentary hesitation. "What about her?"

"What's she doing right now?"

"Watching me. Just a minute, can you hold the line for a moment, Shane?"

"Yeah, sure."

He could hear Cedric lay the gun down on what sounded like a wooden surface. Next there was the squawking of a piece of furniture being pulled across a floor before the receiver was picked up again.

"I'm back, buddy."

"Good. When can I talk to Ginger?"

"Just a minute."

Shane could clearly hear a woman's voice, and he felt a rush of relief. At least she was still alive. Straight on the heels of that he could hear what sounded like a struggle. What was Cedric doing to her?

"Cedric?"

No answer.

"Cedric, are you there?"

"I'm back."

"What's going on?"

"Just taking care of business."

"What do you mean by taking care of business? Can I talk to Ginger?"

"Ginger can't talk," Cedric said, his voice flat.

"Cedric, why can't she talk?"

"Because she's got the barrel of my gun in her mouth, that's why. I don't think she likes it too much."

239

Shane could hear her crying.

"Why do you have the barrel of the gun in her mouth?"

"So she knows I mean business. Like all of this is make believe. I know the gun gets her attention so that's how I had to deal with it. You should see how wide her eyes are now."

"Cedric, I've been honest with you throughout this whole thing, right?"

"I guess so."

"Good, and I know you want to be honest with me too."

"I'll be honest with you."

"You said you didn't want to hurt Ginger, so I'm going to ask you to take the gun out of her mouth. Can you see where I'm coming from with this?"

There was a hesitation. "Yeah, I can see where you're coming from, but I got to keep her in line."

"You have to keep her in line?"

"If I'm going to marry her I have to know she's going to do what I tell her. I have to be able to trust her. I can't have it that if I turn my back she runs off or something like the other one did. You have to keep a firm hand with women. You have to show them who's boss. You have to keep them scared."

"You have to keep them scared?"

"Happy and scared."

"Can you take the gun barrel out of her mouth, please, Cedric?"

"I already did that. But she's right over here by the phone so do you want to talk to her?"

Finally.

"Yes, I do. Put her on the line please. I only need to talk to her for a few seconds."

"Okay, here she is."

Shane could tell that Ginger was now near the receiver because he could hear her sobbing. The poor woman wasn't frightened enough. She had to go through the ordeal of having a gun barrel shoved in her mouth. That would be a nightmare for anyone. Being alone at the hands of a lunatic would be an experience like no other.

"Ginger, this is Shane again. I just wanted to hear your voice so I'd know you're still okay."

"I'm fine," she managed to get out between sobs.

Cedric came back on the line. "See? She's fine, she just told you that herself. Probably hasn't had this much excitement in years. Sorry I was joshing with you earlier about her being dead, I like to get people going sometimes. Have some fun. But ole' blue eyes here is doing okay. I wouldn't kill the woman I'm going to marry, would I? I wouldn't unless I had to. Now, I told you before, I want us to get married tonight, so that's my condition. I want you to bring a preacher here to my property so he can marry us."

An especially brilliant flash of lightning lit the sky for miles around, followed by an impossibly loud clap of thunder. The phone line went dead.

"I've lost connection!" Shane barked to tech support.

"We're on it," the radio guy assured him. "Just give us a few seconds and we'll patch you back in."

It was close to five minutes before he heard Cedric's phone ringing again and thankfully the hostage taker picked it up with a cheerful hello. "Where did you go? I thought you gave up on me."

"No, never that," Shane told him. "It's this darned storm, but we're hooked up again and hopefully it holds."

"So did you hear what my demand was before the line went dead, or do you want me to go through it again?"

"Go through it again if you would," said Shane, stalling for time, the best friend of law enforcement in all of this. "That would be great."

"I said I want a minister to come and marry Ginger and me."

"Why do you want to get married, I mean what's the hurry anyway?"

"Why not? She loves me, she just told me so a few minutes ago."

"Okay, but what's the hurry if she said she loves you?"

"When people are in love with each other they are supposed to get married."

"They're supposed to get married?"

"Yes. So that's my one condition. Just get a preacher here, but you have to get a licence first."

"You have to get a license first?" asked Shane, continuing to mirror the suspect in an effort to keep him talking. The last thing he wanted was to stall the conversation. He had to keep reassuring Cedric; validate him.

Cedric laughed, his mood having swung once again to the sunny side, like a pendulum on a clock. "I take it you never got married because you need a license before you can do it. You need a license to do anything. But since Ginger and I can't go to City Hall and get the license ourselves, someone will have to take care of that for us. Did I tell you what happened when Annabelle and I were going to get married? When we went to get our license?"

"No, tell me what happened."

"Annabelle was pregnant you know, so we didn't have a lot of time to waste. We didn't want the stork to beat the preacher to the wedding as they say. Her old man was already pretty mad at me for getting his little girl pregnant. Well, she wasn't a little girl. She was seventeen, but anyway, off we go

243

to City Hall. Annabelle goes into labour on the drive in, so instead of going to City Hall I started for the hospital as fast as I could. Our son, Stilwell, was born not a half-hour later."

Shane knew all about Stilwell Gourney. He was even more erratic than the father if that was possible, a real chip off the old block. He had also been to prison, no doubt because of the explosive environment he'd grown up in. He was always fighting with someone and like his father he was an expert woodsman. He'd been taught well. He'd done time for a fight outside a bar and the guy died. It was one unlucky punch. Ordinarily it would have ended like any other bar fight with the combatants battle scarred and hung over, but that one punch had knocked the guy off his feet and he'd hit his head. Cedric and Stilwell had that in common too. They'd both served prison terms for manslaughter.

"So anyway," Cedric continued, "Annabelle and I got our license a few days later and we got married. She wasn't feeling too well and didn't feel like going anywhere so I did the same thing that time. I said bring the preacher to the house and he came and we got married in a hunting wedding during deer season. Sometimes you just have to bend the rules a little to get what you want. So what about it, Shane?

Are you going to get the preacher to come here? Now?"

"I'm sorry, you want to bring a preacher out in weather like this?"

"Sure, they're used to being out in bad weather, they…."

Shane heard a door open and close hard in the background. Had Ginger made a break for it? Was she trying to escape on her own?

"Cedric, talk to me. What's happening there now? Where's Ginger?"

"She's right here beside me like I told you. Getting ready for her wedding day. So about that preacher…."

"Are you and Ginger still alone?"

"We're like two ships that sail in the night. That's what we're going to do tonight, sail off into the sunset. So if we come out of here after we get married, are they still planning to take me in? It wouldn't be much fun to spend my wedding night in jail."

"I heard a door slam in the background. Are you sure Ginger is still there with you?"

"I'm looking at her right now."

"I heard a door slam. Did someone come in?"

"Oh that! That's my son, he just got up and came out to get something to eat."

Shane heard Ginger scream.

Chapter Twelve

A negotiator's worst fear was losing control of a situation when innocent lives were at stake. There was now a second man in the house, although it seemed that Cedric was the main perpetrator. It wouldn't help that Stilwell Gourney was also on the scene.

"Cedric, talk to me," Shane said calmly. "Tell me what's going on."

Shane could hear heated words being exchanged. Stilwell had outstanding warrants because his whereabouts had heretofore been unknown. Now it seemed he was furious with his father for bringing the police to the house. Shane had succeeded in calming Cedric and negotiations were proceeding very well toward the nonviolent termination phase … the hostage released and the hostage taker surrendering quietly. Now things were ramping back up, fast.

Suddenly a voice barked in his ear. It had to be Stilwell. "Who is this? Is this a cop?"

"This is Shane, who am I talking to?"

"I don't know anyone by the name of Shane, so good-bye."

Shane kept his tone of voice even. "Why would you want to hang up on me?"

"Why would I want to hang up on you? Because I don't know who you are, that's why."

There were sounds of a tussle and Cedric apparently won because it was his voice that next came over the line. "Sorry about that, Shane. My boy always wakes up in a bad mood. He's like his mother."

Stilwell shouted from the sidelines. "I am not in a bad mood. I want to know who you got on the line, Dad. Who is it and what does he want?"

Cedric coughed. "Shane is a friend of mine and he's going to help me out. Miss Ginger and I are going to get married tonight and Shane here is going to make that happen."

Stilwell did not seem to be appeased. "Hang up the damned phone. I don't want the police snooping around here."

Cedric was adamant. "I'm not hanging up the phone. This is none of your business."

Stilwell remained close by, maybe waiting to commandeer the telephone from his father again. "It is my business. Let me talk to him, okay?"

Cedric apparently gave in as Stilwell came on the line again. "Why did you come to this house? I want you to tell me that."

Shane kept his voice soft, low and reassuring. "We're here because Ginger would like to leave and your father wants her to stay. If she's allowed to come out, and your father surrenders, this whole thing will be over. We will go away, but not until that happens."

Stilwell turned from the phone to speak to his father again. "I don't know why that bitch is here, but get rid of her. Let her go, and the police say they'll leave."

Cedric was not agreeable to his son's suggestion any more than he was with that of the hostage negotiator. "No, she stays right here with me."

Stilwell sounded like a man who had zero patience. "Get her out of here, now!"

Cedric was exhibiting remarkable forbearance with his son. Could it be that he was scared of him? "She came to do a story on me for the newspaper."

Shane listened carefully before he spoke. It was the cornerstone of the entire process. "Stilwell?"

Stilwell returned his attention to the phone. "What?"

"How are we going to get Ginger out of the house safely?"

Stilwell shrugged. At least Shane supposed he had with what he said next.

248

"Just let her walk out, I guess. How else?" He then turned his attention to Ginger. "Go on, bitch, get out of here and don't come back. Is that your stuff on the table?" She must have nodded. "Okay then get it and go and don't you never come back to this house. I don't like newspapers, I don't read them and I don't trust the people who write that crap. You all print lies, so get on your way and if you write even one thing about my father, I'll sue you. Now go, and tell the police to leave when you get down there. If all they wanted was you to come out, then go out and they have no more reason to stay." He turned back to the telephone. "There, Shane, problem solved. Now leave us alone."

Cedric however was having none of it as he roared at his son. "She's not going anywhere! We're going to get married!" His attention must have turned to Ginger. "Sit back down, 'darlin'."

Things were beginning to escalate, and Shane had to think fast. "Stilwell?"

"Yeah, what?"

"Can I talk to your dad?"

Stilwell remained agitated. "No, you cannot talk to my dad. You're talking to me so anything you have to say from here on out, you can say to me."

"Okay," Shane nodded. "How do I know that Ginger is still alright? I heard her scream."

Stilwell chortled. "She screamed when she saw me, all right? I got my face messed up in a fight. I didn't lay a finger on the chick."

Shane wasn't bothered that the hostage situation, which seemed about to be over, could now for all intents and purposes continue well into the night. The longer it took, statistically, the more likely it would end peacefully. It was also textbook that hostage takers were more volatile during the early part of the episode. The longer things dragged on, it meant more time to work things out without bloodshed.

"That's good," Shane said in a quiet, even tone in an effort to reassure Stilwell. "There is no need to harm her."

"Look man, she's not my hostage. I'm not into this at all, it's my old man's thing. I want her gone. But since we are in the middle of something now, I have a demand that I want you to meet. I know how these things work. I've seen them on TV. So I get to make a demand, right?"

"I'll have to get back to you on that." Shane as a negotiator always referred to himself as an intermediary, never the guy in charge because it allowed him more time to resolve things.

It also kept the hostage-taker in suspense, seeing the negotiator as a mediator. And now Stilwell, because he was currently the one making demands, was unwittingly involving himself in the crime.

Stilwell's mood had not improved any. "Yeah, you go right ahead and get back to me. You do that."

Shane kept talking. "Stilwell, you said you were banged up in a fight. Do you need to see a doctor do you think?"

Stilwell hesitated. Good. "I don't know, I can't see out of one eye and my nose is busted."

Shane pressed on. "It sounds like you really might need to see a doctor. You don't want to lose your eye, that wouldn't be good. It would be a terrible thing to lose your sight just because you can't get yourself checked out."

Stilwell seemed open to suggestion, which was excellent. "You're probably right. I wouldn't want to be blind in that eye or anything and it is hurting something awful."

"I can do that for you, Stilwell. I can arrange for a doctor to look at your eye. I know the chief would permit that."

"You think he would? Why would the police care if I lost the sight in my eye or not?"

Shane adjusted to a more comfortable position. "We want to help you."

"So you would get a doctor to come and take a look? Is that what you're saying?"

"Absolutely, but first why don't you let the woman come out, safely, and we can

251

make sure your eye gets looked at by a proper doctor. We will make that happen."

Stilwell remained undecided. "I don't believe the police would do that. I don't like the police. All they do is put people in jail that shouldn't be there. They locked me up before for something that wasn't even my fault. It wasn't my fault that the guy at the bar hit his head. It wasn't my fault if he had too much to drink. It wasn't my fault that he had a big mouth and was always running it. That's what got him into trouble in the first place. I just gave him some of his own medicine."

It had been a half hour or so since Shane had heard any sound from Ginger. With Stilwell seemingly having taken over the telephone, what was she having to contend with from Cedric? Just because he hadn't heard any sign of distress from her didn't mean Cedric hadn't silenced her in some way.

"Stilwell?"

"Yeah?"

"How is Ginger doing?"

"Sitting there gaping at me."

"So she's alright?"

"She's alright. Why, you worried about her?"

"I want this whole thing to end peacefully and I think you do too because you didn't bargain for any of this."

"You're right, I didn't bargain for this. Here I was having a good sleep and all the yelling woke me up and what's the first thing I see? About a million police cars on the property. Not a good thing to wake up to. We just mind our own business back here. We don't ask for no trouble but the police still come nosing around trying to get something started. I didn't know there was going to be some reporter asking questions or I would never have agreed to let her come here. Look at the trouble she brought with her. And now apparently my old man wants to keep her, but you guys say he can't. A man should be able to decide if he wants a woman or not. There's no law against that. She should be allowed to stay."

"She should be allowed to stay?" Shane asked, mirroring Stilwell.

"Yeah," Stilwell agreed, still on a roll. "That's between two adults. They know what they want. Anyway, I didn't ask to be woke up to all this."

The tone of Shane's voice never varied. "You sound like you're still tired."

"I am still tired," Stilwell whined. "I didn't get to bed until almost noontime, so I don't need this."

"Sounds like you just want all of this to be over," Shane emphasized.

"Of course I want it to be over."

"How do you think we can make that happen?" Shane asked him.

Stilwell didn't miss a beat. "By letting the woman leave."

Shane nodded. "That's right. Just let her come out so she can go home."

Stilwell was in full agreement. "Great, I'll send her out right now."

"No!" Cedric could be heard shouting in the background. "She's not going anywhere!"

"Let her go, Dad, and the police will go away. Problem solved."

"No!"

Stilwell was in a fighting mood. "Okay, you don't want to let her go? I'll get rid of the police my own way. I'll set the dogs on them. Where are they anyway?"

Cedric stood his ground. "They're in the back room and that's where they're going to stay until I say otherwise. This is my house and I get to say what happens around here. They'd just as soon stay in out of the weather. If I need them I can get them myself fast enough, so don't worry about it. You send them out there and they're as good as dead. They'll shoot them."

"They were going to get someone to look at my eye!" yelled Stilwell. "I can't see out of it. Don't you care if I go blind?"

Cedric was still in the background. "Go on down there then and see a doctor. They got no reason to stop you. You've got nothing to do with any of this, so stop sticking your nose in."

Stilwell was apparently as stubborn as his father. "I don't like all that heat hanging around. How did the police come to be here anyway?"

Cedric was still agitated. "Ginger called them is how. I was mad as hell at first but we've managed to get past that. The police won't leave though, even though she told them she wants to stay."

Stilwell sounded exasperated, impatient. "If you don't want the police here, maybe I should take that gun of yours and do some target practice."

Cedric was all but shouting. "Don't do that, stupid! You go anywhere near that window they'll pick you off sure as not. Your eye's fine, now go into the kitchen and get something to eat and leave me and Ginger alone.'

Shane could hear the conversation going on between father and son, but Ginger was wisely remaining silent. Hostage negotiation usually proceeded at a snail's pace. However there was always the concern that the longer things went on, the hostage might think the situation would never be resolved. They could become impatient and attempt to take matters into their own hands; try to escape. That move would surely see Ginger get shot. Things did move agonizingly slow, from the hostage's point of view he was sure, but as long as they were still talking there was hope for a nonviolent resolution.

Shane had to determine who was on the phone with him. "Stilwell?"

No answer, but he could hear someone beside the telephone. Then Cedric came on the line. Stilwell must have left the room to do as his father suggested and get something to eat.

"Shane?"

"I'm here, Cedric. What's happening?"

"I want to apologize for my son. He can get a little hepped up at times. He's a good boy though and I don't really want him involved in this. He's never really forgiven me for his mother dying like she did. He still holds it against me. But a man has a right to move on with his life, don't you think? I mean you're probably married, so I'm sure you can understand why I want to do the same. Why can the rest of the world do what they want to do? When poor old Cedric Gourney tries to do the same, half the police force shows up with guns drawn," he complained. "All I want is be happy, but there always seems to be someone who tries to stop me from doing that."

"Do you think Ginger wants to get married?"

"Well not right now maybe but she'll come around. It's my job to convince her that she'll be happy here. You take

Annabelle. Her old man told me to stop sniffing around once he saw the direction things were going when we were kids. He told me to get lost, but him and her mother came around after a while and saw things my way."

Shane was trying to keep Cedric in a positive frame of mind so he'd be more likely to relax, as though this was just a friendly chat when in fact it was a deadly situation. The tables could turn at any moment.

"Did I ever tell you about my mother?" Cedric continued, now apparently in the mood to talk.

"What about your mother?"

"First of all everyone always thought our family was weird. I could tell at school that's the way they thought because we were really poor. After Dad died it was just my mother and me, and she acted like it was my fault that my father was gone. It was as though she didn't want to be stuck with a kid to look after. Late at night, when I couldn't get to sleep, I would hear people coming to the house. I looked through the floor grate one night to see what they were doing. After a while I got so I'd wait until the action got going and then I'd sneak downstairs and watch. Hell, it was better than television. And then the next day I'd act all innocent and never say a thing, but I looked at her different after that. Here she was getting after me for every little thing and what she was doing was a lot worse. I think if I'd ever said I knew what was going on, she'd have crowned me. After a while I understood what people were saying about us. I was big for my age and I beat up a lot of kids who said things like that about my mother, but they were true.

"I didn't trust woman after that either. They pretended to be all angelic and everything and then when the lights went out they were just as bad as anyone else. Women will do that to you, you know."

"It sounds like you had a hard time growing up."

"I guess. My mother always cooked and cleaned all right, but it was the night time stuff that I didn't like. No guy wants his mother to be like that. The kids said my mother never had a job, so where did the money come from for us to live on? It was embarrassing. So that's why I decided to do something about it."

"What did you do?"

"One night I refused to go to bed. She was begging me to go upstairs but I kept on sitting there until the first guy came and then I tried to throw him out."

"Sounds like you'd had enough."

"That's right! I'd had enough, but he was a lot bigger than me and I got a fat lip out of it. So I got my gun and I put a bullet in him."

"What happened to the man?"

"He never died if that's what you're asking. I gave him a flesh wound, something to think about. It worked too and he never came back because I told my mother I was going to shoot every one that came through that door."

"What happened then?"

"I eventually made it so that nobody else came to my house after dark. They were too scared to. So what did my mother do? She went out and got a real job at a diner and made pretty good tips. She never forgave me for what I did, but at least she cleaned up her act. She was not a bad woman, only desperate I guess. Lonely maybe. Women do crazy stuff sometimes."

Cedric yawned noisily.

"Sounds like you'd like to have a nap."

"I am tired. I was up all night cleaning this place so it'd be good for when Ginger came. When a man's courting everything's got to be just perfect."

"You sound to me like a man who wants this whole thing to be over."

"I do, but I'm not ready to say that yet. After we're married is when I'll give myself up. Not before. How are you making out getting a preacher?"

"I'm working on that," said Shane.

"It can't be that hard to get someone to come and marry a man and a woman. All you need to do is get a marriage license for us."

"How am I going to do that at this time of night, Cedric?"

"I do know that the man and woman need to go themselves and make out the application. I do remember that much, so that would have to be done before we can get married."

"It sounds to me like you've really given this a lot of thought."

"I have, but maybe in this case the preacher could marry us and we could take care of the everything else later."

"How would that work?"

"I haven't really thought about it. We could promise to get the license, bring it to him later and he could update his paperwork. We could do it that way."

The storm seemed to be intensifying, the rain coming down in torrents. The wind whipped the tall trees surrounding the property. They swayed two and fro like dancing pick-up sticks, branches furiously askew.

"How could a preacher stand out in this rain and marry someone?" Shane asked reasonably.

"That's right," said Cedric, unexpectedly agreeing. "I don't know too many who would do that."

"That's true."

Stilwell had apparently come back into the room because Shane could hear his voice and it sounded as though he was speaking with food in his mouth. "You know, Dad, this wedding thing is about the stupidest idea I think you've ever had. To start with you're a lot older than she is. Face it, you're an old man. Not much wonder she doesn't want you."

Cedric apparently didn't appreciate his son's scathing assessment. "You mind your own business! This is between Ginger and me."

Stilwell laughed out loud. "She don't look like a willing bride to me. She looks scared to death. Supposing they do get the preacher. How do you plan to get her to say I do? She'll never do it, let alone let you touch her. You're nothing but a dirty old man and she's young enough to be your daughter." He laughed. "That makes you an even dirtier old man."

"You shut your mouth!" Cedric shouted, his temper reignited. "What Ginger and I do is no business of yours."

Stilwell laughed even harder. "You and Ginger! Ha! Look at her! She's freaked out of her tree. She's more my age and maybe she'd rather be with me than with you. Did you ever think of that? What do you say, Ginger? Want some real sugar?"

Shane could hear Ginger whimpering and he guessed sonny boy had made a move on her. That was confirmed a moment later when Cedric bellowed his disapproval.

"Leave her alone, she's mine! I saw her first! You go and get your own woman and leave mine alone."

Stilwell was still laughing, clearly egging his father on. "I think I'll take this one. She's more my style."

Cedric refused to back down. "A few minutes ago you wanted her out of here and now you want to try to take her away from me."

Stilwell's voice came across the line, loud and clear. "You know I'm not in a good mood when I'm hungry. Now I've had something to eat and I'm in the mood for a little loving. Come on now you pretty little thing, don't look at me like that with those big blue eyes of yours. I didn't say I was going to kill you, just … love you."

Cedric sounded as though he was about to blow a gasket. "You stay away from her! She's mine I tell you. I'll kill anyone who gets too close to her."

"How do you plan to do that when you're sitting in jail?" Stilwell taunted him. "They'll take you in and Ginger and I will have some fun. You won't be able to do one thing about it."

"You stay away from her!" Cedric hollered at the top of his lungs. "She belongs to me I tell you! I've had my eye on her for a long time. You go and get your own woman."

Shane was now dealing with two unstable suspects. It was a toss-up who was worse.

The line went dead. The situation was ramping up yet again. Force was always a last resort in anything like this and it was Shane's job to make the suspects understand that there was an alternative to violence.

He called Cedric's line again, and it was Cedric himself who answered. "Shane, is that you?"

"Yes. What's happening?"

"I've got my hands full right now because Stilwell is causing problems. He's always causing problems, which is why I don't want him here. He's done nothing but give me trouble his whole life. I never have any problems until he's around."

Stilwell was still in the mix. "You're one to talk, old man. You're the one who started this whole thing today. I'm only trying to think of a solution so that you don't have to go to jail, you old fool. If she gets out of here in one piece then everything goes back to normal. And how that happens is that she decides she wants to be with me, not you. Then she's not being held against her will anymore. I have a way with the ladies, so it's all up to little blue eyes here. Why don't we get her on the phone so she can tell them she's changed her mind about needing help."

"Cedric?" Shane prompted.

But Cedric wasn't interested in talking to Shane, he was likely ready to do battle with his son.

Stilwell was now in the thick of things. "What do you say, sugar? Go over and talk to the nice policeman and tell him that everything is fine. You've changed your mind about needing their help. Then they can all get out of the rain and go back to their nice little warm houses and not have to be out here bothering us. Come on, tell Shane over there you want to call the whole thing off."

Shane heard Ginger for the first time in long minutes.

"I just want to be let out," she whimpered. "I want this to be over. I want to go home."

"Cedric...." Shane tried again. "Why doesn't everyone just take a step back and calm down. We can work this out."

The negotiation had been in progress now for some seven hours, as the hands inched closer to one o'clock in the morning.

Cedric was breathing hard. "I hear you, Shane. Why don't I let you talk to my son? See if you can talk some sense into him. I certainly don't seem to be able to."

Shane kept his mood positive, upbeat. "Sure, put him on. I'll talk to him."

There was the sound of Cedric passing the phone to Stilwell.

"Yeah? What can I do for you?"

"Stilwell, how are we going to get this resolved, peacefully?"

"Everybody go home, that's how."

"Including the hostage," Shane said reasonably.

Stilwell snickered. "She's not my hostage, she's my old man's. I'm not stopping her from leaving, I'm just having some fun with her. It's the old man who won't let her go. He's the crazy one."

"Who're you calling crazy?" Cedric yelled in the background.

Shane persisted. "It sounds to me like you're ready to walk away from this, Stilwell."

"What's the weather like out there?" Stilwell asked. "It doesn't sound very good."

It seemed Shane's patience was inexhaustible. "I think the rain's starting to taper off a little actually. It's a good time to come out and get this thing over with."

Stilwell sounded apprehensive. "Do I have to be arrested?"

Shane stayed pleasant yet assertive. "We have to take you in to get everything sorted out, yes. Do you have a weapon on you right now?"

"No," said Stilwell.

"That's good, because you'd need to leave all weapons in the house for

265

everyone's safety. Are you ready to come out?"

Stilwell's tone told Shane he was serious about leaving the house. "You say its stopped raining?"

"It's starting to ease off."

"What about the girl?" asked Stilwell

"Let her come out first."

Stilwell seemed ready to act on his decision. "Okay, I've had enough of this. I'm coming out." He then spoke to Ginger. "Okay, Ginger, you're coming outside with me."

Shane interrupted. "Stilwell?"

Stilwell sounded almost conciliatory, but obviously not someone interested in making friends, with anybody. "Yeah?"

"Ginger comes out first," Shane told him, "and then you come out after she's safely with us. Just listen to what we tell you to do. Okay? That's the way it has to be."

"She's not going anywhere!" Cedric yelled and then a crash as Stilwell dropped the phone. It sounded as though he and Stilwell were wrestling with one another, knocking over furniture.

Ginger had obviously seen this as the moment for escape because Cedric shouted: "She's getting away! Let go of me, I'm going to get the dogs!"

Chapter Thirteen

Shane's muscles tensed. This was a bad development and it didn't seem like anyone was listening in the house at the moment. At least the line was still open and that gave him ears in the room as he heard Ginger shout: "Don't send the dogs! I'm not going! Look, I'm sitting in the chair. Please don't set the dogs on me! Please!"

Shane could hear frenzied barking, but at a distance, which would seem to indicate that indeed the animals were still in another room. He could also hear by the amount of racket that Cedric and his son were still locked in battle, the dogs adding to the commotion. He could also hear Ginger crying.

Then a gunshot rang out followed by a man's scream, although he couldn't be sure who had been hit. The dogs were going into overdrive, then more shouting, the voice of the hostage unable to be heard above the din. She was likely keeping as quiet as possible to avoid drawing any unnecessary attention to herself.

Shane could hear Cedric shout a command, the dogs falling silent in the back room. Then, miraculously, Cedric came to the phone, startling him when he yelled into the receiver.

"I shot my son! I had to do it!"

Shane took a deep breath and let it out slowly so that he himself could continue to convey calmness. "Is he badly hurt, Cedric?"

"I don't think so."

"Where is he hit?"

"In the arm, his upper arm. I didn't want to shoot my son but he gave me no choice. He was fighting me for the gun. I'm sure you could hear that from where you are."

Shane figured from the loudness of the report that it had been the .357. Stilwell was very lucky to even still have an arm because one strike from a handgun of that calibre could do massive damage. It could be a serious injury if the bullet had struck an artery. He could bleed out without the proper attention.

"He shouldn't have been fighting with me! He knew I had the gun in my hand! It was a stupid thing to do. He...." He hesitated. "Don't you do it!" Cedric shouted as it seemed there was yet another sudden turn in the situation. "Don't do it Stilwell! Don't you dare shoot me!"

"Cedric!" Shane called to get the man's attention. "What's happening now?"

"He's got hold of my rifle and he's aiming it at my head. I can see it in his eyes that he means to pull the trigger."

"Is that weapon loaded?"

"Yes! Stilwell, don't you shoot me or I'll kill you first! I can do it and I swear I will. Put the gun down, boy. You know I'll do it."

Shane raised his voice slightly to get Cedric's attention. "Cedric, tell him to put the gun down, that we've already got an ambulance on the way to take him to the hospital."

Cedric turned from the phone. "Stilwell, lay the gun down. They've got an ambulance coming for you. Lay the gun down! Lay it down! Now! Please!"

There was the sound of another shot, and Shane's guess it was the rifle this time. Amidst all those bullets flying in there was that poor reporter who was hopefully still not harmed. Cedric and Stilwell were shooting at each other. Still … the situation continued to escalate dangerously.

"Cedric, talk to me," said Shane. "What's going on?"

"Stilwell has laid the rifle down, it's lying on the table. He just shot over my head to scare me. I'm okay."

"Is he losing a lot of blood?"

"Yes!"

"Can you bring him out with you?"

"He can walk out on his own if that's what he wants to do."

"Why don't you let Ginger go and walk out first, then you and Stilwell come out; him first. I think you're ready to end this thing."

"I'll bring Stilwell out but I'm not giving up my gun to do it because you'll either take me out or take me in."

"What about Ginger?"

"She's fine right where she is. Hold the line a minute, I've got to go settle those dogs again. Ginger doesn't like them barking. It scares her."

An ambulance pulled onto the property, maintaining a safe distance behind the established perimeter.

Shane could hear that Cedric was back and had picked up the receiver. "Cedric, we have an ambulance ready. Is Stilwell able to handle those stairs on his own?"

"Are you ready to go?" Cedric asked his son. "They got an ambulance in the yard and they're waiting to look after you. Just go on out there and don't give anybody any trouble."

Shane could hear Stilwell speaking to his father although he couldn't quite make out what he was saying, until Cedric unwittingly clarified.

"No, leave both of those guns here and get going. You take one of those guns with you and they'll shoot you dead. I know they will. So just go. You're bleeding all over the place. You don't want to lose that arm. Go!"

Cedric then returned his attention to the negotiator. "Shane? I gotta go. I got to help Stilwell. I've got to get something wrapped around that arm and then he's coming down the stairs. He won't have any guns on him, so don't shoot. He's afraid that you tricked him and that you'll finish him off as soon as you get the chance. So you listen to me. If you do shoot him or harm him in any way, I don't think I have to tell you what happens next. I tell you too, it won't be pretty. Am I making myself clear? If you want Ginger to see the sunrise in a few hours, you'll keep that promise."

"I hear you and they won't shoot your son. I promise you that. Just tell him to keep his hands where we can see them. When he gets into the yard they'll direct him as to what to do and then they'll put him in the ambulance and take him to the hospital."

"All right then, I'm going to hang up now."

"Don't hang up. Just lay the receiver down and go take care of his arm and get him to the door. Once he comes into the yard we'll take it from there. He has nothing to worry about if he's unarmed."

"Again, Shane, I want your word on that. He's my only boy, such as he is. I don't want to see him killed."

"You have my word."

Shane heard the phone being laid down. He wondered how badly Stilwell was wounded given his moans and colourful language as his father tried to patch him up. By the sound of things it might be doubtful the injured man would be able to make it down that steep stairway and into the yard under his own steam. But from what he could hear, things seemed to be progressing in that direction. There was still plenty of fight in him.

He also heard Cedric warning him not to take either of the guns that were in the room with him and Stilwell retort: "I'm not going to take any damned guns with me. Okay? Now shut up and get out of my way."

Cedric must have gone to the window to watch his son leave. If that's what he was doing, he'd be able to see Stilwell being taken into custody by the support team and helped into the waiting ambulance. It was important that Cedric see how easily it was done; that a peaceful surrender was possible and no one had to get hurt. Maybe the father would want to follow suit.

Minutes later Cedric picked up the phone again. "I'm back. Thank you for keeping your word, Shane. I was watching. If anyone had taken a shot at my son I would've gotten at least a half dozen of you guys from my vantage point. I might not have gotten all of you, but I would have taken out enough to hurt you."

"We did keep our word about Stilwell, and that's the same word that I'm giving you, Cedric, for when you come out. A peaceful surrender is possible for you too. You don't have to go through any more of this. Just send Ginger out and then you leave your guns in the house and come on out into the yard, like Stilwell did. We'll take care of everything from there."

"I see it's stopped raining. The stars are out."

"It's all cleared off. That was some storm, but it's over now."

"I want you to know that I didn't mean to shoot my son. It was an accident. He tackled me and tried to take the gun away."

"I believe you."

"And then my own son tried to shoot me. I'll tell you I'm right good and mad now. If any of your men, or women, ever try to get into this place I'll kill them. I will kill them where they stand, so don't even think that someone can sneak in here. You pass that along; tell them to keep away. They've got no business being here anyway. If my son wasn't so stupid, they wouldn't have him right now either. He's just like his mother was, gets all excited over nothing. And look where it got her. And look where it got him, in the back of an ambulance although I swear I didn't do it on purpose. You can ask my future wife the same question. She'll tell you it was an accident."

273

"Okay, put her on the phone."

"No! She can tell you from where she's sitting. No more tricks!"

"I've been up front with you and I've kept my word. I'm not playing tricks. Okay, she can tell me from where she's sitting in her chair."

"Okay, Ginger," Cedric told her, "yell out to Shane here that me shooting Stilwell was nothing but an accident. Go ahead, do it."

"It was an accident," she shouted loud enough for him to hear. "Stilwell tried to take the gun away from Cedric."

"Tell her thank you," said Shane.

"He says thank you, hon. That was good that you told the truth. If you ever lie to me again you'll end up no better than my boy in the back of that ambulance, only yours won't be an accident. You understand that, right?"

Shane could hear her agree in a more subdued tone. At least she was still okay, although she did sound as though she was tired and had been crying. If he'd been allowed to speak to her on the phone he'd have told her to sit tight and allow the police, him as a negotiator, to do their job. It was a bad scenario when she tried to make her own escape. She could very well have gotten herself shot, given that there had been two unpredictable men in the house with access to guns. And then there were the dogs. If they'd been let out they'd have

274

had her before she ever made it to the door, or down the stairs.

* * *

Ginger straightened up in the chair and arched her back to try to stretch some of her aching muscles. At least she felt wide-awake again having drunk some of the coffee Stilwell had made earlier. Up now for more than twenty-four hours, she'd been fighting drowsiness at one point; terrified to drift off. She had no wish to be asleep and defenceless in the company of Cedric Gourney. But it was a double-edged sword because a large cup of coffee meant she had to pee again, the need for release becoming evermore urgent. She'd been allowed to go to the bathroom a few hours ago. Cedric had refused to let her close the door although she was grateful that he'd at least turned his back. Just when she thought there was not a gentlemanly bone in his body, he at least showed her that courtesy.

She could only imagine too that the dogs were in need of relief, having been locked up in that back room for hours. They could drown the place for all she cared.

One thing she did remember from the piece she'd done on the hostage negotiator, and the subsequent research, was the time involved in something like this. There was no quick fix, given the time it took to talk a hostage taker around. That fact had seemed perfectly logical when she'd written that story, but now that she was the hostage, the wait was pure torture. She never ever thought she'd at any point in her life be a hostage, but here she sat at the mercy of Cedric Gourney's warped mind.

She thought about her mother a lot during this ordeal, and knew somehow that she was watching over her, giving her strength to get through it. She had to believe that. Her mother had died relatively young and she still missed her. Heather Martel had been a wonderful parent, stepping up when her father had left the family when Ginger was still a child. It had not been easy for her mother as a single parent, but Heather had never complained. She just got on with things and looked after her three girls. It wasn't fair that she'd been diagnosed with liver cancer in her prime, but thankfully hadn't lingered long before the angels came for her.

Her attention swung back to Cedric who was still talking to Shane. She assumed it was the same negotiator. She knew they worked in teams and often switched off after long sieges like this one. And sometimes things went off the rails completely, like with the Stockholm Syndrome. She'd used that in her piece about crisis negotiators. What happened was that hostages developed sympathy for the man who'd taken them captive during a six-day standoff following a bungled Swedish bank robbery. Those hostages had ended up helping the bank robber; the police becoming a common enemy of both the robber and the hostages. One of the hostages had even married the guy when he was in prison.

Well, there was no chance of that happening in this case, not even close. The sooner she saw the last of Cedric Gourney, the happier she would be. But she knew very well that she wasn't out of the woods yet by any stretch of the imagination. One minute he wanted to kill her, the next, marry her. The man was unstable and could fly off his handle at any second. His son seemed to be the same way. When the two of them were here together she had truly thought her number was up. But she was still very much alive and praying with everything in her she would stay that way, with nothing worse to have to deal with than a good fright and a few bruises.

She listened to him asking the hostage negotiator, Shane, where the preacher was that he had ordered hours ago. Would they really go through with that? She couldn't imagine such a thing being allowed to take place, and what would it accomplish anyway? She would say I do, as much as it galled her to do so, just to stay alive and get out of this. It wouldn't be legal. Cedric seemed oblivious to all of that he was so fixated on making it happen.

Then for whatever reason Cedric hung up the phone and she seized that moment to request bathroom privileges once again. When she was seated back in that now hated armchair, he brought a kitchen chair into the room and sat down a few feet away.

"You know, Ginger, I never get tired of looking at you. I can't believe I've got someone great like you here with me."

What could she say to that? She never wanted to see his ugly face again, those beady snake-like eyes, but she had to continue to play the game.

"Cedric, it seems like you've made a good friend in Shane there on the telephone," she said, changing the subject and motioning with her head toward the instrument that now sat idle. "It's hard to find someone who's honest, someone who'll tell you the truth. So when you have a chance to talk to a person like that, it's probably a good idea to listen to what he has to say, don't you think?"

"He's a cop. You know that, right?"

"I know that. But I don't think he has misled you through any of this. I think you'd have to agree with that."

Cedric was quiet for a moment, and she had to say he looked exhausted. She

278

wondered what were the chances of his drifting off to sleep? But as soon as the idea came to mind to perhaps try and make a run for it again if he did drift off, she dismissed it. She'd already tried that and had a close call, much too close for comfort. He might fall asleep, but he was too wired to stay out for long. If she double-crossed him again, he would probably flat out shoot her.

"You're right, darlin', he hasn't lied to me."

"So why not listen to him? There are too many police out there, this isn't going to work out and I think it's better to let me go. Not everything in life works out the way we want it to and we can't force it to because we've got a gun in our hand, or dogs that can chew people up. Do you really want to see me get hurt because of this? I've done nothing to harm you. I came here in good faith to do a story, I didn't ask for all of this. To be terrorized by dogs and threatened with death. Listen to Shane, Cedric, he's only trying to make it so that everybody can go home with no one getting hurt."

"Stilwell got hurt."

"Okay, so nobody else gets hurt."

He looked at her and she could see a parade of emotions march across his face. Had he been a victim at some point in his own life? What had happened to him to damage him so badly that he thought he

279

could go around acting like he did? The man had killed before and it chilled her how easily he could kill again. She had to cling to the idea that he might still respond to reason. He hadn't killed her yet, so maybe there was a spark of decency in him. He'd been rough with her, but he hadn't tried to sexually assault her. The thought of him trying something like that was so repugnant she barely stifled a shudder.

This whole thing had been terrible. Being forced at gunpoint to stay in this house, having the dogs guarding her, the son coming into the picture, shots fired. … It was like something out of a really bad late night movie, one she'd have no wish to watch, let alone endure.

"So why don't you do as Shane is asking? They know what they're doing; you know there's no way out of this. There's no way you can win." She smiled, attempting conciliation. "So if we can't be together, wouldn't you rather I remember you as the man who showed me kindness and let me go home?"

"You should never have called the police. You should not have done that. I was taking care of things, doing what I knew was best for both of us. See, I knew you could be happy here, but you wouldn't trust me and that made me mad."

"I was scared. It was all very new to me. Surely you can see that now."

"Maybe. I think I moved too fast but you were pushing to leave and that's not what I had planned. I had to make my move or I would have lost you."

"I see."

"Now I think you might be more trouble than you're worth. You're awful stubborn and you talk to me when I don't feel like listening. Annabelle was like that."

She felt a rush of adrenalin at this new turn. Was she imagining it, or was he actually telling her he had changed his mind about wanting to marry her? She had to choose her next words very carefully. Being compared to the woman he'd killed, because she had also wanted to leave, was chilling. She sensed a weakening in him and plunged ahead on gut instinct.

"I am stubborn, and I do like to get my point across."

"There's nothing about you that I can't fix but now I want you to be quiet. Shane said he'd call back and I don't want to miss his call for you yakking."

She nodded, not daring to utter another word lest his hair trigger temper be reignited.

The phone rang and Cedric leapt at it as though he was waiting for a call from a long lost friend.

"Shane, is that you?"

"It's me. How are you doing?"

"I'm doing fine. We've been at this a long time."

"No problem as long as everything ends peacefully. How is Ginger doing?"

"She's okay. I'm taking good care of her so you don't have to worry. As long as she behaves herself, she's fine. Have you heard anything about Stilwell? Is he going to be okay?"

"The last I heard he was in surgery, so that will probably take a while. You can't go too fast with that kind of thing."

"That's what I was thinking. I'll say again that I did not want to shoot my son. I had no intention of doing that at all."

"I believe you."

"He came at me like a madman and I was afraid the gun was going to go off, and it did. I would never shoot my own son unless he gave me no choice."

"I know you wouldn't hurt your son on purpose. It seems like you feel as if this is all starting to be too much and you want it to be over."

"I'm not tired of talking to you because you're a nice enough guy, but none of this is turning out the way I thought it would. I had it pictured a lot different in my mind. I thought Ginger would be happy that a man like me wanted to take her for my wife. Give her a good home. That's not the way it worked out though."

"Sounds to me like you're ready to let her go home."

"I'm thinking about that. And I suppose you still want me to surrender even though I might be changing my mind about getting married? People don't have to go to jail because they changed their mind do they?"

"You would have to surrender, yes, so that we can get everything sorted out."

"What about my dogs if I decide to give myself up?"

"Do you know someone who can come and take care of them?"

"My Uncle Joshua. He lives over on the ridge. He comes here sometimes and they like him. He's known them since they were pups, but I don't think they'd want me to go anywhere. I will not go back to jail, Shane."

"Do you have a telephone number for your Uncle Joshua so we can give him a call and have him come here? It would be good to have someone to take care of them so they wouldn't be alone too long. What do you feed them?"

"I've got lots of food for them but I don't want to leave them behind. My life is with my dogs."

"Your uncle can look after them for you. They're smart dogs, they'll probably understand that things are going to be different for a while. Sounds me like you feel comfortable leaving them with him."

"I do, but, Shane? I repeat, I'm not going back to jail," he announced before he recited Uncle Joshua's telephone number. "But you go ahead and call Josh."

"Okay, I'll do that as soon as you've come out of there. You said he didn't live too far away, so he should be right along when I explain to him that you want him to see to your dogs."

It sounded as though Cedric was close to tears.

"It seems like you want this to be finished. That you're ready to let Ginger come out."

There was no mistake about it, Cedric was crying now. He was likely exhausted and certainly disappointed that the woman of his dreams did not want to marry him.

"Cedric? Can you let Ginger come out? All she has to do is walk out of the house and come down the stairs. Tell her not to carry anything, and keep her hands where we can see them."

Cedric turned to Ginger. "You can go now, Miss Ginger. I think this is all for the best. He said not to bring anything with you, just go down and show them that your hands are empty."

Ginger, her legs unsteady, slowly got up out of the chair and made her way through to the kitchen. She felt like she wanted to run. But just as prey should never run from a predator so as not to trigger the predatory instinct to pursue and capture, she resisted the urge. Also, considering Cedric's penchant for abrupt mood shifts, she wondered what second a bullet was going to slam into her back. It all seemed too good to be true that he was actually letting her go free after all this time.

Trembling, she made it to the back door. It felt like she'd receive a nasty surprise and find it bolted shut but it opened easily enough. She held onto the rail for support as she slowly descended the stairs one at a time, feeling as though she would never reach the bottom. At any moment she expected her captor would come barrelling after her, or she'd hear the dogs barking in hot pursuit. But he didn't and the dogs didn't come. Now, in the gently gathering light of early morning, she held her hands out from her sides and walked unsteadily toward the lights at the perimeter of the property. There she fell sobbing into the arms of the tactical officer who came out to meet her and hurry her to safety. She was once again a free woman.

Chapter Fourteen

After being checked out at the hospital and finished giving her statement to the police, Ginger savoured the blessed peace and quiet of her apartment. Her bedroom was her oasis, a welcome respite from the edge-of-the-seat flight she had withstood for all those hours, interview time included.

There were messages from her sister Naomi who lived on the other side of the city, and also from her sister Alexandra in Toronto. Bad news travelled quickly, so despite the fact that she was having trouble keeping her eyes open, she wouldn't make her sisters wait. She spoke with both, promising a longer conversation within the next day or so with all of the sordid details of her ordeal.

She thought about her neat, orderly world. She liked it that way; liked her life in Franklin. She and her sisters were born in Toronto, but the family had later moved to the east coast, the birthplace of both parents, and stayed put following the defection of her father for parts unknown.

Alexandra had returned to Toronto for her work in the Canadian film industry. True stardom had so far eluded her, but the name Alexandra Martel was beginning to be known in all the right circles. Naomi was doing her thing as a computer programmer with her own company, and of course she, Ginger, was the office manager at Pratt & Sons Distributors of fine arts. She loved her job but any free time was dedicated to freelancing. The way she felt right now though, she didn't even want to think about doing any interviews.

A half hour later she climbed wearily into the shower and let the hot water sluice over her until it ran cold, trying to scrub off Cedric Gourney and everything to do with that horrible man. Fat chance of that, and when she finally crawled beneath the covers, there it was waiting for her to be thought about. It was hard to imagine that it had only been a few hours since she'd made that joyous walk to freedom. Nothing had ever felt so good as those policeman's arms around her, hurrying her out of Gourney's line of fire. In a significant way she was frightened of sleep, because Cedric would probably be there, lying in wait for her.

She too had heard the single gunshot just minutes after she'd made it to safety and it really didn't come as a surprise that he had turned the gun on himself. The

287

entire thing was horrible from beginning to end. She'd lived a nightmare and once everything had been hashed out, and she'd gotten it out of her system, she never wanted to hear the name Cedric Gourney again. He probably roamed the spirit world now, her imagination taunted her, toying with her tired brain. She dismissed such thoughts. It was bad enough he'd wreaked so much havoc on this side of things.

Despite her exhaustion, sleep seemed inclined to avoid her. But it was still nice to be able to stretch out in bed, luxuriating in the caress of warm, soft sheets. Her apartment felt like a safe little hidey hole now, the doors securely double locked, and no one about to pop out with a gun. No dogs slavering to get a piece of her.

Her phone jangled on the bedside table. Scooting closer, she answered and her heart sank when she recognized the voice of her editor.

"How are you feeling, Ginger?"

"Beaten up emotionally, mentally. That's how I feel."

"We need to do a story on this, you know that, right?"

"Ahhh, Mr. McDougall, I'm not interested in writing a story about what happened to me. It's too soon, if ever. I couldn't relive what happened to me, I just couldn't."

"Now's the perfect time, Ginger, while everything is still fresh in your mind. Memory fades quickly."

"It can't fade quickly enough to suit me because I want to forget the whole thing. I won't be able to forget, but I certainly want to move ahead, not dwell on it. I could have died! For several hours I thought I would!"

"I'm sorry for what you went through of course, but as a journalist you owe a certain amount of loyalty to this paper. This is a headline story for sure."

"I know that and I know I can't stop you from writing it, but I don't want to be involved in that end of it. I'm sorry, but I can't write it."

"So you'll agree to be interviewed by one of our other reporters?"

"I really don't even want to do that. It was horrible, Mr. McDougall, and I'm trying not to think about it. And I have to ask you, were you aware that Cedric Gourney had a criminal record?"

"There was some stuff, way back...."

"And you knew I was going there."

"There was that thing with his wife years ago but at the time a lot of people thought he was innocent and I was one of them. And the incident with the telephone repairman was just a misunderstanding. Cedric could get a little worked up but I thought you could handle him, Ginger, or I never would have allowed you to go. I

289

apologize, considering the way things turned out, but this is a big story. Just think of talking about it as part of the healing process. That would be a healthy way to look at it, don't you think?"

She couldn't believe he was actually asking her to do this after what she had just endured. Foster McDougall was hard-boiled, it was true, but she never thought him to be insensitive. And now the scoop, the story, was more important than her feelings.

"I'm a very private person, Mr. McDougall. I could give you a statement that says it was an ordeal but that I'm doing okay. It was a terrifying experience, and the wound is still just too fresh to shine a light on it. Do you know what I mean?"

"I know what you mean," although she doubted he grasped the depth of the whole thing, other than a great headline. "So just write a statement and send it along. I don't suppose there's any way you could have that for us by the end of the day? We put the paper to bed tomorrow and we absolutely must have the hostage taking crisis on the front page."

She sighed, mentally exhausted. "I will definitely have it for you by the end of the day, but that's all I feel up to at the moment. I need to get some sleep."

"What about your notes from the interview?"

"The police have my notes and tapes and also my camera; they want to look at them. I suppose it's because Stilwell Gourney is still very much alive and could be seeing the inside of a courtroom with regard to this. They want to see if I have anything pertaining to him. I would imagine I'll be involved in that, but whatever happens, happens. If it comes to that I'll do what I have to do and it'll finally be over."

"You've got people you can talk to haven't you, Ginger? It wouldn't be a good idea to keep any of this bottled up inside. You went through a life and death ordeal and you need to get it out."

"I have my sisters to talk to and believe me, before we're through, it will be well and truly talked out. I appreciate your concern though."

"And if you need to talk to me I'm only a phone call away. I think of everyone associated with this newspaper as family. I hope you know that."

Perhaps she had misjudged him because the bottom line was that he had to keep the newspaper in business. She reminded herself that she was not in the best frame of mind at the moment to pass judgement. She thanked him for the call before she hung up. She might write for the press, but the last thing she wanted was to be featured in it. Something of this nature was way too invasive and she'd had enough invasive since yesterday to last a lifetime. That's why she wasn't interested in mainstream journalism. She had nothing against people who did the job. She understood how difficult it was and the difference they'd made in the betterment of this world. It just wasn't in her to chase after people and suffer the inevitable slings and arrows. She liked the lighter stuff. That was her thing. She had pursued it doggedly but never against the wishes of the interviewee. Their permission had always been given up front, and she refused to blindside anyone.

She knew one thing that had to be taken care of first thing tomorrow morning. She'd have to call the office and let them know she wouldn't be in for work. She had vacation piled up like crazy. The owners, Bill Pratt and his son, Grant, were always after her to take some time off. Well this looked like that sometime although they might not appreciate it that she was doing it so last minute. But it couldn't be helped and she desperately needed some time to herself.

The phone rang again and she reconsidered taking it off the hook. This time it was Grandmother Bridger, her mother's mother, on the other end of the line. Sylvia Bridger was a force to be reckoned with even into old age.

"Ginger! Thank God you're okay, darling. I've been beside myself since

Naomi called and told me what happened to you. That must have been dreadful. Were you raped? I think they call it sexually assaulted these days."

That was Grandmother Bridger, straight to the point.

"No, Gram, I wasn't raped, and yes they do call it sexual assault. It wasn't like that at all. He held me there against my will, which was horrible, but he never touched me."

"Never touched you at all? You expect me to believe that?"

Ginger chuckled. "He pulled my hair, pushed me around and stuff like that, but never anything sexual, and thank God for that. Believe me!"

"So he did touch you, I mean he was rough with you. I don't see why the police couldn't just storm in and get you. That's the way I saw it done on TV and they got the woman out safe and sound. They didn't make her wait for hours and hours. I tell if I had known about it I'd have gone there and got you out of that house and make no mistake about it. That's why Naomi didn't tell me until it was over I suppose."

"I'm glad she didn't tell you until afterwards because I wouldn't want you to worry. I think they did it the right way. Storming in like that could cause someone to get killed, and that someone could have been me. It was awful, but it's over."

"Don't the police have guns? They could have gone in and brought you out."

"Gram, Cedric had guns too and they couldn't take the chance that I could get hurt. I'm deeply grateful to that hostage negotiator. His name is Shane and that's all I know. I spoke to him on the phone a few times because he kept trying to make sure I was all right. He was very good at what he did because he got me out, unharmed."

"Well, he kept that nut job from killing you, so he has my everlasting gratitude."

"Mine too. Those negotiators don't have an easy job. It's a tremendous responsibility to keep everyone safe. They have to stay calm, and keep the situation low-key. He wore Cedric down, and that's how I got out safely."

"Did the negotiator, Shane, have a nice voice?"

"He had a great voice! If I was a hostage taker I think I'd keep things going as long as I could if I thought I'd get to listen to that voice for a few hours. Whew!"

"Ginger!"

"Just kidding! But really, Gram, he had a very sexy voice. I don't know what he looks like, but I could listen to him forever."

"Didn't they let you meet him after going through all that?"

"No, unfortunately. I was so worked up when I got out of there they were trying to get me to calm down. I tell you, even though that Cedric guy agreed that I could leave, I thought every step I took would be my last. That he'd change his mind. He was good at that. One minute he'd be going in one direction, and the next, a sudden turn and he was off in another direction. But anyway, I kept thinking he was going to shoot me in the back. Even going down the stairs I expected him to change his mind and set those dogs on me, the three German shepherds. I still can't believe he let me walk out of there in one piece. I tell you, it was only because of Shane that I'm alive today. I firmly believe that. Can you imagine that Cedric guy wanted to marry me!"

"Well I do want you to get married," she said with a chuckle. "You're getting too old to be alone. That's what I tell your sister Naomi too, although she at least has a steady boyfriend so there's some hope for her."

"Gram! Bite your tongue! I would rather marry one of those dogs than that awful man. I wouldn't marry Cedric Gourney if he was the last man on earth. Ugh! Horrible!"

"Okay, I'll stop pulling your leg. I want you to get married and have a family, yes, but not to a maniac like that! I'd shoot him myself before I ever allowed you to go through with the wedding. I want you to get married to someone nice, a man who'll be a good partner for you."

"You don't have to worry about me marrying Cedric Gourney because he's gone now anyway, but he had a son...."

"Ginger Martel! You're giving me some of my own medicine? Seriously though, keep your eyes and ears open, dear, and you'll meet a nice man someday. Just always remember that he has to be someone who is worthy of you. Your father, wherever he may be and I hope he stays there, was not worthy of your mother. He left her alone with three young children to raise. He should have been horsewhipped for what he did to her."

"Mum was a wonderful mother."

"She was, and I miss her desperately to this day. And I love my granddaughters, all three of you, but please, I want to see at least one of you get married before my time is up."

"No pressure though, right?"

"Certainly not. You're beautiful young women, all of you. I guess I have to satisfy myself that the right one will come along – and honey, wait until he does. I'm teasing you, there's no rush. There's plenty of time yet to get married and have children. Look at me, I never met my Robert until I was almost forty and I had your mother the next year. She never got pregnant until she was thirty-seven, so lots of time. Oh how I wish you girls could have known your Grandfather Bridger. He was something else, that man. But the good Lord saw fit to take him not ten years after we got married. I still think about him every day too. But let me tell you something, the first time I saw your grandfather I knew he was the one. Sounds silly I know, but I just knew. There were fireworks. It's good to know someone before you marry them of course, but I really believe when you know, you know. Your mother knew your dad for three years. She thought because she'd known him all that time that getting married was the logical next step, but it was a huge mistake.

"Anyway, girl, I've kept you long enough. I would imagine you haven't gotten much sleep in the past twenty-four hours or so and here I am keeping you awake."

"I couldn't sleep anyway," Ginger rushed to assure her, "so I was just lying here, my mind going back over everything that happened."

"Well you're safe now and I'll thank God every day for the rest of my life that you are. Now hang up this phone. Turn it off maybe, and try to get some sleep. You're more tired than you know and sleep will be like a healing balm to you. Bye, bye, sweetie."

Ginger adored her grandmother, was closer to her than the other girls. She was a riot too, no grass growing under her feet. If she had something to say, she got it said, no matter how it landed on the other end. If

Cedric Gourney had fetched up against her, he would likely have run out of that house asking for police protection. If there was a showdown it was Gram who would come out on top. She'd bet good money on it. Ginger wished she had half the spunk her grandmother did.

Her mind eventually drifted back to those hours spent with Cedric ... and for a time with both he and Stilwell. If ever there were two people a woman would not want to spend time with, it was those two. Both of them were certifiable, and she seriously questioned her judgement to have mistaken colourful for ... that. But again, she reminded herself reasonably, there was indeed a fine line and it was an easy mistake to make.

She thought again about the hostage negotiator. She'd like to meet him and thank him for saving her life. She knew it was a team effort and there was plenty of police power at the scene, but it was Shane who was with her the whole time. It was him on the other end of the line that gave her hope, and without it who knows what might have happened? Things might have had an entirely different outcome. She definitely wanted to say thank you and also put a face with the voice. The trigger was pulled more than once in that house last night, and it could have just as easily been her that was either injured or dead.

The last thought she had before eventually drifting off was how she was going to go about thanking Shane in person. She'd give herself another day to unwind, but first thing Tuesday she'd look him up.

* * *

Shane stood under the hot punishing needles of water in the shower, feeling some of the tension that still coiled inside him begin to ease away. It had ended with Cedric's suicide. However the end goal had been reached in that they were able to save the hostage. The woman had naturally been upset when she'd finally gotten out of the building and away from that madman and his dogs. The EMT's had seen to her onsite and run her into the hospital to be checked out. She'd been fine once she'd calmed down and was released an hour or so later he'd been told. She'd also given her statement, and he thought she was a trooper to be able to take care of that after everything she'd been through. They'd taken her back to the scene where she'd picked up her car and other belongings, and driven home. He'd liked to have met her though, put a face to the voice he'd heard on the phone. There was always something satisfying about that, otherwise he was plugging stuff into a black hole.

Switching off the jets he grabbed a towel and stepped out of the shower, dried off then wrapped it around his waist. He wondered if he could ever again take a shower without thinking about that last day he'd had with April and her flipping out over a stupid wet towel. Oh well, he wasn't going to go back over all that again.

He studied himself in the mirror. Now that he planned to start dating again, it was a sobering thought that a potential date could see him with his shirt off, naked … eventually. He hadn't hit the gym in a while but he was still well muscled, broad shoulders and chest tapering to a slimmer waist and hips and long legs. He wasn't twenty-five anymore, but he was holding up okay. After running his hand over his face he reached for the shaving cream and razor and made quick work of the scruff of the past twenty-four hours. He liked to be clean-shaven, no moustache or beard for him. And he kept his blonde hair short, not a buzz cut, but not over-long either. Like his father. Maybe he emulated him more than he realized. He was sure he'd noticed that when he stopped by to see him yesterday, and appreciated it, imitation being the highest form of flattery.

Later, in bed, he stretched out between the cool sheets, still in the guest room. His mind wandered back to the hours of Cedric Gourney's hostage taking. He didn't drill down on anything too much, but it was impossible not to reflect, grade himself as it were. There was always room for improvement with crisis negotiating, but he wasn't surprised when Cedric had turned the gun on himself. He'd seen it coming. Thank God he waited until the reporter was well away from the house before he did so though. Still, it was a life lost and the violent conclusion that they'd all hoped to avoid. But they'd done the best they could, he'd done the best he could. Nevertheless you could only take things so far. Then serendipity, or whatever you wanted to call it, took over and that was beyond the control of anyone.

He eventually slept, and it wasn't until ten hours later that he woke up, groggy at first because he wasn't precisely a morning person either, and pulled himself out of bed. It was Monday, garbage day. He quickly found clean jeans, socks, underwear and a pullover. The garage was full of garbage that he wanted to get rid of today, a mountain of stuff in blue bags from his clean-out of the other night. If he didn't get rid of it today it would be stuck there another week and he had to get the house ready for showing.

He also carried the clear plastic bags out for goodwill. With any luck the whole works would be gone before one o'clock when the realtor was coming to look the place over.

He'd just finished carrying the last of the goodwill bags to the curb when his phone rang and it was his father on the other end.

"It was on the news about a hostage taking on Saturday night. Were you the negotiator for that one, Shane?"

"Yep, that was me. It didn't last long though, only a few hours."

It was funny, only a handful of crisis situations made the news. People assumed that hostage negotiators just twiddled their thumbs the rest of the time, only rarely getting to utilize their skills. Of course he had his regular police duties and unless he worked for a much bigger force, that's the way it was for most hostage negotiators.

"You do that much, hostage negotiation?"

"From time to time," he said evasively, not overly interested in going into it with his father or anyone else for that matter. He had always played his cards close to his chest, did what he did but didn't feel the need to talk about it much. "There are three of us at work who do that."

"Why three?"

"Because being on a team, there's always a negotiator ready to step in when the circumstances call for it. One negotiator usually doesn't handle the whole thing by himself. The other team member listens in, provides suggestions, that sort of thing, switching places if necessary."

"I see. Well this was a bad one, wasn't it? There was a hostage and everything."

Shane smiled to himself. There usually was a hostage involved when a hostage negotiator was called in, otherwise the Emergency Response Team would deal with the barricaded person. Negotiators had a situation not long ago where a husband had held a gun on his wife for most of the evening. Somehow that had escaped the media, maybe there were bigger stories that day. That was okay with him. Everything didn't need to be on the six o'clock news. He'd just as soon go quietly about his work than answer a bunch of dumb questions from reporters. He had nothing against reporters, exactly, but sometimes they didn't know where to draw the line. Like this Ginger person, a reporter. How could she not know that Cedric Gourney was a head case before she went to his home, in a remote location no less? Her editor knew about Gourney but to be fair, maybe she didn't. Whoever was at fault, score one for bad judgement. Still, he knew she was probably a well-intentioned person who got in over her head.

"Yes, there was a hostage; thankfully only one, and we got her out safely."

"And the perp shot himself I understand?"

Shane smiled at the insider lingo. With television, everyone was a cop or a wannabe, knowing all the slang. Only real police officers didn't normally talk that way. But this was his father, and he was only trying to be nice; show interest in his son's work.

"He did."

"You weren't in any danger, were you son?"

It was not well understood that any situation that involved loaded firearms was dangerous.

"I was fine," he said, knowing his father had always underplayed the edgy stuff he'd faced as a firefighter. "You don't have to worry about me. I've been at this police thing for a while."

"Still. Just called to see if you were all right; glad to hear your voice."

They chatted for a few more minutes before they hung up and he was glad to talk to his Dad. It was nice to know he cared. It was new to him, this feeling, and he knew he had to allow it to happen. Let his father in where he had for so many years shut him out. His father was trying, that was all that mattered, and so would he.

On Tuesday Shane went in for the day shift, stopping at the coffee shop for his usual cup of Joe before heading to the office. There was plenty of paperwork waiting for him following the hostage incident, always that, and he saw his day pretty well laid out in front of him. He actually hoped it was quiet so that he could finish up everything that needed to be done. He liked to keep a clean desk, well as much as possible anyway.

Merle Brewster stopped by his desk in the squad room a few minutes later, looking like a man on a mission. The older police officer hung around with Shane some. They went to hockey and ball games together from time to time since Merle got divorced. Other than this casual friendship, both men were known to keep to themselves. Merle never said much, but today he certainly looked as though he had something on his mind and eager to share whatever it was.

"I've got two things to say to you, buddy," said Merle with a smile. "First of all a bunch of us are getting together tonight at the Squeaky Eel for a few drinks because as you know Chris Brantly is retiring. And since his old lady never lets him out of her sight, this might be the only time we have to get together with him. So are you in?"

Shane grinned. "If Chris is allowed out to play, then I'm all in. What's the second thing you want to tell me?"

"Just that there's a pretty girl waiting for you downstairs at the desk, and I mean pretty. She says she wants to thank you for saving her life on Saturday night. I take it she was that reporter who was held hostage."

Shane shrugged. "I don't know, I never laid eyes on her. I would've liked to have a word with her, but they had her out of there so fast there wasn't time."

"Well she's here now and like I said, she's pretty."

"I'm kind of busy at the moment, Merle."

"Are you serious right now?"

Shane didn't enjoy being the centre of attention and he didn't need some reporter falling all over him with gratitude. If all she wanted to say was thank you, then that was fine, but she probably wanted to do a story about it or something. That was a non-starter as far as he was concerned. No way did he want to be in any newspaper. Besides if they brought her up here, all the guys would be gawking. Then the ribbing would start and it would take a very long time before he was out from under it, but okay, whatever. If she was nice enough to come all the way here to say thank you, he could at least let her do it. But that was all though. No stories.

"I'm serious, can't you see I'm up to my neck in paperwork?" he asked, trying his best to look put upon before relenting good-naturedly. "All right, bring her up and we'll get it taken care of."

Merle's smile got wider before he disappeared down the hall and minutes later was back with said reporter. Shane lifted his head as she came through the door and his mouth dropped open. He couldn't help it. He was now face to face with the beautiful woman he'd been eyeing at the coffee shop.

Chapter Fifteen

Ginger was aware she was staring about the same time she realized he was staring at her. Neither said anything, and there was a room full of people watching this whole thing play out. She found her voice.

"I just wanted to thank you, I...."

The negotiator appeared to recover himself too. He suggested they step into a small boardroom nearby to have this conversation, for which she was grateful. Once they were inside and the door closed, he pulled out a chair for her and then took one himself a short distance away.

She knew she was staring again, the words of her grandmother ringing in her ears: she would know the right man when she saw him. This guy was gorgeous by any account, tall, blonde, smouldering grey eyes, nice white teeth although he didn't seem inclined to smile often. That was her first impression, that he was a quiet guy, but when he spoke ... oh, that voice! She was mesmerized.

She started again. "I want to thank you, officer...."

He did smile this time and he had a great one, lighting up his face. "I guess you know my name is Shane from Saturday night." He reached to shake her hand. "I'm Shane Elliott."

She took his hand in hers. "And of course I'm Ginger Martel."

His smile was contagious and she felt herself relax. "I wanted to say thank you for saving my life. Those were the longest hours I've ever spent, and knowing you were on the other end of the line helped me keep my sanity. It was almost unbearable being in that house with him, and then his son ... those dogs. That was the worst thing I've ever been through. I don't know what I would have done if you hadn't been keeping him in check."

"It's just what hostage negotiators do."

She was still smiling. "Well, I for one am glad you do what you do. I did a story a few years ago with one of your colleagues. He's retired now, Kenny Ferguson. Never in my wildest dreams did I think I would ever be in a situation like that myself."

His eyes never left her face. "And I never thought, after seeing you every day in the coffee shop that I'd be helping you out like that. It's a small world, isn't it?"

Her brows knit. "This is the first time I've ever laid eyes on you, offi … er … Shane."

He nodded as though he understood. "What I meant was that I see you every day, well just about every day. That doesn't mean you noticed me."

He was way off base on that one because if there was a coffee shop and he was in it, she would notice him.

She shook her head, perplexed. "I'm sorry, I have no idea what you're talking about. What coffee shop are you referring to?"

"The Daily Grind in that strip mall on Lexington Avenue. That wasn't you? You look just like the woman I see in there all the time although her hair is long and yours is short. Otherwise you look the same. I thought you got your hair cut or something."

She laughed, nodding. "Of course! You likely saw my sister, Naomi."

"Don't tell me you're twins."

She chuckled, remembering the confusion they used to cause, although it had been a few years since it had happened. "No, there's another sister in Toronto. I'm one of three. We're triplets."

"Triplets!" He laughed and she really loved the sound, deep and sexy as it pushed its way up out of his chest. "Are you serious right now?"

She was laughing too, immensely enjoying this conversation. "I'm the oldest of the three by seventeen minutes. Alexandra is next and she's twelve minutes older than Naomi, which I assume is the woman you've been seeing in the coffee shop. We're all identical, although eighty percent of triplets are actually fraternal ... and sometimes two can be identical with one not looking like the others at all. Just a little triplet lore for you."

"Wow! That's unbelievable! And you said one of your sisters lives in Toronto?"

"Alexandra does. She's an actress. She's been on television and everything. Her last part, even though it wasn't very big, was in the mini-series Frontiers. That ran a month or so ago. She played the part of the King's sister, Sunda. That character got killed in the first episode."

He looked at her incredulously. "I saw that show and I think I know who you mean. That's your sister?"

"The pride and joy of the family."

"I think I remember her because she reminded me of the woman in the coffee shop. You're sure there's only three of you?"

"Just three. It sounds like Naomi really caught your eye."

She knew he saw her checking out his ring finger, but that's okay because she'd seen his gaze dart to hers. For once in her life she was thankful it was bare as the northern tundra in a January deep freeze.

"Yes, I mean she's ... you're ... beautiful. Quite a few heads were turned I would imagine, not just mine. But I saw her holding hands with a guy one day, so my guess is that she's taken."

She nodded, happy to tell him he was right. "Her and Ritchie have been going together for about five years. I don't think they'll ever get married though. Naomi was in love with this other guy, but he up and married someone else. She treads very lightly in the romance department."

"Sooo... are any of you, the triplets, married?" he asked and she liked his candour.

"None of us are married, much to the dismay of our matchmaking grandmother."

"What about you, Ginger, are you seeing anybody?"

She shook her head, her eyes meeting his. "No, I'm not. And you?"

He grinned, not looking at all displeased that the conversation had taken a personal turn. "Not at all." His smile slipped a little. "My wife died three years ago, and it's only been in the past little while that I've felt like I'm ready to move on with my life. Meet someone, start dating again." The shadow passed. "So ... would you like to go out ... with me?"

She smiled, aware that she was glowing. She could feel it. The last thing she'd expected when she came here today was to be asked out on a date ... by Shane. She couldn't believe it.

"I'm sorry, I'm kind of rusty with the dating thing," he continued. "I didn't mean to pounce on you like that. It's just that...."

"I don't feel pounced on at all," she told him, unable to stop grinning. "Besides, I'm a bit rusty myself seeing as how I haven't been out on a date in over a year. We can be rusty together."

The way he was looking at her made her heart do funny things. Was this really happening? Apparently so.

"Are you up for dinner tomorrow night, and maybe a movie if there's anything decent playing?" he asked, looking way too anxious for her to say yes, but she didn't care. "If there isn't, we could watch something at my place if you'd be comfortable with that. We'll keep everything casual if that works for you. I'm not much into anything formal."

She found herself nodding before he'd even finished speaking, obviously as interested as he was to get together and it made him smile again. If this was love at first sight, then sign her up. It was sad that the poor man had lost his wife, and at such a young age, but relieved that he felt ready to start dating again.

"Do you have children?" she asked him.
"No, you?"

She shook her head no. It was not something she gave a lot of thought to other than she believed everything would all fall into place someday. And that was before she met anyone great, like she just had. Who knew what the future held?

They talked for a few more minutes before he walked her back to the front desk, amid the shameless scrutiny of his colleagues. They didn't even try to hide their curiosity and she imagined as soon as she was out of the building they'd start in on him. But he looked like he could handle it. She got the impression that not much would rattle him, and of course she'd heard that for herself on Saturday night. She couldn't believe she had a date with the hostage negotiator! Of all things! She felt sure she was going to burst with happiness as she walked back to her car, her feet barely touching the ground.

She spent the rest of the day shopping for a new outfit. He'd spoken the one word that was dear to her heart, casual. She liked her jeans! So chose a soft black turtleneck and faded slim-fit denims which would look great with her faux-alligator boots. Could a woman ever go wrong with basic black paired with interesting accessories? The turtleneck might make her come across as a prude, but this was a first date and she didn't expect anything more than a kiss. No home runs for this girl on day one, although she felt as if they already knew each other a little bit.

Glad that she'd found something great to wear, she considered seeing if her stylist could fit her in for a trim but ultimately decided against it. Her scalp was just too sore. It had hurt to wash her hair in the shower. Instead she splurged on a massage and manicure at the spa. That made her feel so good she wished the date was tonight instead of having to wait another twenty-four hours.

That night she soaked in a luxurious rose-scented bath, after lighting candles to complete the relaxing mood. She was ready for sleep when she drained the tub, dried off and slipped into bed a few minutes later. She wasn't long dozing off. She had no idea how long she'd been asleep when she awoke feeling as though she couldn't breathe, her heart pounding, paralyzed with fear. As she lay there in the dark she could swear she'd heard something in the next room. Was it Cedric? Was it the dogs or Cedric's son? Was she even awake? Her whole body shook, and she was soaked with perspiration, filled with dread. Dear God, what was happening to her? Terror held her in its icy grip as she lay there, hardly daring to breathe. Her chest was clutched in a painful twist, her heart racing.

As minutes passed she realized she was indeed awake and alone in her apartment, as the fuzziness in her brain slowly began to clear. It had all been a terrifying nightmare. She should have known. She'd done a story on that too. It was a follow-up to the hostage negotiator piece, outlining how victims of horrible crimes or other bad things, very often experienced PTSD. Could that be what was happening to her? If she remembered correctly, the people she had interviewed had described feeling the same way she was feeling right now. Why had she thought she'd be immune? It was ludicrous to think she'd skate away from what happened without a second thought.

Being held captive by Cedric had been absolutely petrifying; having the dogs sitting not a foot away from her, so close she could smell their breath was agonizing. Not knowing what minute Cedric would give them the command to attack after one of his mood shifts. Or maybe they'd have jumped on her of their own volition. The possibility was torturous. Dogs were obedient to their masters, but they also had a mind of their own. Given her level of fear, she couldn't imagine how they resisted acting on that primal urge.

She switched on the bedside lamp as her heart rate began to resume its normal rhythm, and her breathing slowed to a more comfortable level. But one thing was for sure, she wasn't interested in getting any more sleep tonight. If that's what was waiting for her, she'd tough it out and stay awake with coffee. Maybe since she didn't have to go into work in the morning she'd try to get a couple of naps tomorrow, in the full light of day. She didn't want to look half asleep when Shane picked her up.

* * *

On Wednesday night, ready or not, her doorbell rang at exactly six-thirty and she tried not to appear too excited when she hurried to let him in. He did casual well, his jeans snug in all the right places, a light grey shirt that matched his eyes to perfection and a soft black leather jacket. And he smelled great too with barely a hint of cologne, something masculine like leather and some sort of sexy spice. What was that silly thing she'd said about first dates? She wanted to lead him straight to the bedroom, she thought naughtily, and see if he looked as good out of his clothes as he did with them on. Her guess was that he did, but time would tell if that's the direction this budding relationship would eventually go.

She could feel his eyes on her.

"Sexy," he said, a slow smile lifting the corners of his mouth and telling her he too liked what he saw.

She smiled.

"Are you hungry, Ginger?" he asked as he helped her into her jacket. "I didn't ask what type of food you like, but I took a chance and made reservations at Franconelli's. I hope you like Italian. Have you ever been there?"

"No, but I've always meant to try it because I do love Italian. Actually, it's my favourite."

* * *

Once there and having placed their orders, it was as though they were alone in the room. The chatter of nearby diners faded away as they watched each other over the flame of a single candle in the centre of the sturdy wooden table. She felt something touch her hand and glanced down to see that he had placed his hand over hers on the checkered tablecloth. She loved the warmth of his fingers against her skin. She felt a quivering in her stomach, and this was only dinner, and before a glass of red wine from the carafe that had just been delivered.

She was not surprised that this didn't feel at all like an awkward first date. It felt like already being in love, which was foolish, because they had known each other for such a short time. Perhaps becoming acquainted in that way during that wretched experience, took them further along than they realized.

The spell was broken, albeit temporarily when the server brought them their appetizers and they reluctantly began to eat.

"I don't know if you had a chance to check out what's playing locally," he said as he dipped a piece of warm focaccia bread into a bowl of spiced olive oil, "but I didn't see anything that great."

She was doing the same, savouring a nibble of the delicious bread. "I did take a look, but I honestly didn't see anything that interested me. I was going to say though that if you found something, I'd go along with it and maybe like it once we got into it. Sometimes you don't think you'll like a movie at all and then it turns out to be great."

"Like I said before, you could come to my place. I have a service so we could probably find something to watch that we'd both like. That's if you don't mind coming to my house. It is a first date and I'll understand if you don't feel comfortable doing that."

How could she come right out and say, sure, I'll come to your house but there's no way I'm sleeping with anyone on a first date? She'd sound like a nervous teenager, but she still had to be true to her values.

He smiled as though he knew what she was thinking. There was that darned face of hers again, so easy to read. She felt a warm flush beginning to spread over her, hoping he would assume her heightened colour was because of the wine. "You have very expressive eyes, Ginger. They're the most beautiful big blue eyes I've ever seen, and let me say I'll behave like a gentleman if you want to come over and watch a movie together. I want us to get to know one another, not move too fast and ruin what might turn out to be a good thing. I'd like to take it slow and see where it goes. You?"

She was sure the relief must be playing across her face like a neon pixel sign. "That's what I was thinking too," she said.

With the obvious chemistry between them, she wondered just exactly how they were going to accomplish that, unless they sat on opposite sides of the room. That didn't sound like much fun at all. Getting even closer to him would be unbearably exciting; maybe just a touch or two ... or three.

Sitting across the table from Shane Elliott was like nothing she'd ever experienced before, in terms of the man/woman thing. She'd been on dates, lots of them, and of course at twenty-nine had even had a couple of serious relationships. However, anything that had gone before paled by comparison as to how she felt right now. She couldn't stop looking into his eyes. They were almost hypnotic, and his hands were well shaped and strong. It would feel absolutely wonderful to be touched by him. Her hand was still tingling from before, so what chance did she stand at keeping her distance?

The meal, as delicious as it was, seemed to be interminable. On the other hand the time flew by, and soon they were back in his vehicle and headed toward Franklin's east side. His home was lovely, obviously well cared for and she noticed the for sale sign. He probably wouldn't have much trouble selling it because it was a very nice property. Again she wondered about his late wife and if she should say anything about that. He'd said he was ready to move ahead with his life, but he must have loved her very much. It was incredibly sad that he had lost her at such a young age. She would never ask the details of such a personal matter. If he wanted her to know, he'd tell her all in good time and she'd wait for him to bring it up when he was comfortable doing so.

"Is there any particular time you want to be home, Ginger?" he asked courteously as he unlocked the door, turned on the light and ushered her inside. Dispensing with their coats he directed her to the spacious living room.

"Not really, I'm off this week, but I'm sure you have to be to work early tomorrow morning. You probably work shift work, do you?"

"I don't go in until four o'clock tomorrow afternoon so a late night won't bother me."

Ginger had never been accused of being a wallflower, somewhat like her grandmother. When ice needed breaking, she didn't mind taking on the job. So she winked, affecting a sassy tone. "Me either, I'm over eighteen so I'm allowed to stay out past midnight."

He look surprised, then laughed that sexy rumble again. "Good to know, so at least we won't have to watch the clock. We can relax and watch a movie instead. Ladies choice."

She chose a romantic comedy and he either went along with it because he was a good guy, or it was something he enjoyed too. There was no way to tell since they were both on their best behaviour.

She sat in a comfy armchair while he settled onto the sofa, leaned back and crossed his legs at the ankles. He glanced over at her and catching his eye she smiled, knowing without him saying so that he wanted her to join him on the sofa. That was a no-brainer.

"I don't bite, Ginger, come on over," he said with a lazy grin. "I think you can see the TV better from this angle anyway."

She joined him, then cursed herself for stifling a yawn. Way to go, Martel! Very sexy move indeed! Now he'd think she was bored. But no, he was more concerned.

"Let me guess, you didn't sleep well last night."

She looked at him. "How do you know?"

"That wouldn't be surprising considering what that idiot put you through. Nightmares?"

She nodded, furious that his kind soothing voice brought tears to her eyes. She willed them to dry up and go away. Instead they shimmered on her lashes threatening to fall. Perfect! Now he'd think she was a bona fide head case who was going to dump all over him.

When he slipped his arm around her it was nearly her undoing. "I was going to ask you about that. I think you should see someone, discuss what happened to you. That would be the healthiest thing for you to do. Don't underestimate what you went through. You were terrorized for hours and it's bound to have an effect."

"But I'm very strong. I'll be okay, I need a little more time. I'm sorry, I'm embarrassed about this," she told him, wiping at her eyes.

"Don't be embarrassed, Ginger, just think about what I said. No use suffering if you don't have to. Look, we could watch this movie another time, if you're interested in getting together again that is."

"Of course I'm interested. I am having a very good time. I don't know where that other came from. I'm sorry."

"First of all stop apologizing, there's no need to because I completely understand. And second of all that's what I'm talking about. If you don't get some counselling to deal with this, it will be right there waiting for you for a long time, maybe always. Trust me, I know. So, why don't I drive you home so you can get some sleep? There's always another time."

No way did she want to leave the warmth of his arms because she couldn't think of any place she'd rather be. That included alone in her bed thinking what a dork she'd been to blow the entire evening with him because she couldn't keep it together.

"I'll sleep later, we've got a movie to watch right now. We had a deal," she joked, and was rewarded with that sexy chuckle of his again.

"Okay then, let's watch the movie. Have you seen this one before?"

"I have, and I really like it."

"Me too. Okay I like this part when she goes into the restaurant and he doesn't know she's there."

"That's crazy funny," she agreed, but was aware that she sounded breathless. Being this close to him was having its predicted effect on her already heightened senses. This guy should come with a warning label.

He clearly picked up on her vibe that said I'm enjoying being this close to you, as he too suddenly lost interest in the movie. His arm tightened around her and she snuggled against him. She felt his lips against her ear and her stomach did a spectacular somersault, Italian feast and all. This wasn't supposed to be happening, not on a first date. Suddenly her turtleneck felt like it was made of boiled wool with her steaming inside of it. Their lips met, tentatively at first, but the fire that was spreading between them needed no fanning. The kiss quickly deepened as their response to each other threatened to set the room ablaze, which might be a problem because his house probably wasn't insured against spontaneous combustion.

He pulled away from her long enough to shift her onto his lap. Then his hands were on either side of her face as he looked into her eyes and kissed her again. Her hands found their way to his chest which was much more dangerous territory. This thing was getting out of hand fast. How did they think they could sit this close and ignore the mega tonne of electricity crackling between them? It was like that for some people. They couldn't come anywhere near each other without starting a forest fire.

"I don't think we're going to watch the movie, are we?" he whispered when they both finally came up for air. "I couldn't care less about it at this point in time."

"It doesn't look like it's going to happen but, Shane, I didn't come here to sleep with you."

"And I didn't bring you here to try to change your mind about that, but it's obvious there's something hot between us. You really turn me on and I think I'd better take you home before I break your first date rules, and mine. Okay?"

"Yes," she agreed reluctantly. "I don't want to jump into anything too quickly, is all."

"Me either, believe me, but something tells me it's going to be different with us. What do you think?"

She nodded, her head still cradled against his chest. "You're probably right."

"I've always been a slow mover when it comes to relationships, Ginger, intimacy, believe it or not. But I not only want to get to know you, I want to make love to you too. Sorry, but there it is."

"Right back at you," she said. "I don't want it to be all about sex though, I'm not looking for that. I'm looking for a relationship that could lead somewhere someday. I have to be honest with you."

"I couldn't agree with you more. I'm not into one-night stands. I want something more stable than that too. I want you to know I'm not a player, okay?"

Her heart soared with happiness because he was saying all the right things.

"So do you want me to take you home, or can we behave ourselves do you think?"

"I say stay awhile. I was really enjoying those kisses. Maybe we could have a few more of those."

"Deal," he said. "We don't have to be in a rush, we've got lots of time."

* * *

When he finally drove Ginger home, he walked her to her door and kissed her goodnight. He left a happy man. This was a woman he could get serious about. There were single guys at the office, and married ones too, who bragged about their conquests. Getting as many women as they could seemed to be a game with them. There were always lots to choose from because a uniform was a chick magnet as he'd often heard it described. But that wasn't for him, it never had been. A roll in the hay was a roll in the hay to some guys. When he took someone to his bed he didn't want to wake up in the morning wondering why he'd brought her there after the push for easy sex had worn off.

When he woke up in the morning he wanted the woman beside him to mean something to him. He'd loved waking up next to April, but of course that was in the past and he was determined to leave it there. Funny, it was just about how Hank had described it. When the space opened up beside him, someone had been found to fill it pretty fast. He had great hopes for a future with Ginger. It was crazy, really awful how they had met, but met they had and he looked forward to getting to know her. Have her get to know him. He couldn't imagine that it wouldn't be some of the best fun he'd ever had.

He slept in late the next morning and woke relaxed and happy. About noon he heard from his real estate agent telling him she had a showing scheduled for tomorrow, and one for the day after that. Things were starting to move in the right direction although there was a part of him that would be sad when the house was finally sold. If this thing did work out with Ginger, it wouldn't be right to expect her to move into a house where he had lived with another woman. He knew it was done all the time because it wasn't always economically feasible for everyone to make that kind of a change, but he had no intention of doing it. He was glad he'd made the decision to get rid of this place and find something else.

He actually caught himself singing in the shower when he was getting ready for work. Singing in the shower! What was next? Parading up and down the street with a goofy smile carrying a sign that said I think I'm falling for Ginger Martel after just one date? He'd be laughed out of town. That's how he felt though, as crazy as it was to try to explain, especially to himself. Had Mr. Careful finally met his match?

On the way to work he stopped for a take-out coffee and then again for a pack of gum at Georgia's Variety, a corner store a block away. Even though it'd been a while since he'd quit smoking, he still liked to have some gum in his pocket in case he felt the urge for a cigarette. He was at the counter paying for his purchase when he heard the bell ring over the door indicating another customer had come into the store. He glanced over his shoulder to see who it was and saw the gun. Before he could react he felt the bullet, branding iron hot, tear into his back. He spun, going off balance, the floor coming up to meet him with an angry smack.

Chapter Sixteen

Ginger finished reading the book then set it on the coffee table. It had been fairly interesting, but the last few chapters had more or less been a wasted effort because nothing sank in since all she could think about was Shane. The thrill of his lips on hers last night, how wonderful it was to be close to him, to be held in his arms. She'd never felt so completely swept away ... never imagined it could be this strong, or fast. How could she, a grown woman, be pining for someone she'd only gone on one date with? Ridiculous! Never one to rush into these types of things, it seemed her heart had done a complete about face. She was well and truly smitten with Shane Elliott. What was so great was that it felt like they were both in sync with this; to take things slow and see what came of it. And they did seem to be well matched, but wasn't that the case with everyone when love was new? Both she and Naomi had a cautious nature, and that included matters of the heart. Alexandra was the rebel of the family.

But Shane was the real thing and she didn't want to mess it up by jumping the gun, not that she didn't want to tackle him and have her way, she thought giddily. That was more than tempting because he was so sexy with those bedroom eyes of his. But no, they would wait for each other if for no other reason than to see if this thing was going to go anywhere.

It was six o'clock and still at loose ends, she flopped back in the recliner and switched on the television. A commercial was ending and the intro started for the evening news. The anchor, a portly fellow who seemed to enjoy the sound of his own voice, was checking his notes before looking seriously into the camera.

"Good evening, everyone. We begin tonight with a breaking story out of Franklin, New Brunswick," he said, and that got her attention. "Police are on the scene of a shooting at a convenience store on Lexington Avenue that occurred late this afternoon. In what appears to have been a robbery gone bad, a police officer was gunned down and is currently in hospital undergoing surgery. From what we have been able to determine, the victim is currently in stable condition. We have a reporter outside Bayview General Hospital. Rod?"

The veteran reporter came onscreen, standing in front of the hospital and holding a microphone. "John, this is a rapidly evolving story. Police have confirmed that it is one of their own who was shot, and he has just been identified as thirty-six year-old Corporal Shane Elliott. His father, Weston Elliott, has agreed to speak with us on camera," he said turning to an older man. "What can you tell us about your son's condition, Mr. Elliott?"

Ginger became aware that she wasn't breathing. It was as though she had suddenly turned to stone, her eyes riveted to the television. She watched in horror as the report played out. Shane had been shot? No! There had to be some mistake she reasoned wildly, but there was no mistaking that the picture on the screen was Shane. Her heart was hammering as she listened to Shane's father, the older man explaining that his son was hanging in there and they'd know more when he came out of surgery. The man looked stricken, of course, and she made note of his name at the bottom of the screen.

Anger began to spiral through her. He had to make it through this. She couldn't meet someone like him, a potential happy ending, only to lose him in some random shooting.

Poor Shane! What he must be going through at the moment. Her immediate reaction was to go to him, but then really, she had no status in his life. Who was she to him? To his family? Not even a girlfriend. It sounded crazy even to her own ears that she could go to the hospital and tell them she had dated the man once and needed to be with him. No, the cold reality of it was that she was a nobody in his life right now, just someone he'd met and said he liked. Her spirits sank even further. What if he died? She pushed that horrible thought away and knew she had to come up with a way to see him. She couldn't just sit here!

Then she thought of her grandmother. She didn't want to upset her of course, but she had to talk to someone and she could think of no one stronger than Grandmother Bridger. Naomi would always lend a sympathetic ear, but would likely tell her to stay strong. Meditate. Pray. Gram might say the same things, but she'd put some meat on the bones; come up with some sort of action plan and that's what was needed now. So she dialled her number and was grateful that her grandmother answered on the second ring. She immediately wanted to know what was wrong when she heard Ginger's tearful voice.

"Gram, remember I called you this morning and told you about the great guy I went out with last night?"

"Of course I do, dear. He was the hostage negotiator who was trying to get

333

you released, right? I'm delighted you two went out together and I've got my fingers crossed that it turns out to be the real thing. What was his name again? Don't tell me he stood you up! Is that what happened? You sound upset."

"No, nothing like that, and his name is Shane Elliott."

"Shane Elliott! Wasn't he the one I just saw...."

"Yes! He's the one who was shot in that convenience store hold-up this afternoon. It was on the news."

"Oh dear me! Ginger! I'm so sorry, darling. Are you going to be okay? Why don't you drive over and spend the night here so you don't have to be alone."

Ginger was crying now, she didn't even try to hold back. "I want to go to him, Gram. I feel like that's what he would want. I know it's what I want. He helped me when I was in trouble and now I want to go to him. I have to!"

"Then go to him."

"I can't! Who am I in his life? A nobody!"

"You are not a nobody! Now you dry your eyes and go to that hospital and tell them whatever you need to so that you can get in to see him."

"You mean lie?"

"Aren't you listening, girl? I said do whatever you need to do so that you can see him. It just might be the most important lie you ever told in your life."

"What if they won't let me?"

"Cross that bridge when you come to it. I don't mean to try to force your way in, the quiet rational approach is always better. Who wouldn't have sympathy for a young woman in love? Now, wasn't that his father I saw on the television a few minutes ago?"

"That's what they said, Weston Elliott. I've already made a note of it."

"Good! Now you know who to ask for and he did look like a nice man, so get yourself there and meet him. You'd likely be meeting him sooner or later anyway, so this just moves it up a bit. Now's a great time to get to know him and unless I miss my guess entirely, he'll be glad to meet you too. He could probably use the company if there are no other family members there. I do recall you telling me that Shane is an only child."

"Yes, he is. Oh, Gram...." She broke down again.

"Ginger, dry your eyes, girl and get going. Don't waste any more time, and let me know how you make out. I'll be waiting for your call telling me you were able to speak with him. Make it happen, Ginger. You'll never regret what you're about to do, that much I promise you."

The drive to the hospital seemed excruciatingly slow. Every traffic light turned red as she was approaching. At last though she pulled into the crowded hospital parking lot, and hurried to the Emergency Department where she asked for Weston Elliott. She managed to look the nurse in the eye when she told him she was Shane Elliott's girlfriend and had just gotten a call to come to the hospital. Really, was that such a stretch? She was a girl, well a woman, and she was his new friend, so her conscience eased a little. The part about the call was an outright lie though and she asked for forgiveness even before it left her lips. She had to see Shane! The nurse took her to where Weston Elliott was waiting for word on his son, along with several police officers standing nearby in a show of support for their fallen friend.

Weston looked surprised when the nurse led her to him. He probably knew his son's relationship status and wondered where she'd come from. He seemed friendly enough though as he indicated the empty chair beside him and invited her to sit.

"I'm Ginger Martel, Mr. Elliott, and I'm afraid I told a bit of a white lie when I said I was Shane's girlfriend." She wouldn't repeat the one about the call because that might upset him, and she had not come to make things worse. "We actually have just started to go out, but I want to see him and I know he would want to see me," she said, whereupon the tears started to fall again. She didn't seem to be able to hold them back.

Weston was studying her kindly. "I spoke with Shane a day or two ago and he didn't mention you."

"I know, because like I say we're just new. So if when he comes back from surgery and says he doesn't want to see me, I promise I'll leave with no problem. Okay?"

A shadow of a smile passed over his still handsome face. "It's a deal then. We'll let him decide."

"Thank you, so much, Mr. Elliott! I don't suppose you know anything yet about his condition?"

He ran his hand wearily over his face. "No, but they said he might be in surgery awhile. They have to determine the extent of the damage and then fix him up. They have to get the bleeding stopped first." He drew a shaky breath. "The guys said there was a lot of blood at the scene, so it's hard to tell how bad it is,"

She laid a hand on his arm. "Shane is a big strong man," she said tearfully.

Weston nodded. "He's a fighter, and that should make a difference. It's just the waiting…."

"Can I get you anything? Coffee or tea or maybe a soft drink?"

"No, hon, I'm fine. I honestly couldn't get anything down right now anyway. I just want to know that my son is okay." He sniffed and looked away. "I was always afraid this day would come, him being a cop. It's a call you're always afraid you'll get. I was a firefighter, so now I know what I put my family through; them worrying about my safety although we didn't have to contend with guns."

"I know being a firefighter is a high risk occupation too. Are you still on the job?"

"I retired a few years ago. So how did you and Shane meet?"

She sighed, not wanting to rehash the whole Cedric thing. She'd just hit the highlights.

"We met on the job you might say."

"You're a cop too?"

"No," she said quickly. "There was a hostage taking the other night. Shane was there as the hostage negotiator, and I, unfortunately, was the hostage. We met when I went to thank him for saving my life."

"No way! You were that hostage? The reporter?"

She nodded. "Your son is a remarkable man."

Weston smiled. "You're right, he is. I'm so proud of him I could bust. He's done well for himself, but my son has been through a lot in his life. He didn't deserve this."

"Where was he shot? Did they tell you that?"

"The doctor said he got hit in the back, just below the ribcage on his right side," he explained, his voice tremulous. "Not a great place to take a bullet. Of course there's no good place to get shot, although some are worse than others."

She almost wished she hadn't asked as her stomach, still sour with shock, continued to threaten full revolt. She'd imagined, hoped, that it was maybe his leg or arm, or like in the movies, the shoulder and they just shook it off and rode away. It was a much different story in real life.

"When the doctor comes, I'll step away so you can speak to him in private, Mr. Elliott. That's not going to be a problem. Then if you want to include me, we can go from there, okay?"

"Thank you," was all he said as he folded his arms stiffly across his chest, his body rigid.

She felt sorry for what he was going through. She knew how frightened she felt, she couldn't imagine what a parent must feel like.

She glanced up as a white-haired man made his way slowly toward them, stopping to speak with the police officers first, their number having grown. Then he approached Weston.

"My name is Hank Peterson," he told Shane's father. "When I heard on the news what happened to Shane, I had to come and see for myself how he was doing. I take it there's no word yet."

Weston shook his head as he took hold of the other man's hand, first introducing Ginger. "We're still waiting, but I'm hoping it'll be soon. I don't know how much more of this I can stand. It seems like forever since they took him into surgery."

Hank nodded sombrely. "I can't imagine going through something like this, but at least if you haven't heard anything that means they're still working on him. As long as he's alive, there's a chance. Anyway, there are a lot of people here pulling for him as well as elsewhere. Please tell him when he wakes up that I was here and that I'll be in touch as soon as he's feeling a little better. In the meantime my wife and I will be praying for his recovery."

Weston's tears did fall then as Hank embraced him, and nodding to Ginger in that unpretentious way of his, he left.

Another hour passed as they sat in silence until they spied a surgeon in green scrubs striding toward them purposefully. Ginger got to her feet to leave, but Weston reached out and touched her arm. "Stay, please. If the news is not good I'd like to have someone with me if you don't mind." He glanced at the officers who'd also seen the surgeon and moved closer to hear what he had to say. "It's wonderful to be surrounded by friends."

She nodded, too close to tears to speak as she reclaimed her seat.

The doctor arrived and stuck out his hand to Weston, smiling, which was in itself an encouraging sign. "I'm Dr. Harrison, and you are Shane Elliott's father?

"Yes," Weston confirmed, "and this is Shane's girlfriend, Ginger Martel. What can you tell us?"

"I can tell you that your son is one lucky man for starters. The bullet was a twenty-two calibre and entered just below his right ribcage. It nicked a kidney and missed other vital organs by a fraction of a centimetre and lodged in muscle, otherwise it might have been a totally different outcome. There was minimal damage to his kidney and we removed the bullet and patched him up. He'll be down from recovery in about an hour. We should only need to keep him for a few days. He'll be in ICU for the first twenty-four hours though, so only family tonight and short visits. A nurse will let you know when you can see him."

Weston shook the doctor's hand, unashamed as tears trickled down his cheeks.

Ginger herself was making good work of her hanky and when she saw a news reporter headed in their direction, she excused herself to go to the washroom. Her own picture had been on the news, so the last thing she wanted was to be recognized. When the coast was clear she returned to where she'd been sitting.

Another hour dragged by until a nurse came and summoned Weston. He had generously included her as family and she now waited patiently until her turn came to see him. That is if he even wanted to see her. There was always the possibility that she had misjudged this whole thing entirely. Maybe he said the same things to every woman he met. She sincerely doubted that was true, but still…. And then there came Weston, smiling, and telling her that Shane wanted to see her.

She suddenly felt shy as she approached his bed, stopping to look with distress at all of the devices he was hooked up to. He managed a weak smile and reached for her as best he could considering the attached tubing. She needed no further invitation as she hurried to his bedside and gently took hold of his hand.

He tried to squeeze her hand, but it was a feeble attempt. "I'm so glad you came, Ginger. You are a sight for sore eyes."

"Are you in any pain?"

"They've got me juiced up pretty good. I don't feel too much at the moment, really. I imagine I'd know about it if this stuff wore off. It hurt like hell before they put me under."

"I heard about it on the six o'clock news and I was shocked. They said they were investigating what took place. Did you try to break up a robbery or something and the guy shot you? Is that what happened?"

Shane shook his head, the movement barely perceptible. "Nothing heroic like that. It all happened so fast, really. I dropped in for a pack of gum and I heard someone come in. I turned to see who it was because a cop always watches his back, and the kid let me have it. And the stupidest part of it is that my Kevlar vest was in the SUV or I probably wouldn't be lying here right now. That'll be a big thing too when the reporters get going with this. Why wasn't he wearing his vest! It was a stupid move on my part. I was running late so I just threw it in the vehicle and left."

"But you didn't go in 'til four, right? Wouldn't you be off duty?"

"It's part of the uniform so I should have had it on. Anyway…."

"I don't understand why he shot you if you only looked at him. Did you know him?"

"I know who he is and he's a bad dude. His whole family is. I'd say he came to rob the store and didn't expect to see me there. I never even had a chance to react. I took the hit and went down."

343

Ginger could feel tears coming again, and they fell despite her best efforts to prevent them from doing so. She wasn't normally weepy. It was obviously because of everything that had been going on over the past few days. Her emotions were on overload, and then of course almost losing Shane. This time last week her romantic prospects for the future looked dim; this week she was in love.

"Come on now," he said sill holding her hand, his voice barely above a whisper. "I'm okay. You have to be strong, Ginger. This is always a possibility with a police officer. There are hazards that go with the job; with wearing the uniform."

She sniffed, comforted by the fact that he was alluding to the future, with her in it. If it did work out between them, she'd have to make peace with the danger he'd be in on a regular basis because there was a well-established criminal element in Franklin. There were a lot of big players in the drug trade. It was something she hadn't even thought about until she listened to the newscast tonight, and then it had been brought into very sharp focus. Of course the job carried risks, although there were police officers who served their entire career without so much as a work-related scratch. But things did happen and it would be something she would have to make peace with if they did indeed move forward together.

"I guess I should have known that," she said, "but a person would never be ready for when it happened. Thank God you got lucky."

"Yeah, lucky since I was so damned dumb, but I'll take the break and run with it. I'm certainly going to hear about not having my vest on though. I should've been wearing it."

"The doctor said you'd only need to be in the hospital for a few days, so that's good. But you can't go back to your house all by yourself can you? I mean until you're better."

He tried another weak smile, obviously tired. "Why, Ginger, do you want to come and play nurse?" he teased.

She blushed, loving it. "Any day," she winked, "but seriously...."

"I've already agreed to go to my Dad's until I'm back on my feet. What with them showing my house and all it wouldn't look good to have an invalid shuffling around inside. But you can come over to my father's. I hear you two have met. He likes you, told me I was lucky."

She smiled, aglow from the compliment. "Your dad and I have met and he very generously included me when the doctor came to talk to him after your surgery. I thought that was so sweet of him.

345

He's a very nice man and loves you very much."

"Yes," was all he said, his eyes drifting shut. She bent over the bed and gently brushed her lips over his, and his eyes flew open.

"Wow, way to revive a guy. Thank you for that, Ginger, but it's a good job we decided to wait because I won't be good for much more than a kiss or two for a while. Then look out."

She laughed with him, then seeing he looked exhausted turned to go, promising to be back again tomorrow.

True to the doctor's prediction Shane was in the hospital for only a few days, and during that time she saw him as often as she could. Weston Elliott, understanding that theirs was a love in early bloom, gave them every opportunity to be alone together. They were as comfortable with one another as a couple who'd been dating much longer.

She called her grandmother one night shortly after she got home from visiting Shane at his father's.

"Well, Ginger, do you still think he's the one?" Grandmother Bridger asked in her usual forthright manner. "I haven't talked to you in a while now and you've both had enough time together to see where each of your faults lie. So do you think you can live with what's wrong with him?"

Ginger laughed. "What's wrong with him?"

"The stuff you must have noticed by now that could be irritating if you didn't believe you were in love."

"Oh I'm in love all right, we both are."

"So, what about his faults? Let's have them, because I won't believe you if you say there aren't any."

"Honestly, Gram, the only thing is that he's an assertive, take-charge kind of guy. I'm assertive too so I expect that at some point we could butt heads, but really, that's not a fault. I like that about him … me too. Oh, and I don't think he's so hot on reporters because he's very private, but that's okay. He's entitled to his own opinion."

"Do you know each other yet in the Biblical sense?"

"Gram!"

"Well?"

"No!"

"Why not?"

"Gram, you're outrageous, but that's what I've always loved so much about you. We have to wait because the doctor told him he could tear something from his surgery."

"And if you did things properly, you would."

Ginger was laughing. "Gram!"

"Has he said anything about marrying you?"

"Well hardly."

"What do you mean, hardly?"

"We've only known each other for a very short time. It's a little early to start picking out a dress and china pattern, don't you think?"

"Well, keep an eye on that."

"I promise I will," she agreed with a chuckle. "One good thing is he sold his house. His father and I packed his stuff and arranged to have it stored until he finds a new place. Shane was very happy it went so quickly. And he asked me to help him pick out a new one. He said I had good taste so he'd appreciate the help."

"That's encouraging."

"It's just a friend helping another friend. I'm not going to read anything into it because I doubt he's thinking of it in that way."

"I doubt that you doubt that, but anyway, darling, I've got to go. Mavis and Connie are coming over for tea in about twenty minutes, so I have to get everything ready. It was wonderful to talk to you, as usual. Remember, I'm still waiting for an invitation to meet your young man. Then I can properly size him up for myself."

After they'd rung off Ginger sat for a few minutes and thought about Shane meeting her grandmother. Of course it would happen eventually, but she shuddered at the impact that could have. Gram had her own mind, and Ginger doubted she'd ever had an unexpressed thought in her life. She remembered one time she'd brought a guy she was dating over to meet her grandmother. It had proved to be a disaster because Gram had disliked the guy on sight and told him he was no good for her granddaughter. She really couldn't blame him when he split, and she and her grandmother hadn't spoken for a while. In the end Gram had been right because Ginger discovered he'd been cheating on her. It had been hard to do, but she'd called her grandmother and apologized, and they had quickly mended their rift. There was no doubt about it, Grandmother Bridger was a major driving force in her life, and she was glad to share this whole Shane journey with her.

* * *

Ginger missed seeing Shane during the day now that she was back to work. She enjoyed her job, but the time did drag almost unbearably until she could be with him. As far as her freelancing went, she'd decided to shelve that for a while, with her editor's blessing. He was simply running previous columns in her allotted space until she felt up to interviewing again. And it would be a while, because every time she even thought about going to someone's house her heart began to speed up. She simply wasn't ready. Also, on Shane's advice, she was seeing a psychologist to help her work through the ordeal she's suffered at the hands of Cedric Gourney. And it was working. Her sleep had improved dramatically since she'd begun the sessions. She agreed with Shane that therapy was a healthy option. When someone had suffered any kind of trauma and didn't get help, the tendency was to rely on friends and loved ones to help make them whole and that wasn't fair. While they could be sympathetic, they were not trained professionals with the tools to help her heal. It was just a plain fact of life.

As time passed she could see that Shane was beginning to become restless to get out on his own again, but when he did return to work he'd be at a desk until cleared for regular duty. She knew what it felt like to climb the walls when confined due to illness, having had mono a few years ago. That had made for cabin fever, big time. So when she suggested he come to her apartment for the weekend, he seemed only too happy to accept her invitation for a sleepover.

"Geez," he said when he'd stopped for a rest at the top of the small flight of stairs leading to her front door. "It's going to take me a while to get back in shape. I didn't think a few steps would take that much out of me."

"Take your time, there's no rush."

"Good job there's not, or I'd be in trouble."

Unlocking the door they went inside and Shane took the first chair she offered.

"It's only been a few weeks since you were shot. Give yourself time."

"I'll be okay in a minute," he said, spurred on by the inevitable male ego. "You've got a nice place here, Ginger. This is a heritage building isn't it? I like the look of that wainscoting. I think when I look for another house I'd like to have something with a little more style and substance, like this one. What do you think?"

"I think older houses are beautiful. I love this place. The only problem is that the bedroom was way too small for my taste, so I actually sleep in the dining room."

"Cool."

"Yes it is cool, unless you lit a fire in the fireplace. Then it might not be too cool."

"You've got a fireplace in your bedroom, or I guess it was the dining room?"

"You bet. Get your breath back and I'll show you."

He studied the beautiful marble fireplace in the living room within view a few feet away. "Is it as nice as this one?"

"Nicer, I think. This one's dark," she said pointing to the ornate fireplace and mantle, "and the one in the bedroom is white."

He stood up, obviously eager to see it. "Okay, I'm fine. Come on, show me."

They walked up the carpeted hallway and turned left at the bedroom, stepping inside. "It is beautiful! Look at that workmanship. That does it, I'm definitely going heritage this time around."

"I think that would be a good choice. I do know though that if the property is in a designated heritage area, any improvements you might like to make have to be historically correct and approved by the Heritage Conservation Board."

He shrugged. "No worries. I wouldn't want to do anything that would take away from the historical value of the property anyway; take away any of its charm."

He looked around the room appraisingly, then raised his eyebrows playfully as he looked back at her. "So, Ginger, you say this is a one bedroom apartment?"

"There's just the one and you're standing in it."

"And so I take it there's only one bed, or does the sofa pull out?"

"The sofa doesn't pull out."

He grinned. "So that means…."

She chuckled, joining in the fun. "That's what it means, Shane."

He did a fake yawn. "You know, Ginger, I'm suddenly feeling very tired. What do you say we go to bed and catch up … on our sleep. What do you think of that idea?"

Her stomach was doing those somersaults again, like tumblers in a three-ring circus. "Yeah, that'd be a really great idea. But the doctor said…."

"The doctor isn't here right now and if you don't tell on me, I'm not going to say anything. It'll be our guilty little secret, what do you say?"

"I say it sounds like a good idea, but seriously I don't want you to strain," but he was already kissing her neck and then her earlobe.

As always when he kissed her, he took her breath away so she had none left to take her point any further. She guessed they'd play it by ear.

And so they did, and it was surprising how much could be accomplished without straining anything. The doctor's orders were still intact as they lay holding each other later, still glowing.

"I don't think this will come as any surprise," he said, "when I tell you I'm falling in love with you. I swear, you're all I can think about, Ginger. How'd I ever get so lucky?"

She snuggled in closer, trailing her lips over his shoulder. "I feel exactly the same way, Shane, I...."

Just then the doorbell rang, a discordant jangling noise she always thought sounded exactly like the fire alarm at her old school. It never failed to make her jump.

"Are you expecting someone?" he asked, frowning.

"Oh my gosh, my grandmother! She wanted to meet you so I said come over around three, and it's around three. I forgot all about it."

"Your grandmother!"

"Yes, and if I remember correctly, I think she has a key. I used to have a cat and she'd drop in to feed it if I was working late. If I don't answer right away she lets herself in."

"She lets herself in?"

She nodded. "She does and I would imagine she'll be inside any second now. She's really looking forward to meeting you. I told her what a gentleman you were."

"For crying out loud! I've got to get my pants on, ouch!" he yelped as he moved too quickly in an attempt to grab his clothes off the floor.

"Shane, it's okay," she said as she jumped out of bed and hurried for the bedroom door, locking it.

He stopped what he was doing and watched her getting dressed. "You're really beautiful, Ginger."

She smiled and they both heard the front door opening and closing and her grandmother calling out, asking where she was.

"We'll be right out, Gram!" she answered. "You can wait for us in the living room if you want."

She passed Shane his clothes and he swung his feet over the side and pushed back the blanket, slowly getting dressed.

"She'll think I'm some gentleman," he groused good-naturedly. "in bed with her granddaughter in the middle of the afternoon."

"We're not teenagers, and besides, Gram is about as open-minded as they come. You'll love her."

Minutes later they walked hand in hand into the living room where sprightly Grandmother Bridger waited, her blue eyes cool and appraising as she shamelessly studied Shane from head to toe.

"First of all, young fella, I'm sorry about you getting shot. But I can see it hasn't held you back any, in bed with my granddaughter."

Ginger stifled a giggle as she watched Shane's face light up. "I apologize about that, I…."

"Don't apologize to me, son. I figured you'd end up in there sooner or later and I would say my granddaughter has excellent taste. If I were a lot younger and my granddaughter wasn't interested, I'd take you to bed myself." She looked over at her granddaughter. "You're right, he's the one all right."

Ginger laughed out loud as Shane's mouth fell open in surprise. She'd told him her grandmother was outrageous, but she figured he hadn't thought she'd be that outrageous. As a cop he'd probably seen just about everything by now and if her grandmother could still embarrass him, that was a very healthy sign as far as she was concerned.

Grandmother Bridger still had him in her sights. "So tell me, Shane, what are your intentions with my granddaughter? Do you intend to marry her or just have sex with her and keep her guessing?"

Now it was Ginger's turn to be mortified. "Gram!"

Shane wasn't long getting his swagger back, she could tell by the way he squared his shoulders. It would obviously take a lot to throw him off his game. It was after all what made him a great crisis negotiator, the ability to think quickly on his feet.

She dove in anyway in an attempt to mitigate. "Shane, I…."

He held up his hand with a grin. "It's okay, Ginger, I got this."

"Well, I'm waiting," her grandmother insisted, a twinkle in her eye. "What do you have to say for yourself?"

"Of course I intend to marry your granddaughter," he said as he looked at Ginger and winked. "That is if she'll have me."

Ginger's mouth fell open, but Gram looked as pleased as punch. "Is that what passes for a proposal these days?"

Now it was Shane's turn to laugh and to Ginger's relief, he did look as though he was loving this. "Yep! I thought I'd wait a while, but what the hell? What do you say, Ginger? Do you want to get married?"

Ginger's laughter was mixed with tears as she looked at her grandmother then back at Shane. "Yes, I do … want to marry you! Oh my gosh, yes!"

Epilogue

Two days after the shooting:

Nineteen year-old Boyd Robert Westerhaus was apprehended and charged with the attempted murder of Corporal Shane Elliott. The handgun in question, a .22 calibre Smith & Wesson, belonged to his older brother, Ivan, who was incarcerated in federal prison at the time of the incident. When Boyd was eventually sentenced, he admitted to the court he had gone to "get some cash" at Georgia's Variety and was surprised to find a police officer standing at the counter. He said he believed he had to "take the cop out" before the officer could "get him". Westerhaus had actually fired twice, the second shot missing Shane by mere inches and lodging in the counter behind him.

Boyd was the son of Barnard Westerhaus, a career criminal and a known cop hater. All three brothers had lengthy criminal records, including Boyd, who'd committed his first crime at the age of eleven. He'd relieved a seven year-old girl of her earnings at her lemonade stand.

He received a substantial prison term for his attempt on Shane's life.

One month after Shane met Grandmother Bridger:

Shane and Ginger picked out a beautiful diamond ring together, and it was a perfect fit right out of the tray. He waited until they were alone together before he slipped it on her finger, and when he did, there were emotions on both sides. Later they celebrated by returning to Franconellie's where they'd gone on their first date.

Three months after the hostage taking:

Thirty-two year-old Stilwell Cedric Gourney was sentenced to jail on outstanding warrants. The charges were dropped with respect to his involvement in the actual hostage taking, but did face charges for weapons related offences for shooting at his father. Despite surgical intervention Stilwell lost his left arm as a result of the gunshot wound, as well as vision in his right eye from the injury suffered in the earlier barroom brawl.

Two and a half months after Shane gave Ginger her diamond:

Shane and Ginger found a wonderful old two-storey brownstone just outside the city that had all of the features they loved, including a spectacular view of the river. It had once been the estate of the wealthy Robertson family but had fallen into disrepair over the past number of years. Both were excited to get started on the restoration project in the spring.

Six months after the shooting:
Weston Elliott met prospective wife number five, widow Christina Henderson, a charming retired librarian five years his senior. With four grown sons of her own, she was warm and motherly toward Shane and the two immediately hit it off. She clearly adored Weston, but given his track record, insisted on a two-year courtship before making any serious plans for the future. Weston had clearly met his match.

Nine months later:
Ginger returned to freelancing and scored a wonderful story, interviewing Mamie Lachlan, a fiercely independent woman. She'd not only built all of her own furniture, but sailed solo to the British Isles and then wrote a book about it. She accomplished all of this after raising five children on her own after her husband died young following a heart transplant. Maime was quirky and wonderfully off the wall.

That story won Ginger her second Keith Hassam Media Award for best story by a freelancer in her category. Shane, absolutely gorgeous in formal wear, was the first one on his feet applauding as she took the stage to receive her award. The ballroom of the South Winds Hotel was packed for the gala evening.

One year after Shane and Ginger became engaged they tied the knot in a small intimate ceremony in Weston's backyard on a gorgeous afternoon, with only close friends and family in attendance. Weston stood up with Shane as his best man, and Hank Peterson and Merle Brewster served as ushers. Ginger was a vision in her late mother's peau de soi satin wedding gown, and Grandmother Bridger was at her side as matron of honour in a dress as startlingly blue as the cerulean sky above. Naomi and Alexandra completed the bridal party as bridesmaids, which made for some very interesting wedding photos. Shane couldn't stop smiling.

The End

361

Eden Monroe books published by BWL Publishing

Dare To Inherit
Gold Digger Among Us
Looking for Snowflakes
Sidelined
Dangerous Getaway
Almost Broken
Just Before Sunset
Unforeseen Shadows
Incomplete Truths
Storms in the Valley
Back in the Valley
When Fate Comes Calling
Gold Digger Among Us
Dare to Inherit

Eden Monroe loves giving voice to the endless parade of interesting characters that introduce themselves in her imagination. She writes about real life, real issues and struggles, and triumphing against all odds. A proud east coast Canadian, she enjoys a variety of outdoor activities, her cat, and a good book.

BWL Publishing

bwlpublishing.ca

www.ingramcontent.com/pod-product-compliance
Lightning Source LLC
Chambersburg PA
CBHW070045120726
47909CB00002B/298